Katja Ivar grew up in Russia and the US. She travelled the world extensively, from Almaty to Ushuaia, from Karelia to Kyushu, before finally settling in Paris, where she lives with her husband and three children. She received a BA in Linguistics and a master's degree in Contemporary History from Sorbonne University. *Evil Things* is her debut novel.

# EVIL THINGS

Katja Ivar

BITTER LEMON PRESS
LONDON

BITTER LEMON PRESS

First published in the United Kingdom in 2019 by
Bitter Lemon Press, 47 Wilmington Square, London WC1X 0ET



A CIP record for this book is available from the British Library

ISBN 978–1–912242–09-2
eBook ISBN 978–1–912242–10-8

Typeset by Tetragon
Printed and bound in Great Britain by
CPI Group (UK) Ltd, Croydon CR40 4YY

*To Marguerite*

*"Hell is empty, / And all the devils are here."*

WILLIAM SHAKESPEARE

*The Tempest, Act I, Scene ii*

# *Introduction*

It was only at the time of the Russian Revolution, after almost a thousand years of foreign rule, that Finland declared itself an independent nation. Gone were the days when it was ruled by the Russian tsars; nor was it Swedish Österland any longer. Finland had a lot on its plate – establishing democracy, rebuilding its economy and consolidating its national identity – but its biggest issue was the management of the country's foreign relations. After all, Finland had the questionable privilege of having the longest frontier with the Soviet Union, while St Petersburg, the epicentre of the Russian Revolution, lay just eighteen miles from the Finnish border. That fact alone made Finland the object of close attention from the Soviet bear – and from the Western civilization that saw it as its weak link. Thus began for Finland a balancing act of guarding its independence in the shadow of its terrifying neighbour.

The emancipation of Finland coincided with the emancipation of its women. With men at war, it was Finnish women who fought to rebuild the country, engaging in a number of previously unheard-of activities: driving, factory work ... and policing – another endeavour that was not to everyone's taste, least of all those who, in the 1950s, still viewed female officers as lesser beings who could only be trusted with body searches on female suspects and taking care of children brought into custody. Undeterred, the female police officers took advantage of their country's emancipation to think for themselves. Aloud.

*Evil Things* takes place in Finnish Lapland in 1952.

# MONDAY 13 OCTOBER 1952

# 1

She had to squint hard to see where the village was. Just a tiny speck of grey on the map, buried deep in the crevices of that ancient, frozen land. Surrounded by marshes and hills bristling with low, crooked shrubs typical of the permafrost. Inhabited mostly by Skolt Sami, indigenous people who lived off the land, hunting and fishing. Not exactly a tourist destination.

She must have been out of her mind to have insisted on going there. And to do what? To solve a crime that her boss didn't even believe *was* one.

"It sounds just like an accident to me," Chief Inspector Eklund said, his full lips pursed.

He was standing next to her by the map that hung on the wall of his newly refurbished, obsessively clean office that reeked inexplicably of fish oil.

"It could be a crime," said Hella. She was careful not to sound too sure, too forceful. Eklund didn't like her bossy attitude, as he called it, and for better or worse she was stuck with Eklund.

"An old man, practically a recluse, goes missing from his home. Not a crime. He probably got lost in the forest, or drowned in a marsh. Or went over the Soviet border like they all do, got drunk on local Kremlevskaya and forgot who he even was. There's nothing to it."

"He was born in that forest. He couldn't possibly have got lost. And I don't believe he went binge-drinking with the Soviets either. He left a young child behind. His grandson."

"Oh, that's why!" Eklund lifted an accusatory finger. "He left a *child* behind! Of course, that immediately makes you think he was the victim of a crime. Mind you, I understand why you'd react like this, I really do, but that doesn't make his disappearance a crime. Accidents happen. All the time. And that old man probably wasn't the doting grandpa you imagine."

Lennart Eklund went back to his desk and dropped into his brand-new swivel chair, making it squeak under his weight. For him, this conversation was over. Not for Hella. She went on, her voice loud and clear, all her prudent resolutions forgotten.

"So this priest's wife, Mrs Waltari, writes to the police saying that an old man has gone missing, leaving a child behind, that it's been six days since he was last seen, that she's worried, and you're telling me we do nothing? We just file her letter in one of our neat archive boxes and forget about it?"

Eklund looked up at her, puzzled. "Police work isn't about passion. It isn't about people being worried. It's about doing what is good – what is useful – efficient. It's up to us to decide what's best for this community. Which cases warrant our involvement, and which do not."

"Well, I guess we should just throw it away, then," said Hella. "The letter, I mean. Destroy the evidence. Because if there really *has* been a crime, and we've been told about it but haven't solved it, it will ruin our hundred per cent record."

Her boss shifted uncomfortably in his chair, and she knew she had made her point. For Chief Inspector Eklund, police work held little interest, but he had a passion for neatness and efficiency. Under his direction, the Ivalo police district currently boasted the best crime resolution rate in the country, and even if the crimes they solved consisted only of petty thefts at the timber factory and the odd case of a poisoned dog, it didn't matter. Only the numbers mattered to him.

And now Eklund was hesitating, his plump hands playing with a paper clip, his pale blue eyes fixed on something just above her left shoulder.

"We can write back to Mrs Waltari, explaining that her concern has been noted but that at this time of the year the risk of the police being caught up in a snowfall is just too great. We can tell her we'll return to our investigation, if there *is* an investigation, in May next year, when the snow starts to melt and … at least, there could be something tangible …"

His voice trailed off, but she understood exactly what he was getting at.

"And if there *is* a body, we just find it when the spring comes?" she snapped. "Really? That is, unless that body has been eaten by wolves or bears, in which case we can still carry on pretending there was no crime?" Unable to stop, she added, rather viciously: "Is that your golden standard of police work? Just ignoring cases when the weather conditions are too harsh?"

She had gone too far. Even a placid man like Lennart Eklund couldn't take it any longer. She half expected him to throw her out of his office, or lecture her on the virtues of subordination, but what he said hit her far harder.

"Why are you pushing this, my dear? You're a woman. You can't go out there alone, can you? And both Inspector

Ranta and I are very busy right now. Take my advice, forget about it. I'm not talking to you as your superior, but as an older, wiser friend. There's that ball next week everyone is talking about. Put on a dress if you have one, and go. Or you can borrow a shawl and some make-up from Esmeralda. Her dresses would probably be a bit large in the chest for you, but I'm sure we could find you something ..." He paused, thinking, his gaze summing up her body. "Kukoyakka from the timber factory seems to quite like you. Maybe he just has a thing for women who are" – Eklund hesitated, in search of a word that would describe her best, then brightened as he found it – "angular."

Hella winced. *Angular*. For once, he was bang on target.

And now he was wagging his fat index finger at her, a Victorian father admonishing his irrational daughter, his problem child. "You'd better not miss that opportunity; another one might never come along."

She looked at him in a blind rage, which he as usual didn't notice, or at any rate recognize. "And why is that, may I ask, sir?"

He looked at her in bewilderment. "Well, men have been scarce since the war, you know that as well as I do. For women your age, given your past and, well, your present, finding one would be a miracle. I mean, being a *polissyster* is a very honourable profession and you can quite legitimately be proud of yourself for that, but that's surely not all you're looking for in life."

Hella breathed in, slowly, counting to ten to cool off. This conversation was taking an unexpected turn. Was Eklund manipulating her, acting provocatively so she would forget about the crime and focus on her own inadequacies? Or was he just a hectoring middle-aged fool who really thought that pointing out her bleak future was his duty as her superior?

She could have answered him in several ways. That she was not a *polissyster*, for a start. True, she had trained as one, because when she had started her studies women were not yet allowed to be fully fledged officers, and her ambition had been to join the police. But after she graduated, and other options did become possible, she took an advanced course at the police academy that put her on a par with her male colleagues. She had been an inspector in Helsinki, for God's sake, even though she knew that was not an argument she could use.

Or, she, too, could get personal. She could say she had noticed that his right-hand cuff button was missing and that there was an old grease stain on his tie, that it could mean only one of two things: either his wife, the strikingly exotic Esmeralda, was touring Southern Europe again, leaving her bland Finnish life behind, or else she was beyond caring. Hella could have also told him that she'd rather die than marry Kukoyakka, a fifty-something logging truck driver – a truck driver! – who only had one eye and whose breath stank of decay. But she chose not to say anything. Instead, she turned her attention to the map again, and with her index finger followed the jagged line of the road that led from Ivalo to the village of Käärmela. In October, the timber factory trucks went up north every day, working overtime to get as many pine trunks out of the forest as possible before the roads became impassable. And from the logging camp, she could reach Käärmela by foot in a couple of hours. It was doable. She could even try to convince one of the truck drivers to make a detour to Käärmela. She looked at Chief Inspector Eklund again. He was slumped behind his desk, his weary glance following her movements, his mouth pursed tight as a rosebud. As if powered by their own free will, his sausage-like fingers fumbled through a pale blue folder, the cover of which read, in block letters, STAFF EXPENSES.

"How about I take a couple of days off work and pop to the village?" she asked brightly. "I've always been interested in northern architecture, especially Orthodox churches. Those people are Orthodox, aren't they? The Skolts usually are. Where I come from, we don't have that sort of thing." She looked at him expectantly.

The chief inspector sighed and, with visible effort, forced himself to meet her gaze. She could almost see the little wheels turning in his brain, weighing up the risks and benefits of giving in on this one for the sake of office peace. She wondered, not for the first time, if he was afraid of her. Or maybe not *of* her exactly, but of dealing with her. Then, reluctantly, he said:

"You're a nuisance, Mauzer, do you know that? Your parents must have entertained false hopes when they called you Hella the Gentle. Still, if you have nothing better to do, if you insist, go and see for yourself. Take your vacation, and if you uncover a murder, we'll count it as duty time. If that's the case – and it won't be, I assure you – write every day to inform me of your progress." He paused, staring at her as if she was some previously unheard-of species. "The village is nice, little log cabins with ornately carved windows, if you like that sort of thing. You can stay with Waltari and his wife. I hear she's a great cook. Just don't wander anywhere near the Soviet border – the last thing you'd want is to wake up the Soviet bear, so to speak – and be back before Monday. The winter snow could start any day now, and when it does, the road up north will be cut off. I can't afford to lose one of my agents. Ivalo needs you."

He smiled, in what he clearly hoped to be a fatherly, reassuring manner, and poured himself some water from a plain glass carafe set on his desk. She could see little beads of perspiration on his baby-smooth forehead.

*Of course you need me,* she thought. After all, her boss didn't have much choice. The department consisted only of herself, Eklund and old Inspector Ranta, who spent most of his time at the sauna and whose last solved case dated back to before the war. If she was stuck in Käärmela for the whole of winter, Eklund would actually have to drag his backside out of his comfortable, tidy, overheated office and do some messy detective work. His superiors in Helsinki would expect him to. No hiding behind paperwork, behind regulations and staff reports. And it was not like he had any chance of hiring a replacement for her. No one in their right mind would willingly choose the sort of life they led here. Ivalo, the dullest city on earth, without contest. Buried under ten feet of snow for half of the year.

Aloud, she only said:

"I'll be back as quickly as I can, sir. You have my word. I have no intention of spending six months in a priest's wife's kitchen, getting fat on pancakes and listening to her stories. I'll be back in no time."

Then – because her superiors in Helsinki had once told her that if she didn't learn to rein in her temper she would end up thrown out of the police – she forced herself to smile at him.

# 2

If she was completely honest with herself, she would admit that Eklund had a point. In the coniferous taiga forest, people got lost all the time. Granted, they were usually young children or the very old, and the missing peasant, Erno Jokinen, was neither; but still, it was possible. So why had she insisted so hard that this particular disappearance be investigated? Did she *want* it to be murder, so she'd have something to sink her teeth into?

Hella shuffled down the corridor to her poky little office. From a distance, she heard Anita's clear voice, singing a *joik*. Warbling like some Laplandic nightingale. Anita was a distant cousin of Ranta, which was how she'd got her job on the reception desk, but luckily she and Ranta had nothing in common.

Humming to the tune, Hella reached her office – H. MAUZER, POLISSYSTER read the sign, erroneously – noticed that the door was ajar, and stormed into the reception area.

"Hel-lo there, Sergeant!" Anita cried enthusiastically. "What do you think?" The girl swung round in her chair.

What did she think of what? Anita's pink floral dress, so much at odds with the drab office furniture? She'd already worn it last week. Hella was almost sure of that. Her deerskin boots? Old stuff. Her new hairdo maybe, a French twist with a blonde lock sweeping across her forehead?

Anita came to her rescue. "My lips! Just look at them! It's this new lip gloss called 'Cherry on the Cake'. Someone – a friend – brought it for me from Helsinki. Isn't it *lovely*?" she said, batting her lashes.

"It is," Hella acknowledged. "If Perry Como dropped by, he'd fall for you. Absolutely. Do I have any messages?"

She had been asking this very same question twice a day, every day, for two years now, and the answer was almost always "no". Even when it was "yes", the messages were not what she was hoping for. They were never from Helsinki. Never from Steve.

"I'm sorry, no."

Hella turned abruptly, heading back to her office. She hadn't left her door open when she went to see Eklund. She was certain of that. The door didn't shut properly until it was pulled all the way, and the door handle tilted at a certain angle. She had got used to it, knew its tricks, but Ranta didn't. Each time he crept into or out of her office, he'd accidentally leave the door ajar. She peeked inside. No one. Her colleague – her superior, even – was done with his little inspection. Hella wondered if he'd taken something this time. Ranta never went for big, really noticeable things, but he had a fondness for paper clips, and every once in a while he'd spirit away her comb. She had spent months wondering what he did with them, and if he was a hair fetishist, but the explanation turned out to be very simple: Ranta offered the three combs he'd pinched from her to Anita, as a Christmas gift. Hella had found this out on the first working day of the year, when a blushing Anita had given the combs back to her, whispering, "They *are* pretty, aren't they? Please keep them locked away."

And so she did. She had learned to lock her desk drawer, in which she kept her notes, her unsent letters to Steve and the yellow toy bus. She had developed a habit of scooping up everything that was on her desk and stuffing it in the drawer every time she left her office, even to go to the bathroom. Still Ranta prowled around.

With a heavy sigh, Hella fumbled in her pocket for the key to the drawer.

"Oh, by the way!" Anita again, slightly out of breath. "I nearly forgot. There's a package for you. From Helsinki. Something heavy."

She was carrying a sturdy wooden crate, making a big show of how heavy it was.

"Where shall I put it? Do you want a claw hammer?"

*What if I don't want to open it?* thought Hella, but said nothing. Anita meant well. She motioned to her desk, and together they tore off the lid.

"Oh …" whispered Anita, disappointed. "Gherkins. Is it a gift from your grandmother?"

"Sort of."

Hella lined up the jars on the windowsill, hoping that Anita would go away, but the girl lingered.

"Would you like me to water your plant?" She motioned to Hella's aspidistra, a welcome gift from her colleagues, which was dying by the radiator.

"I'll be away working on a new case, starting from tomorrow," said Hella, just to get rid of the girl. "Could you take care of it while I'm gone?"

Anita could, of course, and would be delighted to. Absolutely. A couple of minutes later, having ensured that the plant, her closest friend in town, would survive, Hella ushered the receptionist away, mumbling words of gratitude. She shut her door and got to work.

She needed to leave everything in order. Order and method, as Eklund would say, for whom these two words took the place of a religion. Order and method. She pulled a stack of files out of her drawer and spread them out on her desk. Red was for urgent matters. The beggar Lahti urinating on Dr Gummerus' doorstep, for example. Dr Gummerus was a pompous ass, and as far as Hella was concerned, deserved Lahti's urine. But of course she couldn't say that out loud. Dr Gummerus was a *respected* member of the local community, and as such had to be treated with *deference.* Therefore, she was expected to (a) investigate, (b) punish Lahti and (c) stop him from doing it again. Exactly *how* she was supposed to deal with the problem remained unclear. They did have a holding cell at the station, a one-room affair with a folding bed and a door secured by a bolt, which was out the back next to the neighbour's chicken coop, but the room had no heating, so she couldn't very well put the beggar in there, even for a couple of hours. The doctor knew that, of course. He even had a theory that Lahti only urinated on his doorstep during the cold months exactly *because* there was no way he could be punished. Well, maybe the doctor was right. Maybe she should threaten Lahti with a deferred arrest, if such a thing existed. Hella decided that she would discuss the idea with Eklund before she left.

She pushed the red file to one side and picked up a green one. Policies, regulations and monitoring. Eklund's favourite, the apple of his eye. *That* file was bulky. Some days, it seemed to her that working on policies and regulations was all she ever did. Monitoring the evolution of the crime rate, broken down by types of crime (misdemeanours, petty thefts, serious offences), by geographic location (Ivalo, Nellim, the rest of Lapland), and its evolution quarter by quarter. Comparisons with the national statistics and those of the neighbouring regions. Beautifully typed reports that no one ever read. She was supposed to finish her latest quarter-on-quarter comparison and present it to a solemn Eklund and a sneering Ranta before the end of the following week. She sighed. Two years and counting, and she was poised to still be working on green files until she retired unless a white knight from Helsinki charged down to save her. Only Helsinki had no more white knights than Ivalo had criminals, so she'd do better to forget about it and focus on more immediate matters.

Her trip to Käärmela, for instance. Maybe she'd been wrong to have insisted on it. Still, now that she had started, she might as well do the thing properly. She leafed through the green file. Eklund had a policy for this, too. Here it was, clearly printed. *Before incurring any expenses, obtain an in-principle approval from your superiors.* That one was easy: she didn't expect to incur any expenses. Next. *Check the background of all involved parties with the Security Intelligence Service.* The Suojelupoliisi. Another one of Eklund's obsessions. Making sure communists, and other dangerous specimens of humanity, were properly labelled.

She wondered if this was really necessary. She was going on vacation, after all. But what if she really found something untoward when she arrived in the village? She supposed she'd better do things by the book.

Hella dutifully inserted a sheet of paper into her brand-new typewriter and typed a short letter to the regional representative of the SUPO listing the names Erno Jokinen, one Mr Waltari, Orthodox priest, and one Mrs Waltari, his wife. Then she carried the letter to the reception area and entrusted it to Anita, who was listening to the radio, her head cocked to one side.

"I'm waiting for the local news," she explained to Hella. "They might say something about the dance."

Hella nodded. The dance was the biggest event of the year for Anita. Her dress, a flimsy, pale green tulle affair, had been ready for months. Although Hella had never seen it – Anita was wary of actually showing the dress to anybody – she still felt she was able to describe every tiny rosebud button, every seam on it.

"I had second thoughts about my hairdo," whispered Anita. "Should I try and wear it —"

Hella was no longer listening. The newsreader's clipped voice cut into her thoughts.

*... increasing tensions with the Soviet Union, which is protesting against what they describe as spying incidents and numerous violations on the Soviet–Finnish border. While the claim is not specific, its undertones are perfectly ...*

"— or even a ponytail," said Anita. "What do you think?"

"A ponytail is a great idea," replied Hella in a voice that left no room for further discussion. "It will give you distinction. Horses are noble animals." Leaving Anita to ponder her advice, she hurried back to her office.

The last two recommendations in the file concerned the proper equipment to take along on an investigation, and the correct procedure when filling in expense reports. Hella closed the file and stared at the aspidistra. The plant was shedding its leaves. Maybe Anita was right. Maybe it craved water. Suddenly desperate to get at least *something* right, she picked up the carafe that stood on her desk and emptied all the water it contained into the aspidistra pot. She then watched, fascinated, as the cracked earth absorbed every last drop of it.

She had never regretted what she had done that day in Helsinki, and she was not going to start now. She had made the right choice, and the jars of gherkins that filtered the pale October light on her windowsill were there to prove it.

# 3

Once again, Irja was telling the little boy who crouched motionless next to the stove that he shouldn't worry, that his grandpa would be back soon, any time now, really. Over the last four days, she'd kept repeating it like a mantra: *don't worry, Kalle, he went to the city, you know how it is, it takes time, and maybe he's been hunting along the way, or else he's bringing you something special.* Kalle smiled absent-mindedly and nodded, but he clearly didn't believe her, and she couldn't blame him for that. What she was saying was a lie. The boy knew it, and she knew it, and all the curious villagers who stopped by her house to inquire about the boy knew it too. Old Erno was not coming back.

Irja looked at the boy, frowning. He hadn't said a word since he'd first arrived at her house earlier that week, brought in by a sour-looking old woman who lived in a crooked little log cabin on the outskirts of the village. Irja barely knew her. Still, the woman had come in without knocking, without even taking her shoes off. She had walked over to the kitchen table, stubbornly dragging the little boy behind her, and had seated herself on the bench. The boy had sat down as well, but he hadn't looked up at Irja nor had he answered her greetings.

Martta, that awful woman, had looked at Irja in defiance. "You're a priest's wife," she said. "You should know."

"I'm sorry," murmured Irja. "Know what?"

"Know what to do with him. Stubborn as a goat, that kid is. Was refusing to leave the house. Had to spank him. And now he refuses to open his mouth to eat. Cries all the time. Screams in his sleep. Wets his bed."

"What is he doing with you?" Irja had crouched next to the boy. "Kalle? Where is your grandfather?"

"Missing," explained the woman, matter-of-factly. "Gone. Surely dead. He" – she pointed at the boy – "he would have been dead too, if *I* hadn't found him."

"What happened to your grandpa, Kalle?" Irja had asked, ignoring the woman. "Do you know where he went?"

The boy had shaken his head without looking at her.

"But still, something happened, right? Is he …?"

She didn't dare ask Martta outright if Erno was dead.

"He won't say a word," the woman had snorted. "He's stupid, more likely than not. Just like his dear grandpa. Had to drag him out of the house, while he was screaming and trying to grab hold of the furniture. I should have just left him there, alone, but the place was freezing and there was no food."

Irja had stared at the woman, appalled. What kind of person was she? Still, she had probably saved the child's life. Kalle and his grandfather kept to themselves, barely venturing into the village. Apart from Timo, no one ever saw them, and even Timo didn't see them often. Weeks could have passed without anyone knowing that the old man had disappeared.

"Do you know where Erno went?" Irja asked the woman. She remembered stories about her. Martta was a relation of the old man, but they were not close. And there were rumours of a conflict, of an old dispute, which, left unresolved, had grown out of proportion and dragged on for decades.

"Don't know and don't care. The Devil can have him if he wants. And *you* can have the boy. Maybe it'll do you good."

The old woman had got to her feet, straightening her grey wool skirt, tugging at her sleeves. She had barely looked at the boy, who sat like a little wooden statue, his back straight, his hands folded demurely in his lap. Only his nose, which was wet, was twitching like that of a little rabbit. Irja's heart sank. Would she be able to take care of the child until the disappearance of old Erno had been cleared up? And what would happen next? His mother had died some months ago. Kalle didn't have a father. Would social services take him? As if he was reading her thoughts, the little boy wriggled nervously on his bench, and a single tear ran down his dirt-smeared cheek.

"Kalle?" whispered Irja. "I'll take care of you. I promise. And I will do everything in my power to find your grandpa, because I know how much you love him and how much he loves you."

She had hugged the boy and held him close to her, whispering reassuring words into his ear. Her old grey cat, Seamus, had sauntered over to the boy and sniffed his hand. Seamus must have liked what he smelled because he had jumped onto the bench and settled next to the child. It was a good sign. Seamus was not the kind of cat to easily warm to strangers. If he took a liking to little Kalle, maybe it would help the boy recover. Animals are great for that sort of thing, soothing the wounded and the sad, comforting those who have lost their loved ones.

After a while, the boy's breathing slowed. He had fallen asleep. Irja had carried him to her own bed and covered him with a bright quilt, with Seamus at his side.

Then, she had pulled a sheet of paper out of the desk drawer and had started to write her letter to the police. She had sent it the very same day, rather like a bottle that a prisoner on a desert island throws into the ocean, but she didn't allow herself to think about that too much. Maybe in some places, in other countries, ordinary citizens could rely on the police to help them. Maybe. She was not so sure the same applied to the godforsaken strip of frozen land they called home.

# TUESDAY 14 OCTOBER

# 4

When Hella was a child, growing up in Helsinki, her teachers had tried to teach her gratitude. They talked about it in ringing voices, like it was the most important thing on earth. Not compassion, not honesty or curiosity. Gratitude.

"You have to be thankful for what you've got, Hella! When you say 'Thank you', it should come from your heart! You are a very lucky little girl; you should count your blessings and address a short prayer to our Lord, thanking Him for all He's done for you!"

Then, usually, seeing that she wouldn't oblige, they'd start recounting her blessings themselves. In doing so, her teachers mixed up some really important things. The new toy she had got at Christmas was mentioned in the same sentence as her grandmother, an old woman with a moustache, who smelled of mothballs and whom Hella was afraid of and never wanted to visit. Most significantly, while they usually mentioned the fact that – in contrast to many children whose fathers had fallen in the wars that opposed the Soviet Union – young Hella still had both of her parents, they never mentioned her parents' professions. It never failed to amaze her. Having parents, just ordinary parents, was one thing. But the family she had was something completely different. Something to be proud of, even though at that time she mostly took it for granted.

*Maybe I should have done as I was told,* thought Hella grimly, her eyes fixed on the desolate landscape outside her window, with its crooked yellowish shrubs and scattered stones. Maybe if she had really been grateful, things would have turned out differently for her. Of course, it was no use thinking about it now. Rearranging the past. Thinking of what she might have done differently. It was no use and it led her nowhere. She'd do better to start packing.

Her bulky pigskin suitcase stayed under the bed. It would be impossible to carry around if she ever had to cover part of the road on foot. As a result, she decided to put all her stuff into a backpack, which meant she had to drastically limit the number of things she took with her. From a pine wardrobe that stood in a corner of her room, she pulled out a couple of sweaters and a pair of trousers. She added some sensible walking shoes, and warm flannel pyjamas. And a coffee pot, adorned with the Paulig company's Paula Girl in her traditional costume, smiling away. She wasn't sure whether they had coffee in Käärmela. Even in Ivalo, she could only buy it with rationing tickets, and only at the beginning of each month.

She wondered where she would be sleeping in the priest's house. Would she have a bedroom of her own, or have to doze off in the middle of the living room? It was possible. She had forgotten to ask if the priest and his wife had a big family. She had heard that the Orthodox servants of God were the ones who usually had the largest families, apparently with the idea of setting an example to their parishioners. She tried to picture herself sitting in a hot, low-ceilinged room, trying to question a suspect while little children crawled all over her, picked up her pen and tore pages out of her notebook. She sighed. What a change from her previous position in Helsinki, where she'd been the first woman ever to work in the homicide squad. Interesting, complex cases, envious glances from her male subordinates, an apartment with a sea view smack in the middle of the city. Real power. But she had decided that she would not dwell on her past. So, walking shoes then. And socks. And a notebook. A small, hand-embroidered bag into which she put her toothbrush and a small jar of face cream, her last concession to femininity. Her hairbrush wouldn't fit into the bag, so she put it directly next to her clothes. She was ready. She had already decided that she would carry her gun on her, in the handgun holster under her parka. The armed conflict in the countryside had ended more than six years ago, but still, you never knew who you might encounter in the woods. And of course there was also the fact that she had to travel to the village with Seppo Kukoyakka. The other logging truck drivers set off early, sometimes before 6 a.m., and she would have preferred to go with one of them, but they hadn't wanted to give her a lift and had told her so to her face. She'd had to settle for Kukoyakka. Because he had just one eye, he left the timber factory much later than the others, once the sun had risen and he could see the road properly.

Just thinking about Kukoyakka and his huge Sisu truck made her shudder. Would he try to push his luck and maybe make advances to her? She struggled to imagine how she would react if he did. She couldn't *shoot* him, after all. Not after what had happened in Helsinki. But then what? She once read a book by the French writer Stendhal where the main character, a young and beautiful girl called Lemiel, had to travel in the company of lecherous men. To avoid being disturbed, Lemiel had deliberately made herself ugly.

The girl had smeared her face with some sort of paste which gave her skin a sore, blistery appearance.

Hella sat down heavily and stared at the oval mirror which hung next to the wardrobe. Should she try something similar? But it was probably unnecessary. It was not like she was some irresistible beauty. A gap-toothed woman of around thirty, bony rather than curvy. *Angular*. All elbows and grit, as Steve would say. Freckled, too, which was really unjust because her eyes were black and her hair dark. How could anyone have a redhead's complexion and not be a redhead? If Kukoyakka was tempted nonetheless, well, it was just too bad for him. She wouldn't hesitate to pull out her gun. Even if it meant that he rushed off to complain to Eklund about her.

This thought made her smile. If it hadn't been for her past, she would have loved for something like that to happen. She could imagine the rumours – the plain girl from Helsinki, the police sergeant, had had to shoot a man who had tried to come on to her. It would prove to them once and for all that she was an attractive woman, that men fell for her, even if one-eyed Kukoyakka was not exactly a catch, with his large behind and his beer belly. Still, he was a man, and, as Eklund kept saying, men were scarce these days, so attention from one of them was something. That would shut them up for good, them being her landlady, Mrs Tiramaki, who had lately got into the habit of clicking her tongue with disapproval each time she encountered her, and Eklund, who kept comparing her to his wife – Mrs Eklund this, and Mrs Eklund that, as if she was a template for all women. Hella had to recognize that he was not alone in his admiration. In this town the exotic Mrs Eklund, with her pitch-black hair (which Hella supposed was straight out of a tube), her long eyelashes and her tiny, upturned nose, was the beauty queen and the trendsetter. When last spring the local dressmaker had got his hands on a stock of crimson chiffon adorned with tiny black dots, the entire female population of Ivalo, from pimply teenagers to toothless matrons, had stormed the shop, ready to pay any price, and even sell their souls if need be, for a chance to wear a flamenco dress, one of Esmeralda's signature styles. Eklund, meaning well, had let Hella have the afternoon off that day. She'd never dared tell him that she had spent that time doing something she never had an opportunity to do when her landlady was present, which was just about always. Locked in her room, the radio set to full blast during *Steve's Music Hour*, she had danced away and cried her eyes out. The swollen eyes had come in useful when she presented herself at the police station the following day, pitifully reporting that the last piece of fabric had been sold to the woman in line just before her. That Hella would rather die than look like Esmeralda Eklund was beyond the chief inspector's imagination, and it was just as well. She had more of an incentive to make things work here than he did.

She cast her mind back to their last conversation, and once again she wondered why Eklund had decided to become a police officer. With his love of neatness and order, with his passion for regulations, he could have made a good accountant. Maybe even a corporate lawyer. But a policeman? Hadn't he had a choice in the matter? Or had young Lennart Eklund been different to the man he had become? She decided that one day she would ask him. Not directly, of course, but she would try to find a way. Even though it was possible that he himself had long since forgotten the answer, absorbed as he was in mountains of paperwork that created for him a comforting illusion of reality.

# 5

Jeremias Karppinen was the tiniest man Irja had ever seen. Which was just as well, because he was also the angriest. Just under five feet tall, wiry and cadaverous-looking, he was the embodiment of pure hatred. At first, she had thought she was provoking this reaction in him. She had wondered whether maybe he was against the Church or in conflict with religion. Or maybe he had his own reasons for hating women. Then she realized that it had nothing to do with her, or with women, or with the Church. It was just the way he was. She understood this the day she saw him drowning his dog's pups in the marsh. Here in the countryside, lots of people did it, out of necessity. But Jeremias Karppinen had taken pleasure in it. He had lingered next to the slowly sinking bag until it disappeared with a soft swish and the muffled sounds of crying puppies could no longer be heard. Then he had walked away, slowly, a large smile spreading across his tiny face.

Now he was sitting opposite her at the kitchen table, his fingers curved like claws around a glass that he had picked up without asking. His nails were black and split.

"Do you have any grog?" he asked her casually, extending the glass towards her.

"I'm sorry, I don't." Irja averted her eyes, afraid he would read her like an open book. *For you*, she wanted to say, I do not have any grog *for you*. He was aggressive enough already; drunk, he would become violent. She noticed that Kalle had disappeared as soon as he had heard Karppinen's deep barking, so incongruous in a man his size. Irja supposed Kalle had climbed on top of the Russian stove, even though the flowery curtains that hid the makeshift bed above the stove were not moving. If Kalle was indeed hidden there, he was lying perfectly still.

"Or dumplings?" Karppinen cast an exaggerated glance towards the stove, the open door of which revealed a cooking pot.

"I'm afraid it's a bit early for dinner," said Irja drily. To her, the Christian tradition of hospitality had its limits, and Jeremias Karppinen was definitely on the other side of that division. "Did you come to inquire about Kalle's well-being?"

Which was a polite way of asking if he had come to snoop around. That was what most villagers did. They dropped by under the pretence of asking how the boy was faring, but all they really wanted to know was gossip. Was it really possible for no one to have any information about old Erno's disappearance? And when were the police coming? And how come her husband, Timo, who had been out and about searching for the old man, had still not found anything?

Some people, a minority, did come with good intentions. They brought her pierogies, jars of home-made lingonberry jam, and warm clothes for Kalle. The men accompanied Timo in his search. The women sat next to Kalle, caressing his hair, telling him everything was going to be all right. Yes, there were good people in the village. But Jeremias

Karppinen was not one of them, and Irja doubted very much that he had come to offer his help.

"I came to offer my help," proclaimed the little man sententiously, but just as Irja was starting to wonder if she had been wrong about him, he spoke again, shattering her illusions. "I have decided that I will buy the house."

He smiled, baring his sharp white teeth, triangular like those of a cat, and waited for her answer. A tiny, muffled sound came from the bed above the stove.

"I beg your pardon?" Irja was not sure she had heard him correctly. "What house?"

"The boy's house," explained Karppinen, his eyes greedy and excited. He was starting to lose his patience. "The boy doesn't need it; he can live with you. So I'm offering to buy the house." He fumbled in the breast pocket of his green army shirt, then pulled out several crumpled banknotes. Six hundred markka. The price of six and a half pounds of fresh fish at Ivalo's market.

Karppinen pushed the money towards her. He was already rising from the bench.

"Deal's done, then," he said. "Your learned husband" – the words sounded like an insult in his mouth – "your learned husband can do the paperwork and bring the documents to me later. I trust you."

"Wait a minute!" Irja rose to her feet, breathless with anger. "There's no deal. I don't even understand what you're talking about. Please take your money back and just ... just go!"

She was much taller than Karppinen; it gave her an advantage. Since he made no move to take the money, she seized it, pressing it into a ball, and shoved it towards him.

"Please go now. It's not a good time to discuss that sort of thing."

Karppinen stared at her in disbelief.

"You bitch! And I thought you were a lady ..." The little man was livid with rage. "You'll regret this! You'll come crawling back to me, licking my boots, asking me to take that house off your hands. Now that old Erno's dead ..."

"He's not dead," cried out Irja indignantly. She was thinking about the little boy, perched above the stove, listening to their conversation. "Erno's not dead," she repeated again in a small voice, tears swelling in her eyes. To hell with her education. She tried to remember the exact intonation village women had when they argued with each other, but could only come up with a weak, "You're talking nonsense. Get out of here!"

Karppinen bared his teeth again, and instinctively Irja recoiled. Out of the corner of her eye, she saw the familiar glint of the samovar. She could use it as a weapon against Karppinen if he became violent. But the little man must have noticed her glance and drawn all the right conclusions. He turned towards the door.

"You'll regret this," he said quietly, looking down on her, which, for a man of his size, was quite a feat. "When you know what *I* know, you will come to me, begging, but it'll be too late. I offered you honest money." He pushed the door, letting in a gust of icy air.

"Too late," he repeated, and then he was gone.

# 6

It was a bumpy road, and every once in a while Hella was thrown out of her seat and against Kukoyakka. Each time she composed herself immediately, but the man kept grinning, as if suspecting her of falling into his arms on purpose.

"Not the kind of roads you had in Helsinki, huh?" He half-turned towards her, even though he could hardly see her. Where his right eye had once been, the skin was sewn over an empty socket, the stitches extending downwards like eyelashes.

"How long before we reach Käärmela?"

She had got into the Sisu at the very last moment, when the engine was already running and the large wooden gates that protected the factory's yard stood open. Hella had never seen a truck that big; the front wheel reached as high as her shoulder. She had to use a ladder to climb into the cabin, and she congratulated herself on her choice of bag. She'd rather die than ask Kukoyakka for help heaving a suitcase into the cabin. With the backpack, she could just about manage.

"The roads are bad because of the logging trucks," he said, as if he hadn't heard her. "Trucks are heavy even when they're empty; but when they're loaded with tree trunks, their weight breaks the road." He paused, his left hand on the steering wheel, the right one resting dangerously close to her thigh. A Grundig radio was sitting on the dashboard; Hella resisted the temptation to turn it on.

"Ever been to this part of the country?" Kukoyakka said.

"No. Yes. Just once, when I was chasing that man who stole from the factory safe."

"Ah, Laukkonen?" he chuckled. "You didn't catch him, though, did you? He went to stay with his stepbrother, up north."

Hella turned to stare out of the window. Helsinki was beautiful at this time of year, tree crowns like liquid gold scattered with glimpses of red, and a mellowness in the air that smelled of candied apples and mulled wine. But here … The trees were grey, all their leaves gone in one night, their naked branches twisted at odd angles. The damp soil, from which the grass had gone a long time ago, was like a fresh grave waiting for new victims to swallow. The locals seemed to find it beautiful. It was their land, after all. Soon the first snow would fall, covering the low branches like a shroud, bringing them to the ground in an ever-repeating act of submission. Snow would be everywhere, ten or twelve feet deep, and it would stay that way until the end of April, maybe even later.

That land, and that snow, were the reasons she hadn't caught the factory thief. She had done a good job, guessing which of the tight-lipped factory workers was guilty of the crime; but then, before she could arrest him, the man had run away. She had chased him relentlessly, following the traces his skis had left in the powdery October snow, but the man was a better skier than she, and he knew the countryside. After two days of incessant pursuit, dead tired, her feet like two pieces of raw meat, she'd had to recognize that she was not able to continue any longer. She had hoped that Eklund would send a patrol to where the man was rumoured to be staying, in a small village beyond the polar circle. He never did. To him, it was an unjustifiable use of administrative and operational resources. As he pointed out to Hella, the money had probably already been spent, or else would never be found, buried deep under some tree unremarkable to a stranger's eye. So what was the sense in pursuing it? The case had been closed, successfully solved. The fact that the criminal was never brought to trial was of minor importance. "What about justice?" Hella had cried, who, at that time, still believed Chief Inspector Eklund could be reasoned with.

"Justice?" He had laughed out loud. "My dear girl, justice in a cold climate is not a natural phenomenon. Snow is. That's something that influences our work more than any idea of justice does."

Since then, she had come to realize that the working methods she had acquired during her days in Helsinki didn't apply in Lapland. To start with, there was almost no technical support – no fingerprinting, no lab technicians in white coats, no staff photographer. The sole autopsy she had seen in two years in Ivalo had been performed by Dr Gummerus, who had his practice on the town's main street and who was at least ninety, by the look of him. Dr Gummerus had cut open the victim's ribcage, peered inside and waved a dismissive hand at her.

"Drowned. Drank too much. It wasn't even necessary to open him up; it was sufficient just to look at him."

"But what if he didn't accidentally drown? What if he was drowned?"

"How would I know?" the man had asked, looking at her in mild surprise.

She had never bothered him again.

"What are you thinking about, beautiful?"

Kukoyakka's hand had crawled still closer to her thigh.

"I'm a police officer on duty," she muttered through her clenched teeth. "And you're driving the truck. Your hand belongs on the steering wheel."

"What hand?"

But he did pull it back a little, and started humming.

*Damn,* thought Hella. And they were only three miles into the forest. This was not getting off to a good start. She needed to get him thinking about something else, to change the subject. Hella had decided before leaving that it was vital to keep him on her side, even if that meant smiling at him when all she wanted was to slap him. Without Kukoyakka and his truck, how would she ever get to that damn village?

"Do you know the place we're going?" she asked him. "Why is it called Käärmela – the snake place? I didn't think there could be many snakes up north."

He remained silent for a few seconds, probably trying to make up his mind about her. Or maybe just pondering the question. He was a slow man.

"Yes, I've been there a couple of times. One of my cousins lives there. Also a man who works at the logging station with me, cutting wood. Kai. He comes over from the village twice a week. But I don't know about the snakes. I've never seen any."

"What's it like?"

"The village? Weird. Like an island."

"An island?"

It was not the sort of answer she had expected, not from Kukoyakka.

"In a sea of ice," he explained, and all but blushed. "I mean, just imagine living in a place that's cut off from the rest of the world for eight months every year. Snow that goes up to your roof, or even higher. Night all day long. We have it in Ivalo too, but it's not the same. In Käärmela, they've got no bars, no shops, just a bunch of Sami, most of them old, and a church. Exactly the stuff you need to go off your rocker."

"What do people live off?"

"The usual stuff. Hunting, fishing, tending to reindeer. Quilting and making rugs. Whatever. In the winter, when they need to buy something, they go across the border, to where the Soviets are. To Svetly. It's just closer. They've always lived like that. As I said, it's mostly like an island. I grew up in a village like that, but I left when I was fifteen. Couldn't stay there a day longer."

He shook his head, as if disapproving of people who did stay a day beyond their fifteenth birthday in those far-removed places that had no bars. Hella shivered. It was getting cold in the cabin, but she didn't think that was the real reason. Suddenly, she wondered if she was being over-confident in presuming she could solve a crime for which she had no corpse and no support from her boss. And Lapland was a strange country. It was nothing like southern Finland, where she had grown up, even though the south had its identity problems too. But here! Part of the Swedish realm until the early nineteenth century, Lapland had become Oulu Province, then the Grand Duchy, an inheritance of the King of Finland, before changing its name again to Lapland Province less than twenty years ago. And this was before the Interim Peace, and the Continuation War, and Operation Barbarossa and the Nazi occupation. Hella had heard that a large part of the population had been evacuated while the Nazis, enjoying their Lapland War to their heart's content, had scorched the earth and blown up the roads and bridges. Ivalo itself had been burned almost to the ground, and each time she gave her last name, which was decidedly ill-suited to this part of the country, people stared at her in apprehension, reliving in their minds the atrocities of the war, trying to guess her links with their former occupant. And she couldn't very well keep telling each and every one of them that her name was just a relic of a long-gone past, that she felt Finnish to the bone, that her parents had been real Finnish patriots who had fought the Nazis and the Soviets alike. That she had been brought up on a diet of the *Kalevala*.

Yes, it was not at all certain that she would be welcomed. And did she really have to stay at the priest's house? Couldn't she find other accommodation? Not a hotel, she knew perfectly well that places like Käärmela had no hotels, but maybe the mayor's house, if there was a mayor? Probably not. She supposed Eklund would have told her.

She turned her head to look at Kukoyakka. He seemed to be concentrating on the road, even though she couldn't see his left eye. With his black, bushy hair, still thick for a man his age, he made her think of the Green Man, Tapio, the god of the forest who adorned Lapland's coat of arms. Tapio was a huge, Neanderthal-like creature wielding a club, clad in only a green loincloth and a matching turban, with a beard of lichen and eyebrows of moss, and as a child, Hella had been terrified of him.

Suddenly weary, she shut her eyes and thought about Steve, about his lean body and his sexy voice. After all this time, she still missed him so much the pain felt physical. A song Steve liked to put on the air for his audience came to her mind. It was sung by Frank Sinatra – not one of her favourites; she liked Perry Como better, or Bing Crosby – but this one song was so true, it cut like a knife.

> I'd tried so not to give in
> I said to myself this affair never will go so well
> But why should I try to resist when baby I know so well
> I've got you under my skin.

# 7

"When do you think the police will come?" asked Kalle in a small voice.

Irja stopped mid-movement. She was chopping vegetables for the borscht. Ruby-red cubes of beetroot were scattered over the cutting board, while a bunch of yellowish carrots awaited their turn. Putting down the knife, Irja pushed a strand of hair behind her ear with the back of her hand. She leaned close to the boy.

"Any time now, Kalle."

Then she remembered it was the same answer she had used to convince Kalle that his grandpa would be back soon. She added hastily: "They're probably packing their equipment. Do you know how much equipment a police officer needs? A lot!"

Kalle stared at her, frowning. The shadows cast by the paraffin lamp creased his tiny features, and for a split second she recognized old Erno in him. His eyes were black marbles, drowned in ice water. It was the first time he had spoken to her, or to anyone, since he had been brought to her house five days earlier. She needed to say the right thing. To establish a dialogue, to not scare him off, but also not to make empty promises.

Troubled, she picked up the knife again and started chopping the carrots, quickly. Her hair fell forward again, covering her face. *I need to cut the onions next,* she thought. Their pungent smell would provide an explanation for her tears.

She had made a mistake in admitting to Kalle that she had written to the police. It had now been three days since Timo had left the letter propped on the letter box four miles from the village, on the road leading from Nellim to Ivalo. When Timo had checked the next day, the letter had gone. Presumably one of the truck drivers had taken it, and delivered it to its destination. But then what?

Irja had no idea whether the Ivalo police would even agree to take on the case. She had only ever seen one of them, several months ago, when she had travelled to Ivalo to report a wife-beater. Before going to the authorities, she and Timo had tried to settle the issue by themselves. The man, a calm, middle-aged former schoolteacher, was courteous to a fault to strangers. It was just that his wife had, according to him, a despicable habit of bumping into things and being careless with lit cigarettes. He had listened to Timo with his head cocked to one side, and denied all involvement. The next day, the wife had four of her teeth knocked out, reportedly in another one of her unfortunate accidents.

Irja had talked to the woman, offering her refuge at their house, telling her over and over that what her husband was doing was not right, that he needed to be stopped. When their joint efforts yielded no result, Irja had travelled to Ivalo, full of hope that the police would know how to handle the situation.

After a long wait, she had been received by an Inspector Ranta. She took an immediate dislike to the man. He never once looked her in the eye. His gaze settled on her breasts, and it was them he addressed when she had finished explaining the case to him.

"Is that any of your business?" he asked her.

"It is." She clenched her fists, willing herself to remain calm. "I can't just sit around waiting until that man kills her."

"You're a priest's wife, aren't you? Why don't you pray for her?"

"I do."

"Then why isn't your God doing anything? Why do you expect us to be more diligent than the Almighty?" He smiled, pleased with his joke, baring a row of crooked yellowish stubs. "Yes, why don't you ask Him, and leave us to do our work as we see fit?"

"I'd like to see Chief Inspector Eklund," Irja replied.

But Chief Inspector Eklund was in a meeting. A meeting that, according to Inspector Ranta's sneering comment, was likely to last for at least a couple of hours.

"Never mind," said Irja. "I'll wait."

And so she waited and waited, unsure of what to do, sitting next to a pretty blonde girl, a secretary or a receptionist, who gave her one dismissive look and went back to polishing her nails. As the day dragged on, it appeared likely, then certain, that Chief Inspector Eklund had no intention of seeing her. She hung on in the reception area until the blonde girl started to turn off the lights, explaining that Chief Inspector Eklund had already left via a back door.

It was Irja's first – and last – encounter with the police, and therefore she didn't expect much of them. She had only written to Ivalo because she needed to do something, because she had to busy herself until Timo came back from the church and set up a search party.

Irja didn't think Kalle had heard her talking about it. But she was wrong.

She slid the carrot cubes into the pot, then looked up. Kalle was gazing at her wide-eyed.

"What kind of equipment?"

Images of Sherlock Holmes popped, unbidden, into her brain. Unable to think clearly, Irja muttered, "A magnifying glass. And special powder for fingerprints. And, and … books on criminalistics."

"And police dogs," he added.

"Of course," chirped Irja, fingers crossed behind her back. "They've probably already started their inquiry. Sometimes they prefer to make up their own minds before questioning witnesses."

Kalle turned to stare out of the window, a slow smile spreading across his face.

"They'll bring Grandpa back in no time."

It wasn't a reproach; but still, Irja took it like one. She bit her lips and busied herself with the borscht. The room was quiet, its silence only troubled by the loud ticking of an old clock and the chopping noise made by her own knife.

*If ever the police come,* she thought. That would be a miracle. And now Kalle was waiting for them. If only Timo was here! But she barely saw him these days. When he was not searching for old Erno, he was engrossed in church work, serving Mass, receiving the parishioners and painstakingly restoring the fabulous church icons he claimed were so precious. She understood. Of course she did. But it still hurt, feeling so alone.

Kalle shuffled on his bench, his nose pressed against the window. "I think someone's coming. Can you see? There's a shadow there, by the church. It's moving. It's not Father Timo; he balances his arms as he moves. This one's carrying something."

Irja leaned towards the window. Kalle was right. There was someone out there, barely visible in the faltering daylight. As the shadow progressed towards them, Irja made out a tall angular figure, dressed in a parka, a shaggy *chapka* hiding its face, a bulky bag worn on its back. After getting to the corner of the church, the figure stopped for a second, hesitating.

Then it strode towards their house.

"It's a woman," whispered Kalle in disbelief.

# 8

Some things looked exactly like Hella had imagined them. There were ornate window frames, and cornices, and wooden benches by the doors. There was smoke coming out of chimneys and frozen vegetable patches on which decrepit scarecrows sat looking down at birds they no longer frightened away. There were furtive glances and moving curtains which accompanied her progression through the village. There was a church, a wooden thing with a blue onion-shaped dome and a cross to top it off, but she didn't stop to look at it. Contrary to what she had told her boss, she was not interested in architecture, traditional or otherwise.

And then there was the house next to the church, and the woman who had opened the front door just as Hella was extending her hand to knock. Next to the woman, clinging to her leg, stood a young boy, barely six or seven. At first, Hella thought they were mother and son. They had the same milk-white skin, and the same bouncy, reddish-blonde hair. They also had the same look in their eyes, that of incredulity mingled with disappointment. Then the woman extended her hand, smiling bravely, and dispelled the misunderstanding.

"I'm Irja Waltari, and this is Kalle Jokinen, Erno's grandson. Please come in. Did you have a good trip? You must be so tired!"

*She's not asking me who I am,* thought Hella. *Which probably means that it's obvious I belong to the forces of law and order, regardless of the civilian clothes. Or else no one ever comes to this godforsaken village.*

She wiped her feet on a striped cotton mat and followed the gentle priest's wife through a narrow corridor crammed with skis and anoraks into a wood-clad, honey-coloured living room that smelled of coffee and cinnamon. As soon as they were inside, the little boy let go of the woman's leg and scarpered off to climb on top of a great whitewashed Russian stove that occupied the centre of the room.

There was a scattering of onion skins and carrot peel on the wooden table. Irja Waltari rushed to clear away the mess, before inviting Hella to take a seat at the table.

"I'm Sergeant Mauzer," started Hella, hoping that her low voice and her rank would make a good impression if not on the priest's wife, then at least on the boy who was watching her unblinkingly from his bed above the stove. "I've come from Ivalo police station to investigate the mysterious disappearance of Erno Jokinen."

*Why am I talking like Eklund now?* she wondered. Was it because she felt awkward? Did she really need to impress them that much? Or was it because she was afraid they would question her authority, or her skill, because she was a woman? Would she have reacted differently if the kindly young woman sitting in front of her had looked less maternal, more professional, more like herself? Unable to stop, she went on in a hectoring voice:

"I presume you have reasons to believe that police intervention is necessary? Have you organized a search party yet?"

Irja Waltari blinked, surprised. Hella was clearly not what she had expected.

"Mrs Waltari?"

The young woman nodded silently and turned away, rearranging her skirt, averting her eyes. She had full breasts and glowing skin. She looked like – she looked like Elsbeth, only more luminous. Steve would have loved her.

"Yes, we have. My husband, Timo, and five other men from the village have been combing through the forest. They haven't found anything … yet."

And they probably never would, thought Hella. Unless they knew where the old man was heading when he disappeared. And even then, it was not like there were roads in this part of the country. Just a sparse forest that spread in every direction. You had to be very lucky to find *anything.*

The more she thought about it, the more the idea of an investigation seemed ridiculous to her. Eklund was right. Investigate *what,* for God's sake? For all she knew, the man might not even be dead. Still, here she was, so she might as well do *something.* The little boy was staring at her from the stove. How could she question the woman in his presence?

"Is there a place we could talk in private?"

Irja Waltari jumped to her feet. "Would you like me to show you your room?"

Hella's mood lightened a little. At least she would have her own room. And the house was quiet. Now that she thought of it, she didn't see any small children running around. Was it just the Waltaris and the boy who lived here? Where was the priest? Still searching the forest with his loyal parishioners?

She rose to her feet and followed Irja Waltari out of the room. It wasn't apparent from the outside, but the house was huge. The narrow corridor leading to the bedrooms was at least thirty feet long, with doors on either side. Hella caught a glimpse of the master bedroom – a gleaming copper bed with a lovely patchwork blanket, snow-white pillows, a crucifix on the wall, a candle burning before an icon. These people were living a sheltered life. Murder – if there had been a murder – must be a novelty for them.

She tried to remember the words of Irja Waltari's letter. *A respectable, dependable man ... unexpected departure ... a child left alone ... completely out of character ... It has been six days, and we still have no news.*

The priest's wife was opening the last door on the left. The farthest one from the living room. Very considerate of her. Mrs Waltari's breasts were big, much bigger than Hella's, who had nothing to be particularly proud of in that department, but her waist was not that thin, even if her shapeless green dress and striped apron disguised that fact. Hella raised her chin. She had nothing to be ashamed of. This woman might look like Elsbeth, but she was just an uneducated priest's wife from Käärmela, Lapland.

The room was panelled in pine, like the rest of the house. Another gleaming copper bed. A hand-knitted throw in pink wool. A worn-out pink quilt. A tall pine wardrobe, not a plain one like she had in Ivalo, but varnished and ornately carved. She would have almost nothing to put in it. A shelf for each piece of clothing. She hoped she wouldn't have to stay for too long.

She turned towards the window. A scattering of violets on the curtains, in total disregard for the frozen land outside. The room overlooked a meadow and in the summer, the view must be lovely.

"I'm so glad you came," said Irja Waltari. "We were all hoping someone would. Even though I understand the case might not be a priority for you."

Hella nodded. This woman didn't need to know that it

had indeed not been a priority for Chief Inspector Eklund. Still, Hella enjoyed this indirect recognition of her efforts, even coming from someone who looked like Elsbeth Collins.

"I'll do what I can," she said simply. "You wrote your letter on Friday, right? And since then? No news?"

"No. I've asked everyone I can think of, but nobody knows where Erno was off to. His neighbour, Mr Karppinen – I expect you'll want to meet him – told me Erno was heading east, so that's the direction Timo and his friends have been exploring, but that's about it." She hesitated. "The fact that he's been missing for so long … does it mean anything?"

The priest's wife was asking her whether she thought the man was dead. But how would she know? They teach you at the police academy that if a person has been missing for more than forty-eight hours – and they mean a criminal disappearance, like a victim being led away at gunpoint – then that person is probably dead. But they don't teach you about Lapland, where normal rules don't apply. She thought about what Eklund had said, that the man had probably got lost, or somehow drowned, or gone over the Soviet border, got drunk on vodka and was now lying in a ditch somewhere. Except that, at this time of the year, the ditches were frozen. And if he had been taken by the Soviet forces to sober up in jail, they would have realized by now that he was a Finnish citizen and sent him back. She had heard that the Soviets were tolerant of old Finnish folks crossing the border to do some grocery shopping, as long as they kept quiet and went back to where they came from as soon as possible. They wouldn't have tolerated anyone staying for *that* long.

Irja was looking at her expectantly.

"I don't know," lied Hella. "It's not unusual. Does he" – she almost said "did he", but caught herself in time – "does he have any family in the region? Other than the boy?"

"He has a sister who lives in the village. Her name is Martta – Martta Jokinen. She never married. He had a brother, too, and another sister, but I believe they're both dead."

"If he has a great-aunt in the village, why is the boy – Kalle – not staying with her?"

Irja Waltari hesitated.

"Martta is not … maternal. She's very nice but a bit … peculiar. Also, she has this habit of … collecting things. She's a bit of a hoarder."

So this is how the priest's wife divided her world. On one side, the good, decent, maternal types, to which she so obviously belonged. On the other, the loners, the eccentric ones, the I-don't-know-what-to-do-with-a-child types. As if being maternal was just something you were born with, like blue eyes.

"I'll need to see Miss Jokinen. Tomorrow. And that other man you mentioned, the neighbour."

"Mr Karppinen?"

"Exactly. But now I'd like to see the house where Erno Jokinen lived with his grandson."

"Now?" exclaimed the priest's wife, appalled. "Really? Do you have to? It's getting late."

It *was* late. Hella could barely make out the shapes of things outside. And she was exhausted from her journey. As they reached the Käärmela junction, Kukoyakka had again tried his hand-on-thigh manoeuvre. She had pushed him away, her patience worn thin, and as a consequence had been left at the side of the road and forced to finish her journey on foot while Kukoyakka's truck made a U-turn, roaring towards the logging camp and its makeshift bar. Still, she couldn't really back down at this point. Even if it was more than likely that she wouldn't be able to see a thing.

"Yes, now."

Irja Waltari sighed and, without a word, led her back into the living room. It was the boy she was worried about.

"Kalle, can you stay here alone for a little while? Father Timo will be back from his search any minute now, and Seamus will keep you company."

The boy nodded silently. If only he would cry, thought Hella. Cry out his anger and fear, kick and bite the adults around him, break something. That would make him feel better. But the child didn't move, didn't say anything. *He's like me,* thought Hella. *He keeps everything to himself, but one day he won't be able to any longer. On that day, he'll explode in an outburst of uncontrollable violence.*

A sleek beige and grey cat, probably a Siamese, wormed its way between Irja's legs and stopped, purring, next to the child. Suddenly, Kalle grabbed the cat, burying his face in its fur, holding it tight, his hands white-knuckled. Still holding the cat, he ran from the room and slammed the door behind him.

"Let's go," sighed Irja again. "I'll show you the way."

She wrapped herself tightly in a shawl and slid her feet into felt boots, the kind everyone wore in the countryside. Then she picked up a paraffin lamp and a box of matches.

"It's a thirty-minute walk," she said. "Are you quite sure you don't want to eat something before we go?"

*I hear she's a great cook,* Eklund had said. Ridiculously house-proud, a perfect woman, feminine, long hair gathered in a heavy braid, huge blue eyes and porcelain skin. Was she the one who'd made all those patchwork cushions, too? Father Timo was a lucky man. Hella wondered what he was like. All Orthodox priests she had seen before had dark tangled beards, bulging eyes and no sense of humour. She wasn't particularly eager to meet him. And what was she supposed to call him? "Father" was out of the question; she was not a member of his flock, and never would be. Sir? Timo? The first was too formal, the last not formal enough. She decided she would settle for Mr Waltari. Neutral. Unquestionable. And his wife would be Mrs Waltari.

"Let's just go."

The priest's wife turned obediently towards the door, but at that very same moment they heard voices outside. Male voices, speaking in low tones; she couldn't make out the words. Pushing past her hostess, Hella ran for the door and heaved it open. A young man stood on the porch, a group of five or six others pressed behind him. He had a beard all right, but apart from that he didn't look anything like a priest, unless priests could be athletic and handsome and blond. She couldn't see the cassock, either; he was dressed in a parka, just like everyone else. But of course; he'd just come back from his search. The man looked at her in surprise.

Irja Waltari, who suddenly materialized by her side, extended a hand to him.

"This is Sergeant Mauzer, Timo. She's come all the way from Ivalo. We were just about to go to Erno's house. The borscht is ready, and there's enough for all of you. Why don't you come in?"

Hella thought she could guess what he was going to say. The man was shivering, and under his tan his skin was deathly pale. He was in a state of shock. She read in his eyes a mixture of appeal and another, more basic emotion.

"We found a body," he said finally. "Parts of it."

As Hella's brain struggled to register this information, she looked at him again, at the dark hollows of his eyes and the narrow line of his lips. With a sinking feeling she realized that the other emotion was fear.

# 9

Feeling curiously devoid of emotion, Hella ran down the steps to where a canvas sack stood on the frozen earth, a dark brown stain spread across it like some exotic flower. She motioned towards it.

"Is it inside?"

"An arm," said the priest. "And part of a ribcage. All bloodied and soiled." He paused. "We'll put the remains in the shed, if that's OK with you."

Hella looked over his shoulder, at the old wooden shed that leaned against one side of the house. "Yes, please do. It's so cold now, I suppose we can keep the remains in there. I'm going to need a bucket of water, a towel and a lamp."

The rest of the men that composed the search party stared at her for a long time.

"You heard me," she said quietly. "I need to examine the remains."

One of the villagers, a gangly youth with crooked teeth and a failed attempt at a moustache, ran up the steps. The others followed him inside, casting disdainful glances at Hella. Only the priest stayed at her side. He opened the door of the shed and put the sack on the workbench.

"Where did you find him?" asked Hella. The darkness enveloped them like a shroud.

"Not very far from here. Maybe an hour. East."

"Animals?"

"I suppose so."

Then it was an accident, thought Hella. The old man must have had a heart attack or something, and the animals had attacked him. Wolves. Or bears. She pulled open the string that tied the sack. Father Timo stepped forward.

*He's a gentleman,* thought Hella. *He's probably afraid I'll faint. Ready to catch me.*

A trembling halo of light appeared on the front steps. The young man with the crooked teeth was back, holding a paraffin lamp. Irja Waltari was following him. She carried an enamel bucket.

Father Timo rushed towards them. He didn't want his wife to see this. She heard them talking in low voices, but couldn't catch a single word.

Soon, the priest was back. The lamplight trembled, then settled in a circle. She could start working. The priest was hovering at the door, not knowing whether he should stay and assist her.

"Thank you. You can go back inside now. Will you tell the boy?"

"Yes, I will. He saw us arrive. It's best that he knows."

Hella nodded. No point in hiding the truth.

She waited until the priest was inside the house, then gently folded the fabric back on itself. Her eyes fell on what remained of a ribcage. It must have been a bear, she thought. A hungry one. Almost no flesh left. She counted six ribs on the right side, five on the left; the rest must have been chewed off. The sharp edges of the bones stuck out in all directions, only held together by the sternum. She steadied herself by leaning on the bench, closed her eyes. *I'm sorry, Kalle,* she thought. It was a platitude, but sometimes platitudes were right on the mark. *I am sorry for your loss.* She didn't know about the good people of Käärmela – whether they had lost a brother, a neighbour, a friend – but Kalle had lost his only family. From now on, he would grow up with a shadow at his side.

Now that the priest was gone, she desperately wanted him to be back. Not to be alone, here, in the dark. *Calm down, you idiot,* she told herself. *It's just flesh and bone. Nothing else. You're not afraid of it, are you?* She bit her lip and peered closer at the ribcage. No man-made wounds. A bear. She was not afraid. She wrapped the towel around her hand, took the ribcage out and placed it on a shelf.

The arm now. It was in better condition, but thoroughly soiled, as if the animal had dragged it through the mud. She held it above the bucket and rinsed it, sluicing water over it with her left hand. After a few minutes, when her hand was numb with cold, she peered more closely at it. Still some skin left, and even threads from a light-coloured sweater. A strange arm, actually. The skin was white. No hairs. Hella's heart missed a beat. She looked away, at the lighted windows of the house, saw Irja Waltari moving inside. Serving dinner. She forced herself to look at the arm again. The little finger was still there, dangling from a scrap of skin. She turned the arm over. Erno is a short man, Irja had said. Short and fine-boned. Hella lifted the lamp and brought it closer to the arm. The nail on the little finger was pink and polished. Moving slowly, she wiped her hands on the towel, picked up the lamp and left the shed, closing the door behind her.

The conversation died as she entered the living room. The men were eating. There were mountains of food on the table: Karelian pierogi pie with egg butter spread on top, herring-filled *kalakukko* slices, rye bread and *korvapuusti* cinnamon buns. And the borscht, obviously. Enough to feed an army. Irja Waltari was nowhere to be seen.

Hella continued until she reached the master bedroom. The priest's wife was in there, consoling Kalle. The boy froze when he saw her, his eyes huge, holding his breath. So they'd told him already that the old man was dead. She supposed they had rolled out the usual nonsense about the eternal life, and the resurrection of the dead, and a God's will that doesn't need to be explained, only accepted. About forgiveness, and turning the other cheek. There was no colour in the boy's face. The creases on his cheeks grew deeper, as if he was mimicking the old man's face in a last desperate effort to retain his grandfather.

Hella returned to the living room. "Which one of you knew him best?" she asked the men. Everyone's gaze turned to the priest. "Could you please follow me outside?" she said.

As soon as they were out of the room, she stopped. No sound was coming from the house. They were all sitting there, trying to eavesdrop. Keeping her voice to a whisper, she said, "I need you to look at this arm you found. Looks strange to me, but I didn't know the man. You did."

They went into the shed again. Hella held the light above the cleansed remains. "Pink polished nails," she said. "Didn't he work the land?"

Father Timo was staring at her. His Adam's apple went up, and stayed up while he tried to swallow the lump in his throat. "You're right," he said finally. "It's not his arm. It belongs to a woman, doesn't it?"

Hella nodded. There was nothing to be said. If he knew about a missing woman, from this village or one of the neighbouring ones, he would have told her. And this was no peasant woman, either. She would write to Eklund to check if someone had reported a woman missing after she had left that morning, but she could already guess what the answer would be. No. The woman had been dead for some days now. A week, maybe as much as ten days. She would join the ranks of unnamed victims who were regularly found in the forest and never claimed by anyone. Some death.

# 10

The pendulum clock ticked away seconds that transformed themselves into minutes before growing into hours. Her hands pressed on her stomach, Irja lay on her back, her eyes wide open, unable to sleep. It was still dark, but soon the cockerels would cry out in enthusiasm and welcome another grey Lapland morning. In the meantime, she would need to get up and cook breakfast for Timo and Kalle and Sergeant Mauzer.

She had put the sergeant to sleep in one of the many spare rooms. She had also given her a white bathrobe and felt slippers with pompoms, but now she was wondering if the sergeant would really wear these when she got up.

Irja thought about the day that lay ahead. Before going to sleep, Sergeant Mauzer had written a report to be sent to Chief Inspector Lennart Eklund at the police station in Ivalo. Irja had been instructed to find someone to deliver it to the postbox on the Rajajoosepintie road. From what she understood, Sergeant Mauzer intended to spend the next day searching the part of the forest where that poor woman's remains had been found. It had been an accident, the sergeant had said. The woman had been attacked by a bear. She seemed to believe that explained Erno's disappearance too, but Irja had her doubts about that. Erno was fit for his age. He never went into the forest without his rifle. Irja had said as much to Sergeant Mauzer, but was not certain the policewoman had accepted her arguments. The only witness Sergeant Mauzer wanted to question was Kalle. That was the last thing she had brought up before retiring to her room:

"You do know that I'll need to question the boy, don't you, Mrs Waltari?"

Irja, who was hoping very much that Kalle would be left in peace, acquiesced nervously. "If you absolutely have to —"

"Of course I do," snapped Sergeant Mauzer. She didn't add *you stupid woman*, but the message was clear. *Mind your own business. Don't be a nuisance.*

Irja, who at first had thought that Sergeant Mauzer was a sort of *polissyster*, had to admit that nothing could be further from the truth. Sergeant Mauzer had no experience of children whatsoever. This was obvious. She'd probably be more comfortable running around in the woods after a murder suspect than talking to a child. But apparently the *polissyster*s, whose role it was to deal only with women and children, were a thing of the past. They had female detectives now. And not only in Helsinki: they had them in Ivalo, too. It was amazing, when one thought about it. A recognition that women were as good as men, equally competent, even if they didn't wave their guns around as much. And even though the sergeant was unfriendly, what a change from Inspector Ranta! The woman was not a bureaucrat like her colleagues. What bureaucrat would have travelled forty miles, part of it on foot, just because a priest's wife was worried sick about someone's disappearance?

*It is a pity she doesn't like me*, thought Irja. *She must take me for a boring, dutiful wife with no interests, no personality. All ritual and no substance.* And who could blame her? That's what she looked like, after all. And with Timo's vocation, with their way of life, she couldn't even paint any more. The villagers would probably drop dead in horror if they saw her work. Never mind. Now she had Kalle to look after. Until he was taken away. This was another thing she needed to ask the sergeant, because she couldn't think of anyone else who could answer that question. Did Kalle have to go and live with his great-aunt Martta? She was his closest living relation, as far as Irja knew, but that didn't make her the most suitable one.

"I hope you sleep well," Irja had said to Sergeant Mauzer's retreating back. "What would you like for breakfast?"

"I'll eat what you make. Whatever. I don't care much about food." The door had slammed behind her.

Suddenly, Irja thought of something. She quite liked Sergeant Mauzer, but even so, she didn't want her to find certain things. Quietly, making sure the bed didn't squeak, she got up and tiptoed barefoot to the living room, where Kalle was asleep above the stove. She had tried to lure him to one of the nicer bedrooms, but he insisted on sleeping there. Holding her breath, Irja extended her hand towards the life-sized icon of Christ the Saviour and grabbed a little package stuck behind the frame, putting it into her pocket. Then she quietly made her way back into the bedroom, where finally she fell asleep.

# WEDNESDAY 15 OCTOBER

# 11

They set out at dawn, after a hearty breakfast that Hella devoured without talking to anyone and washed down with coffee. The priest's wife made it Lapland-style: green coffee beans were first fried in a pan, then ground in a coffee grinder, and finally boiled in a copper pot. The resulting beverage was surprisingly good, just like the rest of the breakfast. Three sorts of bread, cheese, two kinds of sausages. Russian *tvorog* cakes. Jam. Eggs. *Maybe the priest's wife cooked all this stuff for me,* she thought. *I have to find a way to tell her that I'm slim – angular – not because I'm malnourished, but because this is what my body's like.* Long, fine bones, and no fat. She could eat cream cakes all day long without the slightest effect. Flat-chested like a boy, her mother used to say. Nothing to flaunt. Christina had been better in this respect, a real woman, with a narrow waist and large breasts; all the boys Hella liked went after her sister. But she had never resented Christina's good looks. And she was not going to resent Irja Waltari either. The priest's wife was much too maternal, much too gentle and meek for her taste, but she was a good woman and she meant well. It was not her fault she looked like Elsbeth.

Outside, the day was still full of darkness. The sun had risen all right, its pale yellowish disc hovering just above the line of the horizon, but its rays seemed unable to pierce the thick fog that surrounded them like grey cotton wool. That was exactly the problem with Lapland. The gloom of the polar nights was compounded by fog. You almost never saw a clear sky.

The gangly youth from the previous evening – Kai, Hella had learned, Kukoyakka's friend who worked at the logging station – was already waiting for them outside, accompanied by two burly men who looked Hella up and down and turned away without saying a word. Father Timo made the introductions.

"Sergeant Mauzer is from Ivalo police station. She's come to investigate Erno's disappearance."

One of the men spat on the ground; the other turned his collar up, and started marching towards the forest.

The rest of the group followed him, a miserable procession surrounded by a colourless infinity. Only Kai stayed at her side. He wanted to talk.

"How come they sent you here?" he asked her. "Weren't there any men?"

"Why?" growled Hella. "I was part of the homicide squad in Helsinki before. I'm competent enough."

Kai looked at her, his eyes wide open in surprise, ignoring her question.

"If you were in Helsinki before, how come you work here now?"

"Liked the climate," explained Hella morosely, as little drops of melting snow started falling on them from a lead-coloured sky. They were close to the forest now. In grim silence, their hoods pulled low over their foreheads, they ventured into the trees. Not another word was exchanged until, an hour and a half later, a big grey rock came into view. It was shaped like a lion's head. Kai motioned to the right of it. "It was there. Three hundred yards down the slope. I went to find a spot to pee, and there it was. I almost stepped on that arm."

At the foot of the hill, they separated. The intention was to comb the area to see if other body parts could be found, something that would allow Hella to identify the dead woman. At first, Father Timo didn't want her to search alone, but Hella glared at him and he backed off. Gun out, safety off, she removed the trigger guard and started raking through the nettles. After a while, she heard a cry. One of the men had found two more fingers. They gathered around him, everyone waiting while Hella wrapped the fingers in paper and put them into her backpack before they resumed their search. After an hour, Hella's back was aching. Soon, she would have to call it off. No more discoveries for today. Go back to the village, warm up, then talk to the boy. If he didn't tell her anything interesting, she would leave tomorrow. She'd walk to the Rajajoosepintie road and wait till someone gave her a lift. Or she could —

"Here!" the priest cried out. Hella rushed towards him. He pointed to something lying under a bush. Hella had trouble making out what it was at first, until Kai, who had materialized at their side, pulled the branches back. It was a head. Much chewed upon, the eyes sucked out, but still unmistakably a head. A woman's head. Short blonde bob, good teeth. And a gaping bullet wound in the right temple.

"Have you seen her before?" asked Hella of no one in particular. No one had. Father Timo recited a prayer, his beautiful, well-modulated voice grave and sorrowful.

The Waltaris had coffee brewing at all hours. Hella held the mug close to her cheek, inhaling the aroma, trying to empty her mind, but the thoughts, confused and terrifying, kept coming back. She was feeling light-headed and at the same time crushed by so much responsibility. There was no doubt about it now. The woman had been murdered. She had a responsibility to solve it. Would she be able to? Would she even be able to find out who the woman was? And what about Erno Jokinen? Had he been murdered too? Or should she consider him a suspect? She briefly toyed with the idea of calling Eklund to rescue her, before deciding against it. From what she knew, Eklund had never solved a violent crime. He would be at a loss here. And there was one other reason. She didn't want him to think she was incapable of working on her own just because she was a woman. Sighing, she gulped down the rest of her coffee, refused Irja Waltari's offer of cinnamon buns and threw her parka over her shoulders. Back to the shed. The head was there, staring at the ceiling with its empty sockets. Once she was done with it, she would ask the priest to accompany her to Erno Jokinen's house.

Young Kai was standing by the gate, smoking. He didn't meet her gaze. Ignoring him, Hella pulled open the door of the shed and lit the paraffin lamp. *Who are you?* she asked the head silently. *We didn't find a ring finger, so we don't know if you're married. If you have children. If they are waiting for you.* The woman was middle-aged, judging by the texture of the remaining skin. The blonde hair had streaks of grey in it. Pity the ears had been chewed off. Ears were useful for identification purposes. With her gloved hand, Hella rolled the head gently to one side, inspecting the bullet wound. It had been made by a high-velocity handgun, not a rifle. That was strange. The locals usually went about with rifles.

Suddenly, Hella caught a glint of something between the woman's teeth. Holding her breath, she leaned in closer. Rigor mortis had passed long ago, and she had no trouble unclenching the jaw. There was a sliver of curved glass in the woman's mouth. Hella extracted it with trembling fingers and held it to the light. She could just about distinguish an inscription. Part of a word: LOROQ, whatever that meant. The curve of the glass itself made her think of a vial. Had it contained poison? Had the woman been forced to take it by her aggressor, or did she break it herself, afraid of being tortured? Hella shivered and closed her eyes. She had done this before. She could manage. She had been trained to solve violent crimes.

A smell of cigarette smoke hung in the air. Maybe it had been there the whole time, but she only noticed it now.

# 12

"My dear girl. A quick word with you, if I may."

The "dear girl" was Hella, in whose memory the scene was playing. The speaker was Jon Jokela, chief inspector in Helsinki's homicide squad.

They were standing outside a gloomy administrative building that harboured the police headquarters. Inspector Jokela was smoking. She was next to him, inhaling the smoke. She didn't dare show that the smoke bothered her, because she was still very young, fresh out of the police academy, and the first woman ever to be admitted to a homicide squad. Besides, she was lost in admiration for this man of great experience, a veteran of the war. She would have never dared say it to him, but he reminded her of her father. He even had the same bristly white hair, combed straight back, and the same military bearing.

"How are you feeling, Hella? Are you comfortable here? With the team, with the work we do?"

As they stood, a group of mostly young men in once white coats wheeled a succession of stretchers into the adjacent medical examiner's office. A stench of disinfectant, mingled with a sweeter, earthier smell, which Hella already recognized as that of recent murder, hit her nostrils. Jokela winced and pulled on his cigarette. The bodies belonged to a family, a mother and four children, ranging in age from two to twelve, all shot in their sleep, or so it seemed. Only one child, a three-year-old girl, had survived the massacre. She was being treated for her wounds in Lastenlinna children's hospital.

"Because it's not for everyone, you know," said Jokela and blew smoke away from Hella's face. "You need to learn how to detach yourself. How not to take things too personally."

Hella shivered in the cold November wind, wondering why her boss was saying this. Was it because her eyes had been wet when, as first officer on the scene, she had peered through the window of a suburban house and seen a little boy cuddled up with his knitted bunny in an armchair, a piece of raw meat mixed with greyish brain where his head had once been? Wasn't that a normal reaction?

"You should follow Mustonen's example," Jokela suggested gently. "Granted, he can be a brute sometimes, but he's a fine officer, organized, meticulous and with an excellent analytical mind. And at least when he goes home to his family in the evening, he's not haunted by visions of crime scenes. He has a normal life, which is something we should all aspire to. Because otherwise you don't last long in this profession. Do you know the story of my predecessor, Chief Inspector Korhonen?"

Hella did.

"Delirium tremens," said Jokela nonetheless. "And he was a good man, a splendid man. But he couldn't bear the pressure, day after day, year after year. The strain of the work, victims crying for justice, the responsibility he felt towards them ... To carry on living, he had to find an escape from his feelings. And so he did. Vodka became his best friend. At first it was only his problem, how he spent his evenings, what he did with his life. But when he started showing up at the station still half-drunk, his clothes crumpled because he had slept in them, his breath stinking like that of a goat, then it became everybody's problem. People didn't want to work with him any more. Officers didn't trust his judgement, because they knew his brain was clouded by alcohol. Victims' families shied away, thinking he was half-mad and as dangerous as the killers he was supposed to be chasing. It was a sad ending to an otherwise very promising career."

Hella nodded. She could understand his point, of course. No one wanted a doctor who was so hysterical about what had happened to you that he couldn't stitch up your wound. Detective work required emotional distance and steel nerves. But wasn't there a middle ground between the compassionate but ineffective amateurism Jokela had just described and the contemptuous indifference Officer Mustonen demonstrated at crime scenes? Wasn't their rigorous professionalism just a façade? She was too young to tell, and they never confided in her. After the day was over, they would all – Jokela included – gather for drinks in a bar on Ratakatu, while she would pack her bag and go to the sad spartan room she called home.

"Maybe you should take easier cases," suggested Jokela. "Or at least cases that don't involve ... families. Given your past."

"I can do this," she said, and looked straight up at him. She had been expecting this sort of reaction, because he knew all about her. He had even known her father. They hadn't been close friends, but they had met on several occasions. "It's very nice of you to be concerned with my well-being. I appreciate it. But I want you to know that I'm fine, and that I'm capable of working on this case."

"Oh, I know, I know," he said, but his eyes were averted and his shoulders were stiff. "Just don't overwork yourself, that's my advice. And keep your emotions at bay. You women tend to get overexcited. Police work requires a rational brain, not an emotional one."

She wanted to protest that she was not getting over-excited, but he had already thrown the cigarette butt in the ditch and was climbing the stairs back into the building.

Following him up the steps, Hella vowed to behave like the young professional she should be. Like a man. Not to be overcome by emotion. Eyes dry.

Which was exactly what she was trying to do now.

She slid the glass into a paper envelope. No one needed to know about it. Outside, Irja was calling her.

"Lunch is ready," she shouted. "If you're hungry. And then Timo can take you to see Erno's place."

As if in response to her words, Hella's stomach gurgled and she realized that she was, indeed, ravenous. She covered the head with a clean towel, locked the door of the shed, and hurried towards the house for a quick lunch.

# 13

At first glance, there was not much to look at. The surprisingly grand log cabin, in which Erno Jokinen lived with his grandson Kalle, stood three quarters of a mile away from the village, in a no man's land of damp soil and crooked shrubs. In the summer, thought Hella, this place must be swarming with mosquitoes. And during the polar winter … Three quarters of a mile is not a great distance to walk, but when the snow reached all the way up to the gabled roof, and one had to shovel one's way out of the house, building crumbling tunnels like a worm in an overripe apple, socializing was not a priority. Erno and his grandson had surely kept to themselves. It was probably easier for them to go into the forest that lay to the east of the house than to the village that was uphill from the cabin.

"Did Erno build this house?" she asked Father Timo, who stood grimly by her side, his hands tucked into the belt of his black cassock.

"His father did. He owned a big chunk of land here, and this was where he built his home. It's a bit like a local manor."

"What about Erno's wife? Who was she, and what happened to her?"

"I heard that she died during childbirth. After that, Erno lived with his daughter, Anna."

"And his daughter —" Hella was about to ask Father Timo if Anna had always lived in this godforsaken place, but checked herself in time and reframed the question. "Was she never tempted to go to the city?"

"She did go to a city. Went as far as Turku, from what I've heard, when she was about eighteen. Came back only a year ago with little Kalle in tow. She never married, so we don't know anything about the father. But you should ask Irja about that. She probably knows local gossip much better than I do."

*But I prefer to talk to you,* thought Hella. Even though she had never liked people of his trade, she preferred him to his wife. Her unstudied perfection, her tranquillity and grace intimidated Hella. She felt awkward and vain, with her police insignia pinned to her ill-fitting, threadbare parka, her hair like straw, and her bitten nails.

Hella turned away, suddenly ashamed of her thoughts. What did it matter what she looked like? Or the fact that she couldn't cook? She was here to do her job. She glanced at Father Timo.

"Mr Waltari, do you have any idea where we can look for the key?"

She had stupidly expected to find the front door open. In her limited knowledge of country life, no one ever locked their doors. But this house stood away from the village, which explained the huge, cast-iron lock that hung on its nail-studded front door. Or else Erno Jokinen had something to hide.

"Yes, I do." Father Timo leaned forward and fumbled under the shutters, producing a key. "It doesn't turn easily," he commented, inserting the key into the lock. "Takes a lot of force to open that door." He looked at her. "This is something I forgot to mention. When Martta brought Kalle to us, she said that the front door hadn't been locked when she found him. The key was inside, on top of the sideboard. She's the one who locked the door and hid the key under the shutters."

A grey cotton runner led from the entrance to a living room-cum-kitchen, lined in pine and devoid of the usual embellishments. It was bitterly cold inside the house, and dark. But of course; there was no one to light the stove any longer. How could little Kalle have survived here alone? Hella looked around, trying to imagine what those six terrible days had been like for him. What had the boy eaten? She noticed a scattering of breadcrumbs on the dining table – he must have had some bread – and a gleaming samovar, so there had been water, too, but this must have been cold. Apart from that, no food except a garland of laurel leaves, a large glass jar full of dried mushrooms and, next to it, a smaller one that must have contained jam but was now licked clean.

A flock of paper planes sat on the windowsill, dozens of them. And a sheet of paper, folded in two, propped against the window, where one couldn't fail to see it.

Inside it, a short, handwritten message: *Erno, Kalle was afraid of being alone for so long, and he didn't want to stay with Martta. He's with us. You can come over to the house any time it suits you. Timo and Irja.*

Strange turns of phrase, thought Hella. No *We've been worried*, no *Please come immediately*.

She refolded the note and put it back on the windowsill. She didn't believe for one second that the old man was ever coming back, but you never knew.

Then she looked around, frowning.

So Kalle had spent six days all alone, waiting for his grandfather to come back. Six days is a long time, very long, for a child. Was he the one who had made all those paper planes? What else had he done? Played hide-and-seek?

Is that why the big stove, its whitewashed belly protruding into the room, was smeared with soot?

She searched a small sideboard, also pine, with its doors primly closed. The insides were empty.

To the right of the sideboard there was a narrow bench covered with cushions; the cushions were torn at the seams. Someone had taken the stuffing out, then replaced it, but hadn't bothered to stitch the seams again. Maybe they couldn't find a needle and thread. Maybe they hadn't had the time.

She continued scanning the room until once more her gaze returned to the stove.

Playing hide-and-seek all alone?

Or hiding from someone?

Or – her eyes on the cushions again – looking for something?

Someone else, not Kalle.

Looking for what?

She called out to the priest, who was waiting for her outside.

"Can you come in? Don't touch anything."

He wiped his feet on the doormat and joined her inside the house.

"You came back here after the boy was brought to you."

It was not a question, merely a piece of information she wanted confirmed. She had seen the message on the windowsill.

"Yes, we did. Irja and me, the day after Kalle was found. We needed to get him a change of clothes." Father Timo thought for a second, maybe wondering whether clarification was necessary or pertinent, then added: "We also took his picture book and his mother's photograph, because he asked for it."

"Look around. Is anything different or out of the ordinary?"

The priest complied with the instruction, his head tilted, his clear blue gaze settling on one object after another. Taking his time.

"No, I don't see any changes. The room was already dirty when we came in. I remember noticing the soot."

Hella peered inside the stove. Empty. Grabbing a two-pronged cast-iron stick from a hook, she fumbled inside, dislodging more soot.

"And to your knowledge, you and your wife were the only ones who came down here?"

"Martta Jokinen also came, the day she found Kalle."

"But if someone from the village had come by, either before you did or later on, would they know where the key was?"

"I'm not sure. The shutters are an obvious hiding place, of course, but Erno doesn't make a habit of leaving his key lying about. He's most particular about security, and he distrusts his closest neighbour, Karppinen. Every time he goes out, he locks his front door."

"So how do you explain the fact that the door wasn't locked when Martta Jokinen came over? Could she have been lying?"

"I don't think so. There was nothing wrong in what she did, was there? Why would she lie?"

"Why was the door left unlocked, then? You said so yourself, the man locked his door all the time —"

Father Timo shook his head. "I thought about that, too. The key doesn't turn easily; it takes a lot of force to open that door. Kalle could never have managed to open it on his own. What if Erno was afraid he'd be gone for a long time, maybe never coming back? He wouldn't have wanted to trap Kalle inside. So he left the door open."

Hella nodded. If that was true, then the old man was probably a murderer, not a victim. But if that was the case, who had searched his house?

"If something had gone missing, would you have noticed? Not only now, but between the last time you paid a visit to Erno and the day you came to fetch Kalle's clothes. You can look around. Take your time."

Father Timo didn't need to look around to answer the question.

"Erno kept a pair of silver candlesticks on the sideboard. A Jokinen family heirloom, given to Erno's parents on their wedding day. They were here when I played chess with Erno a week before he disappeared. But not the last time I came. So those are missing, and also the embroidered tablecloth that Erno kept on the shelf, here, for special occasions."

"And you're sure these things were here when you last visited to play chess but not when you came to fetch Kalle's clothes?"

"I'm sure."

Hella sighed and turned away. The disappearance of kitchen items was probably not meaningful. It happened all the time, of course, people being killed for silverware, but she doubted very much that it was the case here.

# 14

There were maybe ten books on the fitted shelf in the corner of the living room, but these were not the books Hella would have expected to find.

"*Lessons in Pawn Play*, by Reverend E. E. Cunnington. Ernst Brandes' *Social Problems.* Wuorinen's *Finland – An Historical Survey.* Rather sophisticated reading for an uneducated peasant."

"Erno is educated," objected Father Timo, doggedly sticking to the present tense. "Not in a university, of course, but he went to a gymnasium. He likes to read. He's passionate about history, especially recent history. I guess it's the influence of this place we live in. This region has changed hands with every generation, or even more often, and people have had to adapt."

"What about this one?" asked Hella, pointing at a slim, dog-eared volume, stuck between Wuorinen's *Finland* and an encyclopaedia. "*The Woman's Doctor.*" She dislodged the book from its shelf. Published in 1933. "*All you will ever need to know about your health and that of your baby.* Whatever did he have *that* for?"

Father Timo took the book from her hands.

"I've never seen it before. Erno's never been interested

in official medicine. He uses herbal remedies, for himself and for Kalle. I don't believe they ever saw a doctor in their lives."

He paused, thinking.

"It must have been Anna's. Kalle's mother. She died a year ago."

"What of?"

"Pneumonia. She had the flu, and then ... She was a sickly woman, and I wouldn't be surprised if she took a lot of medication. So maybe that book was hers."

Hella wriggled the volume back into its spot on the shelf. She would need to leaf through each of these books, looking for annotations or documents hidden between the pages. But she would do that when she was alone.

Instead, she went to inspect the two bedrooms at the back of the house, motioning to Father Timo to follow her.

"Kalle's room?"

"Used to be. He shared it with his mother for a short time, before she passed away."

So that explained the atmosphere of gloom that hung about the room, in defiance of the two matching yellow bedspreads and the handmade doll that sat smiling on the windowsill.

"Did you know Anna Jokinen?"

"Only a little. Irja cared for her when she fell ill. I administered the last rites to her. I was also the one who buried her."

Hella pushed open the door to the other room.

"So once his mother died, Kalle started sharing a room with his grandfather?"

No matching bedspreads in here. Nothing pretty. It was a room that screamed *men only*. A wolfskin used as a rug. A rifle, certainly loaded, leaning casually against the wall next to Erno's bed. A cloudy bottle on the floor. Hella bent down to smell it.

Aquavit. Home-made. Not Kremlevskaya, whatever Eklund

might think. She could just about imagine the old man downing a glass or two before he went to bed.

She turned towards the priest. "Could Erno have been in need of money? Maybe for Kalle's education?"

Father Timo considered the question. Contrary to Lennart Eklund, he didn't make a big deal out of the thinking process. He didn't search his memory ostentatiously, didn't frown, affecting concentration.

"I don't think so," he answered simply. "He never talks about education. I think he expects that Kalle will stay here, help out, and inherit the house. They don't seem to have any particular needs. The boy is in good health and Erno, though close to sixty, is robust."

Hella closed the door with a soft thud.

"So except for the silver and tablecloth, probably spirited away by that great-aunt you mentioned, Martta, nothing's missing?"

"No."

"Could Martta have been the one who searched inside the stove? Is there, I don't know —"

Father Timo laughed. "A local habit of hiding valuables inside stoves? Not that I know of. But Martta is a strange woman. You never know what might get into her head. Her house is full of so much junk; she just picks things up everywhere she goes. Anything she can find. Old coffee cans, glass jars, rags. So maybe *she* hides things inside her stove. You'll have to ask her, though I doubt very much you'll get a straight answer."

"They weren't on good terms?"

"Martta and Erno? They're like cat and dog, with Martta being the dog. Never got along, not as children, and not as adults either. Although, when Martta sprained her ankle last spring, Erno spent some time caring for her. I doubt very much she would have done the same for him."

"So Martta Jokinen had no reason really to drop in on her brother?"

Father Timo looked at her, his face serious.

"I wondered about that too. But when I asked Martta, I didn't get a satisfactory answer."

"What did she say?"

"That she had borrowed something from him and was bringing it back, as they had agreed."

"What sort of something?"

"That, she didn't want to tell me."

All right, so Martta Jokinen was first on her list. She would also need to go and see the little man who lived in that house up the hill. He might believe that he was being discreet, but Hella had seen him lurking behind his hedge, binoculars in hand.

Who else?

Father Timo was standing next to the window, studying the paper planes. His black cassock inspired a new thought in Hella.

"What about religious icons, Mr Waltari? I haven't seen any. Aren't all Skolts devout Orthodox Christians?"

"Not Erno. He's a non-believer. Likes nothing better than to point out God's perceived inadequacies."

"Doesn't that trouble you?"

"It does."

Hella expected him to add that, no matter what each thought about religion, people didn't kill over that kind of thing. When talking to her, people usually felt the need to justify themselves. But Father Timo didn't say anything. Instead, he went out into the daylight and stood with his back to the house, waiting for her to finish her inspection and join him outside.

# 15

"Martta Jokinen?" asked Hella, even though she had no doubt that the little witch with her curiously shaped, asymmetrical body and her mouse-grey hair through which shone a pink, crusty scalp was indeed Martta Jokinen. Behind the woman's back, Hella could see the two silver candlesticks sitting defiantly on a table piled high with dirty dishes.

The woman didn't answer. She just stood there, staring at her, perhaps wondering who Hella was. Her grey kaftan was stained all over, and so was her floor-length navy skirt.

"Sergeant Mauzer," stated Hella, pointing at the badge pinned on her parka and speaking very slowly. "Ivalo Police. I'm here to investigate the disappearance of your brother Erno. May I come in?"

Still, the woman didn't budge. *She's slow-witted,* thought Hella. *Or deaf.* She almost regretted declining Father Timo's offer to accompany her. She didn't want to stroll around the village in the company of a priest, leading the good people of Käärmela to believe she couldn't do anything on her own just because she was a woman.

Martta Jokinen mumbled something.

"I beg your pardon?" Hella was not sure she had heard correctly. Had the old witch really said "To hell with him"? It made her sound like a story-book villain.

"How do I know where he went and why?" proclaimed Martta Jokinen, louder this time. Her front teeth were still there, but almost all her back teeth were gone, which further accentuated her rodent-like features. "I don't care, either!"

"Is this your brother we're talking about?" asked Hella in her nicest voice. "May I come in, Miss Jokinen?"

"Do I have to talk to you?" asked the woman, not yet ready to give in.

"Yes, you do." Hella wondered what Ranta would have done if he was in her shoes. Or Eklund. Would they patiently wait on the porch? She put her foot between the door and the jamb.

"And how exactly do I know who you are?" the woman said. "That trinket on your coat doesn't mean a thing to me. What if you've come here to steal my silver spoons?"

Coming from someone who had spirited away a pair of silver candlesticks from her missing brother's house, that was a bit rich.

"Miss Jokinen, do you want me to handcuff you and take you over to the police station for questioning? Or are you going to let me in, like the lovely hostess that you are? I can already see evidence of one crime, over there on your dining table. Do you want me to add obstruction of justice to the list?"

The woman glared but stepped back, finally allowing Hella access to a living room which, like its owner, reeked of decay and acrid perspiration. The priest was right; Martta Jokinen was a hoarder. The insides of the living room made Hella think of a junkyard.

"Haven't done anything," muttered the woman grimly, while Hella stood in the middle of the room, not daring to sit anywhere because of the risk of staining her clothes. "Those candlesticks are mine. Father told me so on his deathbed. I was his favourite, too. Erno's been scheming behind my back all my life, trying to rob me of my inheritance."

"Is that so? And, understandably, you felt entitled to recover what you were due as soon as you had the opportunity. Do you think your brother's dead?"

"He is," replied the woman. "One knows such things."

"By reading tarot cards? By having prophetic dreams? Or perhaps by observing someone stalking an old man into the woods?"

"Like you said, I saw it in a dream."

"Tell me about it exactly."

The woman raised her eyes to the ceiling, searching for inspiration. "I just saw something like a shroud, and a coffin, and then an angel with wings and curly hair, telling me my time had come to go and get what was owed to me."

"And so you bravely did as the angel asked?"

The woman nodded.

"You told Father Timo that you went over to Erno's house to give back something that belonged to him."

"He's lying," declared Martta Jokinen, unblinking. "They all do."

"All priests?"

"All men."

"Was the front door locked?"

"It wasn't."

"What about the child? Did the angel mention what you were supposed to do with him?"

The old woman sneered. "That child is a bastard. Why do you think an angel would bother with such a thing?"

Hella clenched her fists, but managed to keep her voice calm. "But still you took him with you."

"Didn't want to be accused of murder, did I? And that little bastard would have died in that house had I not taken him. I deserve a medal for that. Or a reward. You think you can ask about it in Ivalo?"

Hella bared her teeth. "You despicable sleazy scum of the earth. You stole from an innocent child, and you're boasting about saving his life? Give me those candlesticks. Now! And the tablecloth. No, not that one. The embroidered one."

Having stuffed Kalle's rightful inheritance into her backpack, Hella made her way out of the room, while the old woman screeched, cursed and called all of hell's fire on her.

# 16

When Hella returned from her interview with Martta Jokinen, the evening prayer had already started. Kalle was perched above the stove together with the cat, and he was repeating every word. He signed himself at appropriate moments, without being prompted. Yet his grandfather was strongly opposed to religion. How could the boy have learned the rituals so quickly? That was another question she had to ask. What troubled her, though, was neither the prayer nor the little boy. It was Irja Waltari. The priest's wife was acting in the exact opposite manner to Kalle. She pretended to be listening, but Hella would bet her monthly wage that she wasn't. Which was not what Hella would have expected from an otherwise devoted wife. What was the matter with her? Father Timo had noticed it, too; Hella could tell it from the stiffness of his shoulders, from the worried glances he directed at his wife when he thought she was not looking. He rambled on bravely regardless, his beautiful deep voice intoning the prayer, his eyes now set on the Christ the Saviour icon in the corner. Hella felt sorry for the poor man. It couldn't be easy for a priest to have a wife who didn't share his faith.

"Amen," said the priest.

Irja Waltari straightened her skirt and rose to her feet, ready to serve dinner.

"Come on, Kalle," called Hella, in an effort to establish contact. "Climb down."

He did, but without looking at her, and without relinquishing the cat. The priest's wife smiled absent-mindedly and placed a saucer of milk on the floor for Seamus. The animal twisted its nose, making it clear it would rather opt for the meatballs.

There was a new toy in the house, a moose made of rags that Irja had been stitching together. It stood on the windowsill, one of its horns sprawling and proud, the other hanging limply to one side.

"I dropped by the church on the way back, but you were already gone," said Hella to the priest. "I went inside anyway, but it didn't look like anything I'd imagined. It looked ... dark. I don't know why, but I always thought that Orthodox churches were full of light and colour."

"It used to be," said Father Timo, "but it needs restoration now. As you know, the Soviets are against all religion, and this part of Lapland has been invaded. The church had been stripped of its icons and converted into a warehouse. We're lucky they didn't burn it."

Yes, thought Hella. That's what they did, usually. Religion was public enemy number one.

"We've got some new icons from Helsinki, and the villagers have salvaged some of the original ones. I'm restoring them, though I'm not really a specialist. Irja helps a lot."

Probably repainting them in lovely colours, thought Hella. What a nice family business. Pity they didn't have a flock of little children, cute and blonde like Mummy and Daddy. Still, they were young, probably just married, so that would come in due course.

Irja placed food on the table – Russian borscht again – and Hella started eating without waiting for Father Timo to finish saying grace. They ate in silence, Hella wondering what it must feel like to be part of this land that had been torn between conflicting powers for centuries. Did people develop specific personality traits? Did they *adapt* easily? Or did they just cringe and wait in silence until things changed again? She tried to remember what she had heard about the people of Lapland, but nothing came to mind.

She was still pondering the question when dinner finally ended and Father Timo left the house to go back to the church and pray for the dead woman.

# 17

She has beautiful hair, thought Irja, and her eyes are nice, dark grey under sculpted eyebrows. But she's doing everything in her power to conceal her good looks, as if being attractive is at odds with being professional. And her clothes! The lower button of her parka was dangling from a single thread. Irja made a mental note to sew it back on once Sergeant Mauzer went to bed. She also wanted to iron the policewoman's crumpled shirts, but was afraid this gesture might be interpreted as a violation of the sergeant's privacy.

The evening was well advanced and Kalle, exhausted by the day's emotions, was fast asleep on top of the stove, Seamus curled up by his side. Irja was tired too, but Sergeant Mauzer, sitting opposite her, kept tapping on the table with her short, bitten nails. She wanted to ask her something, but she was struggling to find the words. Irja wondered what it could be. She also wondered if Sergeant Mauzer already had a theory about what had happened in the forest.

"About the boy ..." started Miss Mauzer in a low voice. "He seems familiar with your religion. I saw him sign himself just now, in this right-to-left way you Orthodox have. Has he picked it up over the last few days?"

"No," replied Irja quietly. She knew now why Sergeant Mauzer had waited before she asked her this question. She wanted Kalle asleep and Timo out of the house. Irja couldn't hide the truth from her. So she explained:

"Kalle has got into the habit of going to the church over the last few months. I think, in a way, he's been looking for his mother. After she died, someone told him she'd become an angel, and he understood it literally. He would stay there for hours on end, gazing up at an icon of Saint Elisabeth, smiling and moving his lips. He was talking to her, telling her about his life here and asking what the weather was like up in the clouds, and if she could come home one day."

"Your husband encouraged him," said Hella. More of a statement than a question.

"You have to understand he believes that Anna Jokinen is in heaven, and that her son has every right to talk to her, so, yes, he agreed with Kalle."

"Did Erno know what the boy was up to?"

"Timo had asked Kalle about it, of course. And Kalle said that his grandpa had let him attend. Timo had no reason not to believe him."

Sergeant Mauzer paused, pondering the answer.

"Your husband must have thought that it was a consolation for Kalle to keep this imagined connection with his mother. He meant well. Even though he realized pretty quickly that Erno knew nothing about Kalle's visits, didn't he?"

"He was worried about the boy. About the fact that Kalle and Erno kept to themselves so much that Kalle didn't have any friends his own age. The village is small, but there are other children. Kalle never spent any time with them."

"Mr Waltari told me he played chess with Erno once a week."

"He did. Erno was – *is* – a rather good player. He even has a book on chess."

"So they met once a week, and played chess together, and somehow your husband never mentioned that the young boy was spending his days in the church, in total disregard for his grandfather's principles? Because I've heard that Erno wasn't happy with your God, who's allowed so much misery to befall his country and his own family. The last thing he would have wanted was to have his grandson believing in something he was strongly opposed to."

Irja cast an anguished glance over to the stove, but, if Kalle was awake, he gave no sign. She whispered: "I suppose so."

"How did Erno find out?"

"I don't know."

"But he was upset? Mrs Waltari?" Sergeant Mauzer, who was now scribbling furiously in her notebook, raised her head to look at her. "I'm waiting for an answer, Mrs Waltari."

Irja paused, wondering if there was a different way to put what she was about to say. There wasn't.

"He told Timo to leave, and to never again set foot in his house. He also said that Kalle would never be going near a church again."

Sergeant Mauzer jotted down this information. The sergeant had her own disagreements with God, Irja was sure of that. She would now be suspicious of Timo. Would she go as far as to suspect him of murder?

"One last question, please, Mrs Waltari."

Why had Sergeant Mauzer's voice taken that metallic, official note? Irja pressed her hands hard against each other to stop them from trembling.

"When did that dispute, between Erno Jokinen and your husband, take place? Do you remember?"

She could say she didn't remember. That her memory had been like a sieve lately. Or that the argument hadn't really been a big deal, two friends bickering, forgetting all about it the following day. Meeting again, the week after, to play chess. Only it wouldn't be the truth.

"It was on Thursday, the second of October."

Sergeant Mauzer made a quick calculation: "And exactly a week later, Martta Jokinen finds her nephew alone in the house, old Erno missing for at least six days, according to his grandson, maybe even longer."

The policewoman paused, going through her notes. "Well, something tells me we've got a nice motive here, haven't we, Mrs Waltari? Sleep well. We'll talk again tomorrow."

# 18

Some days she hated her job. Hands in the mud, fingers poking around. She had to do it, she knew, leaving no stone unturned, as her instructors at the police academy had called it, but some of those metaphorical stones were way heavier than others and, for all the trouble they caused, often yielded nothing. Deep down, Hella didn't believe for a second that Father Timo would have got rid of Erno Jokinen just because the old man didn't want to play chess with him any longer. But she suspected it was something Lennart Eklund would very easily believe in – or at least persuade himself of – if it advanced the investigation and improved the department's success rate. As he would point out to her, people killed for all sorts of stupid reasons. Oh yes, Miss Mauzer, of course they do. *You* should know.

She raised her glass, which was full of vodka, to toast Lennart Eklund in recognition of his great wisdom. Then she leaned back on her pillow, her eyes set on the scattering of violets that adorned the curtains.

Of course she knew. She had spent her days and her nights looking for a reason why a husband and father would kill his wife and four out of his five children. Had he suspected her of infidelity? Had he believed that the children were not his? That, at least, would have had a perverse, horrifying logic. But as it turned out, it had been nothing of the kind. He had killed them simply because money was tight, and because he wanted to start afresh, with a young girl who admired him, and no children. When Hella realized what had happened, she'd felt as if the sky had come crashing down on her. That fate could be irredeemably cruel, she knew already; but this was not fate. It was a conscious, premeditated act of unspeakable violence by a thirty-year-old man bored with his life.

Shaking off her memories, Hella gulped down the rest of her vodka. She should have taken the whole bottle to her room. Granted, it was not Kremlevskaya, but for home-made stuff, it tasted rather good.

She leafed through her notes. One day into her investigation, and not a clue as to what had actually happened. More questions than answers.

So she had a body, or at least parts of it. One unknown woman, wearing a sweater. Was her death related to Erno Jokinen in some way? Or was it just a coincidence that they had been looking for one body and found another? It was possible, but she didn't believe it. *Bullet wound*, she wrote. *Slivers of glass. Loroq. The stove smeared with soot. The unlocked door.* It didn't add up to anything, did it?

There were two possibilities when it came to Erno Jokinen. One: he was the killer, and he had run away. Two: he was another victim. The fact that his house had been searched seemed to point in that direction, so maybe that was the way to examine the situation. Who would want to kill *him*? What person would be interested in hurting a peasant from Käärmela?

*Property.* The most obvious of motives, and often the right one. What property? The candlesticks? The house? Kalle would surely be the one to inherit it, unless children born out of wedlock were deprived of their inheritance by some stupid law. The neighbour Karppinen, whom she was yet to meet, wanted to have Erno's house; that's what he had said to Irja Waltari. What he wanted it *for* was unclear. Maybe it was just jealousy; he felt entitled to have more than his neighbour. Maybe. With Jokinen alive, there was no way he could have it. But with the old man out of the way? Kalle was too small. Whoever ended up adopting him after Erno's death would probably struggle to maintain the estate. The priest and his wife wouldn't be able to, for instance. They were quite busy as they were …

*Secrets.* Erno knew something, and had to be shut up. What could he have known? Had he witnessed the woman's murder? Possibly. He was out and about all day. But that didn't help Hella in the least, because it placed the spotlight on the unknown woman, with Jokinen simply being in the wrong place at the wrong time. Or could it be the other way around: *he'd* known something dangerous, and the woman had just been a witness? But what could he have known? Spying came to mind, of course. They were close to the border, the woman's body found lying barely a mile inside Finnish territory. But spying on what? Try as she might, she just couldn't imagine what Erno Jokinen's contribution to the spying business could be: betraying such sensitive information as the reindeer population or the cranberry harvest, maybe? Ridiculous. To Hella's knowledge, the closest strategic installations were more than a hundred and thirty miles to the north. Surely, he couldn't have gone *that* far. No, spying on behalf of the Soviets didn't make sense.

Spying on behalf of the Finns, then? Pretending to go out hunting, going across the border, taking pictures of Soviet military installations. If there was no camera in the house, it's only because the Soviets had taken it after they killed him. *Mental note: ask Kalle if his grandpa had a camera. The boy should know.*

She drew a gingerbread man, carrying a rifle in one hand and a rectangular sheet of paper in the other. Having done that, she told herself that she was a very bad artist indeed, and also that her theory didn't hold water. Because Eklund would certainly know about it, if that was the case. He had access to that sort of information. He wouldn't have let her come out here at the risk of her stumbling into something she wasn't supposed to know.

Third idea. Jokinen as a *double* agent, betraying the Finns, betraying the Soviets. A nuclear project in the region that not even Eklund knew about, top secret, burn after reading, and he was a key player in the game. A nuclear physicist in disguise, made to look like Erno Jokinen following extensive cosmetic surgery, working on a new type of bomb that could destroy the whole world and then some. Kalle was a child he'd borrowed from someone to make the story more plausible, the late woman his devoted assistant. And Hella Mauzer was good for an asylum. Next.

Erno Jokinen was killed by his sister. *Jealousy*, dating back to their childhood. *Jealousy* and *property* combined. He gets everything: the estate, the silver candlesticks, the embroidered tablecloth and his parents' love. She gets nothing. She looks crazy, but probably isn't. How hard would it have been for her to trap him in the woods? *But what about the woman?* Hella had asked Irja, and apparently Erno had another sister, whom no one had seen since her twenties, presumed dead. Could she be the one? Seemed rather far-fetched, though.

Hella sighed and slumped back on her cushions. A strong wind was blowing outside: she could hear it wail. And the clouds were low as usual; she couldn't see the stars. Slowly, she drew little circles on the paper, all around the gingerbread man. The circles represented the coins. Next to the rifle, she drew a candlestick with a candle in it.

There was another possibility. What if Kalle himself was the motive? Unbeknown to his grandfather, the child was becoming a frequent guest in the church, and in this very house. The Waltaris made light of it when they discussed it. But could it be more serious than that? Could you kill in the name of your faith, for a child, for the salvation of his soul? She had seen stranger motives than that.

What next? She'd have to talk to the boy. She was sure he knew *something*, even though he might not even realize it. Except that Kalle was not talking much. Not to her, nor to the Waltaris, nor to the village folk who kept popping in at ungodly hours, presumably with the idea of seeing a badly dressed policewoman make a fool of herself. He was not saying "hi", he was not saying "thank you", and he asked no one to pass him the salt. He only whispered into the cat's furry ears. And Seamus, though bright and cooperative, had proved as yet totally incapable of communicating useful information to the police. If she had a listening device, she would have just hidden it under Kalle's pillow. If she had been back in Helsinki, she could have enrolled the help of a psychologist. But in Käärmela, her options were limited. Which was an optimistic way of saying she had none. She could ask for Irja Waltari's help, or she could ask for Irja Waltari's help. Though she was not very sure, after all she had said to the priest's wife, that any help would be forthcoming.

Damn it.

The little boy was terrified. But whether something had scared him, or whether he was simply afraid of being alone, she didn't know.

And now she was back to that day, eight years ago, when she had been older than Kalle, but no less frightened. No less desperate.

The police officer, a large, bulky man with a belt running low in the front, was standing on her doorstep, his right hand raised towards the bell. Behind him stood another man, short and stocky, with bulging eyes and a handlebar moustache. She knew that his name was Kyander and that he was her father's colleague. Hella opened the door dressed only in a bathrobe that reeked of vomit; she had spent her morning throwing up, ill with a virus, or possibly food poisoning. She would never know, although this question would turn into an obsession for years to come. And so she was standing on her doorstep, confused and wishing she had rinsed her mouth before answering the door, and the policeman with the too-tight belt was leaning towards her. He was whispering, afraid of what he had to say.

"Miss Mauzer. I'm afraid I have some very bad news for you."

*Oh God,* she thought. *Oh no. Please no.* As if from a distance, she heard herself answering in a normal, even reasonable, voice, which surprised both the police officer and herself, "Could you please wait a second? I'll go and get dressed."

"Miss Mauzer, please. You don't need to go anywhere. Just listen to me, please. May we come in? This gentleman here is your father's colleague."

"No," she said. "Please no. Just stay at the door." As if stopping them from entering her house could have the power to keep the news at bay.

"Miss Mauzer, now please listen —"

"I'm listening."

After that she would not utter a single word for months.

# THURSDAY 16 OCTOBER

# 19

Jeremias Karppinen was saddled with an obsessive personality. His house was aggressively clean, and it smelled of nothing. The cushions on the bench in his living room were strictly parallel, their covers unruffled. The samovar that was set on the table had probably never been used. Next to the door, a clothes rack, from which hung a tiny parka, and a gleaming rifle. Had he put it there on purpose? As a way to demonstrate that he had nothing to hide? Or to intimidate?

Karppinen let her in without comment, but he didn't offer her a seat. Instead, he stood bolt upright in the exact centre of the room, his little feet, in child-sized boots, planted firmly on the floor. His position was calculated to stop her from getting to the bench. But if he thought he could deter Hella with this attitude, he was wrong. Maybe some fat-headed *polissyster* would have been impressed. Not her. She pushed past him, almost stamping on his foot as she did so, and sat down resolutely on an immaculate cushion. Then she pulled out a notebook and a much-chewed pencil from her shoulder bag, which she then dropped at her feet. The interview could start.

"I've been informed," she started out rather sweetly, "that you were interested in acquiring Mr Jokinen's house. You made this offer while your neighbour was known to have been missing for a week. Do you expect him to be dead?"

"I guess he is."

"Is it important for you to buy this house? Do you like it *that* much?"

No answer. Hella waited. It was a trick she had learned at the police academy. When your suspect refused to answer your questions, you kept silent too. The idea was that people would begin rapidly to feel uncomfortable, and would talk. But she was starting to suspect that whoever had invented this technique had never been to Lapland. Karppinen definitely looked comfortable, and he kept his lips shut tight.

In the end, Hella was the one to break the silence: "Mr Karppinen, are you a friend of Mr Erno Jokinen?"

*That* question took him aback; she could see that. Maybe because the word "friend" was not part of his vocabulary.

Once again, he took his time answering. First, he tugged at his trousers, then he sat down carefully, his bony elbows on the table. "I was his neighbour."

From where Hella was seated, she could see the white picket fence surrounding Erno Jokinen's garden, and a string of clothes he must have hung there to dry before going away.

"For how long?"

"Since I was born."

"So you know him well," she mused. "What kind of man is he?"

"Stupid."

Hmm. Interesting.

"Any precise reason why you would say that, Mr Karppinen?"

"He lent money to his idiot of a sister once. He took in his slut of a daughter to live with him. And he even read books to her little bastard at night."

Which was clearly not something the wise Mr Karppinen would have done if he had been in his neighbour's shoes.

"Wasn't she his daughter, and the little boy his only grandchild?"

"So what? She was a grown woman. Could have fended for herself, couldn't she? But she complained all the time, pretending to be sick. They woke me up once in the middle of the night; their horse had hurt its hoof, and they wanted to borrow mine to get her to the doctor."

"Did you oblige?" asked Hella, knowing full well what the answer would be.

The little man let out a cackle. "Course not. What am I, an old fool like him? So Erno put her in a wheelbarrow and carted her off to the village, knocking on all the doors until someone lent him a horse and carriage."

*This tells me something about Erno,* thought Hella. *But it says even more about you.*

She still didn't know what kind of person Erno Jokinen was, but she was starting to have a good idea of what he was not. He was not a believer in God, he didn't rely on anyone else, and he loved his family.

"So when did you last see him, Mr Karppinen? If I may ask?"

As always, the angrier she was, the more her voice mellowed. This was something that the nuns in her school had insisted upon a lot – being graceful under pressure, concealing her feelings. For the quiet, subdued young Hella, it had never been a problem. But the evil gnome who was sitting in front of her, his eyes gleaming, didn't know that.

"Erno was always out and about. Cutting wood, hunting, whatever. Digging in his garden. Can't remember when I saw him last. I don't spend my time keeping tabs on old Erno."

*I bet you do,* thought Hella. The man had good eyes, too, because otherwise how would he know that Erno read books to his grandson at night? And there was one other thing. He must have noticed the old man had been gone a long time, and that the little boy had been alone, but still he hadn't gone to check on him. Not his business.

"You might know already," she said out loud, "that we have found a woman's remains in the woods. Do you have anything to tell me?"

The gnome fidgeted, but said nothing.

"Mr Karppinen?" Her voice struck an official chord. "You are being questioned as a witness now. I would rather appreciate your cooperation."

No answer.

Hella tried another technique. "I heard that Mr Jokinen had received visitors lately. Did you by any chance see who they were?"

"No," said the tiny man stiffly, but his eyes danced in all directions.

*Lying,* thought Hella. *I'm sure you're lying. There* was *someone.* Hella felt a familiar tingling sensation running down her spine. But Karppinen was not the kind of person who would spontaneously cooperate with the police. Let him think she was not interested.

Hella rose to her feet, dwarfing her host who remained seated, an expectant half-smile on his thin lips.

"In that case, Mr Karppinen, I must thank you for your time. Our interview hasn't been very informative, but then, I shouldn't have expected too much from a senior citizen with poor eyesight. Goodbye, Mr Karppinen."

# 20

The thin manila envelope, addressed by hand to SERGEANT MAUZER, WALTARI HOUSE, KÄÄRMELA, was propped against the milk jug. Every once in a while, Irja stopped to look at it. The letter had been delivered shortly before noon by a middle-aged man who had introduced himself as Sergeant Mauzer's fiancé but refused her invitation to have a cup of coffee while waiting for Miss Mauzer to come back. He had work to do, explained the man. Important work at the logging camp, a busy schedule. So he had left, and Irja had wiped away the muddy traces his big black boots had left on the floor.

So Sergeant Mauzer had a fiancé. Irja was not surprised, not really, even though she would have expected the sergeant to marry some sophisticated city type, a lawyer or a doctor, rather than this aggressively masculine man with a single eye that had ogled her as if she was a thing on display. Never mind. Sergeant Mauzer was probably wondering why *she* had married a priest. She had hinted at it over breakfast that very morning.

"So where did you two meet?" Sergeant Mauzer had asked her. "In church?"

It was an innocent question, decided Irja. Nothing to it.

"No, just on the street. In Turku."

"And you knew he was a priest?"

"He wasn't a priest back then. He was a student."

"So you two fell in love ..."

"Yes," confirmed Irja, a dreamy smile on her face as she remembered that cold October day. "We did."

"I bet at that time you imagined you'd have a good life. A sheltered life," implied Sergeant Mauzer with a nasty smile, and broke the spell.

"I hadn't imagined anything at all," said Irja, pulling herself sharply back into line. Sergeant Mauzer was not her friend. She was just pretending to be one.

"Does your job include helping out in church?"

"It's not a job. It's a vocation. Like a doctor, like a police officer. You cannot do it for money alone."

But Hella Mauzer was not to be deterred. *She has an instinct for half-truths,* thought Irja. For pressing where it hurts.

"So do you feel it? That burning sense of vocation?"

"My husband feels it."

"But you don't."

"Yes I do."

Irja stumbled to her feet, pretending that the pot of milk on the stove required her immediate attention. She took her time, wiping the pot with trembling hands, fanning the fire. But when, some minutes later, she turned back to the table, Hella Mauzer was still staring at her with a sardonic glint in her eye.

"Isn't this house a bit too big for the two of you?"

"That's what rectories are like."

"That's correct," mused Sergeant Mauzer. "Built to accommodate a big family. Hordes of children running around. But you don't have any."

"No, we don't."

"Or rather, you didn't. Because now you have Kalle."

Irja glanced towards her bedroom. Kalle was in there, reading his favourite book, about a red toy plane, to Seamus. At least he had climbed down off the stove.

"Kalle needs us," she said. "He can't live with his great-aunt. You've seen her!"

She fought back tears, angry at herself. She had been far too emotional lately. Crying for no reason. What would Sergeant Mauzer think of her?

But the policewoman was already packing her worn-out brown shoulder bag.

"What you do is your business," she said gruffly. "Your life. I'm off to see your friend Karppinen."

# 21

Hella noticed Kukoyakka's heavy frame as she was turning the corner of the street, and her first instinctive movement was to duck behind somebody's picket fence. But as soon as she was hidden from her visitor's view, she felt stupid. What if he came towards her? Or if someone else did? Her cheeks burning, she emerged resolutely from behind the fence, only to see Kukoyakka's back and meaty thighs. He was already climbing into his monstrous truck.

Hella waited for a moment, then, as the truck switched into gear and trundled out of sight, slowly made her way to the Waltari house. She had a lot to think about.

That Karppinen man was very peculiar indeed. He had hated and despised his neighbour and he was jealous of everything Erno Jokinen possessed. He had a motive – the house. It was a good motive, a sound one. Much more sound than the one she had credited Father Timo with. Much more plausible than any idea of an international spy game that had crossed her mind.

He had opportunity – well, everyone in the village or even out of it had an opportunity, really. In the forest, there was no way of knowing. She would need to search his house for the murder weapon. She would do it on her next visit. Yes,

Jeremias Karppinen was a very promising suspect indeed, and he had lied to her. Had he seen the woman? Was she another one of Erno's sisters? If that was the case, with her white hands and polished nails she must have come from a city.

Smiling, Hella climbed the three steps that led to the Waltaris' front door. She was glad Karppinen was proving to be a better suspect than the priest. She felt a little bit ashamed, too, for the way she'd spoken to Irja that morning.

The floor in the corridor of the Waltaris' house had been freshly washed.

"Oh, you just missed him!" cried out Irja, her hands clutching a grey mop. "What a pity! He so wanted to see you! He left only a minute ago, maybe if you run —"

She stopped in her tracks, alarmed by the expression on Hella's face.

"What?"

"I saw him. From a distance. I don't know what he told you, but it's most certainly not true."

Irja blushed. "Good to hear that. He is certainly a very decent man, but … maybe you are a little bit ill-matched. He left a letter for you."

Hella glanced at the letter. Lennart Eklund's schoolboy handwriting, letters plump, a double bar on the *t*. Why was he writing to her so soon? There was no way he could have already received her letter about the dead woman.

She smiled at Irja, who was hovering expectantly by her side. "I'll read it later. It can wait. There's a number of things I need to do first. I need to talk to Kalle. I don't understand why he's so scared. Also, I need to know if there's a connection between the dead woman and Erno. You told me he had another sister?"

"Yes, but no one's seen her for a very long time. Look, can't you wait before you talk to Kalle? He's still so shaken up. Maybe if you wait a couple of days —"

"Mrs Waltari, I can't wait a couple of days," Hella explained patiently. "This is a murder investigation. And it's not as if I'm going to bully the child. Please call him through."

Irja frowned, but she called out nonetheless, "Kalle! Come over here, sweetie."

"You can stay if you want to," offered Hella. Why did this woman make her feel like a monster? She was just doing her job. She was a good person.

The boy stood trembling before her. She knelt before him, as they had taught her to during the training course. Kalle looked away.

"Kalle, I just want to know two things. And then you can go back and play."

A doubtful expression spread over the boy's face, but Hella persisted, her voice cheerful.

"Did your grandpa have a lady friend? Someone he was close to? Or did your aunt, not Martta, but another one, from the city, come over to see you?"

The boy shook his head, still without looking at her.

"I don't think there was anyone really," chirped Irja, eager to end this conversation. Hella glared at her.

"Are you sure, Kalle? It's a natural thing, you know, to receive visits from friends and family. Nothing to be ashamed of."

"He didn't have a lady friend," whispered Kalle. "And I have no other aunt." Hella had to lean close to him to make out the words.

"All right, Kalle, what are you afraid of? You're safe here."

No answer.

"Aren't you? Safe?"

No answer.

"Are you afraid of your neighbour, Mr Karppinen?"

No answer.

Hella sighed. Having a young child as your only witness is every investigator's nightmare. Even if he says something, how do you know that what he's telling you is the truth? It's hard enough with adults, who tell as many lies as children, and maybe even more than they do, but at least, being an adult yourself, you can have a pretty good idea of how your witness's mind works. Not so with a child. And even if you are convinced that your child witness is not lying, you can never rely on his statements. What if he misinterpreted the situation? Did he even understand your question?

Her course instructor on witness interrogation had made it absolutely clear. Never trust a child witness. Don't even ask. If you have no adult witnesses, work with the clues. But Hella couldn't afford such luxury. For one, she didn't have any real clues. And two, she was certain that Kalle knew a lot about what had happened. He was a bright child. If only he would talk!

Maybe it would have helped if her nephew was alive. She would have learned from being around him. Or – but she barely dared think about it – she could have had a child of her own. With Steve. A lovely, curly, cuddly boy who would have had his father's sly smile, and they would all have lived together happily ever after.

*Of course they would have done. You idiot, Hella.* As it was, though, she had another undoubtedly lovely child standing in front of her, trembling, and she didn't know what to do with him.

The priest's wife must have felt Hella's dismay, for she crouched next to the boy and asked Hella's question in that cooing, soothing voice of hers. "Kalle, are you frightened because you're not at home? Or are you afraid of someone?"

No answer.

"Is it a thing, or is it a person?"

A long, long silence. Hella started to open her mouth to repeat the question when the boy murmured, "A thing."

"Where is it, Kalle?" Irja said, having placed her hand on Hella's arm as if to say *I'm better at this, don't interrupt.* A nasty comment sprang to Hella's mind, but she swallowed it down for the sake of efficiency.

"Everywhere. In the village. In the forest. There are evil white things all over. Grandpa said so. He said he went to battle that evil thing and I was not to go looking for him. I wasn't to tell anyone, either. It was Grandpa's secret. And now the thing has taken him."

He broke down sobbing and ran away. Hella looked at Irja Waltari. Either the woman was an excellent actress, or she, too, was lost as to what these "evil white things" could be. One thing was certain, though, Hella reflected gloomily. She was absolutely not suited to the work of a *polissyster.*

# 22

Every time she went into the spacious guest bedroom, Hella was taken back twenty years, to the house her family had occupied before the Winter War. Her room there had had the same scattering of flowers on the curtains, only there it had been roses instead of violets. The room also had the same floral smell, out of sync with the snowflakes that were dancing before her window. Probably potpourri forgotten on a shelf.

Hella collapsed onto the bed and ripped the envelope open. Lennart Eklund's neat handwriting covered a whole page, and then some.

*Sergeant Mauzer, blah-blah-blah, you will find here attached the SUPO file on Waltari, Timo and spouse. There exists no file on Jokinen, Erno.*

That was quick, thought Hella, surprised. Usually, it took ages to receive a background file from the SUPO on anyone, and here it was ready almost before she'd even asked.

She pulled a yellowish paper file out of the envelope and leafed through it. Jesus Christ! *Timo Waltari, born in Helsinki in May 1925, the fifth son of a university lecturer. Member of the Socialist Party at 15, a student protester and subversive element.* Was it really the same man? She tried to imagine the priest in everyday clothes, armed with a Molotov cocktail, ready to throw it at the police. Was it the same idealism, the same desire to make the world a more equitable place, that had driven him later towards the Church? She read on, with a sick feeling. *On 15 October 1939, Timo Waltari and two accomplices participated in a failed attempt to murder Juho Niukkanen, at the time the Finnish Minister of Defence. A shot was fired, but missed its target. Niukkanen escaped unharmed. While Timo Waltari was not the shooter, he was present at the scene. Following a spontaneous denunciation by one of the members of the terrorist group, the three attempted murderers were arrested and given different prison sentences. Timo Waltari, having played the least active role in the group, was sentenced to four years' imprisonment and released from prison after three years for good conduct. Upon release, he immediately entered a seminary. To the knowledge of the SUPO, since that day he has kept clear of any political or terrorist movements. The church authorities appreciate his commitment and what they call his "good spirit". He asked to be given a poor parish in Lapland, and was sent to Käärmela following the untimely death of Father Nikolai in 1951.*

Hella stared at the file in disbelief. A student protester, that she could believe. But a terrorist? The SUPO wouldn't lie, would they? A short typewritten note was attached to the document: *Irja Teiva, married name Waltari. Born on 11 April 1925.* Almost the same age as her, thought Hella, surprised. She had expected Irja to be much younger. She read on. *Youngest daughter of a bankrupt porcelain manufacturer.* Nothing else on her.

Did this new information change anything? Even if Timo Waltari had been associated with some past wrongdoing, could she draw a parallel with present events? Could an attempted assassination of a politician relate in any way whatsoever to the disappearance of an old peasant from

Lapland? Hella decided that the answer was no. She picked up Eklund's letter again.

*... as you will see from the file, this couple is dangerous, blah-blah-blah. It is very unfortunate you chose to stay at their place. I suggest you find different accommodation ...*

*He's got to be kidding. He* was the one who'd suggested she stay in their house. What was she supposed to do now, go and ask Martta Jokinen if she would take her in as an unpaid house guest?

*... I remind you that strict compliance with the police procedures blah-blah-blah, utmost caution must be exercised, blah-blah-blah, nowhere near the Soviet border ...*

*Been there already,* thought Hella, *found nothing.* Though she would have loved to be able to present Eklund with a nice espionage story and watch him soil his underpants. As it was, though, she had a perfectly good suspect, a man by the name of Jeremias Karppinen. Or rather she'd had one before young Kalle started talking about the white evil. It sounded just like something out of a fairy tale. Could it be that he had misunderstood his grandfather's explanation? That the "evil white things" were something completely different?

*And please do not unnecessarily delay your return to Ivalo,* concluded the letter.

"Just you wait," hissed Hella. "I'll be back when I'm done here, and not a day earlier."

She folded the letter in two and slid it between the pages of her notebook. She needed time to think it over. Then she pulled a page out of the notebook and started to write her daily report to Eklund.

# 23

Kalle's small hand trembled in hers as Irja knelt before the altar. All the villagers' eyes were on them. There was Martta, wearing a garish red dress and no coat, a big smile plastered across her face. Kai, who had spent so many days combing the forest, and who looked more shaken now than when he had found the woman's remains. There was Karppinen, standing apart from the crowd, his tiny features set in a disapproving pout. They had all come, and so had the rest of the village.

Timo recited the prayers in his beautiful voice. She had fallen in love with that voice first, and with the man later. She so much wanted for that voice to sing on a happy occasion. A wedding, a baptism. But there were not many of those in the village. The last wedding had been almost a year ago, the week after Anna Jokinen's funeral.

"Lord Jesus Christ, Son of God, have mercy on me, a sinner ..."

*But will He?* wondered Irja. *And why should He?*

That was a discussion she and Timo kept having lately, and they could never agree with each other. Timo thought that His ways are mysterious, but whatever He does, He does for a good reason, even if we may not know it at the time, and sometimes maybe not even later. But Irja was not sure it was all so simple. For her, God was far, far away, and He had no interest in humans. That was why He let innocent children suffer. Because He didn't even notice they existed.

Irja blinked away her tears. Kalle was not crying, but his mouth was a narrow line and his face was deathly pale. She clutched his hand firmly and bent to kiss the top of his head.

"You're not alone, Kalle. Father Timo and I, we'll take care of you. I promise."

Sergeant Mauzer was there too. She was standing in a corner, not praying, not even pretending to. Her sharp gaze followed their every movement, and the message was clear: she was there to work. Irja wondered whether Sergeant Mauzer felt anything. She had only emerged from her room when it was time to go to church, and she was humming. This probably orphaned child, and the old man who was still missing, and that woman who had been so horribly killed, they were just cases to solve, nothing more, nothing less. *Sergeant Mauzer's life is so different from mine,* Irja realized suddenly. *It's almost like we live on different planets.*

Irja wondered what it would be like to never let anyone influence your choices. To care for no one else's feelings. She thought of the day when, as a girl of nineteen, she had rushed home to tell her parents that her work had been noticed and praised, that a gallery in Paris had offered to exhibit her paintings. That her teacher thought she was really gifted. That she could become a great artist.

Her father, who was reading his newspaper by the fire, took his time finishing the page. He then folded his newspaper slowly and only after that looked up, but not at her. He glanced at her mother, who was hovering anxiously near the door.

"Has she gone mad?" he asked her. "I always thought those art lessons were a bad idea."

Her mother, a small, timid woman, clasped her hands, rather like a Victorian heroine upon discovering that her fiancé has perished at sea. "I never thought that she would ... Rouva Ivanova is such a respectable woman ... How could I ever have imagined ..."

Her voice faltered. Without another word, Irja's father got to his feet and made for the door. He stopped when he reached the doorway.

"You are engaged to be married, young lady. You marry first, and if your husband lets you dabble with paint, it's his business. You will do it under his name, not mine."

Having said that, he left the room, while Irja groped for an explanation and her mother cried silently.

There was never again a discussion about her future as an artist. No more lessons, either – not only did her father refuse to pay for them, he refused to let her attend the lessons, even when Mrs Ivanova offered to teach her for free. A year later, Irja and Timo were wed in a small Orthodox church that had a tree growing inside, its trunk a few steps from the altar, its crown spreading above the roof. Her father, to whom she had not spoken for a year, suggested Irja take care of the wedding decorations, but she refused. And when Timo, her new husband, proposed that she resume her classes with Mrs Ivanova, or even that she go to Paris, she refused as well. She had turned that page in her life. No more art. She would be a devoted wife, an active member of the local community, and a mother, when her time came. It was her destiny, and it was enough. That was what she had decided on her wedding day, and she had kept to her decision with fierce determination. But now she was wondering.

Timo's clear voice filled the church: "Again we pray for the repose of the servant of God who departed this life, and for the forgiveness of her every transgression, voluntary and involuntary. Lord have mercy."

The parishioners, woken from their torpor by the familiar sound of the church bell, wandered towards the door. Out of the corner of her eye, Irja saw Sergeant Mauzer stop Martta Jokinen and whisper something in her ear. The old woman froze, the red dress gleaming in the dull candlelight. Then she whispered something back at the policewoman, and from where Irja stood, it looked like an insult.

"Aunt Irja, are you OK?" whispered Kalle. "Aunt Irja?"

Through her tears, Irja caught a glimpse of her old paint palette; or maybe it was just the multicoloured splendour of the icons. The candlelight was brighter now, it danced before her eyes. A baby screamed, his first raw scream upon coming into the world. Irja smiled and, as other screams closed in on her, and the heat from the candles became unbearable, she fell first to her knees, and then, face down, onto the floor.

# 24

"Kalle, I think you know more than you're telling me," said Hella. "About your grandpa. About where he went, and what those 'evil white things' really are."

Kalle shook his head. *No* meaning *I don't know*? Or was it a *no* meaning *I don't want to tell*?

Irja was lying on the bed in her room, weeping quietly. She had not been injured in the fall, just scared by it. Her husband was with her; he was whispering something into her ear, but his words brought no comfort.

*And here I am, enjoying this opportunity to grill the child on my own,* thought Hella, suddenly disgusted with herself. The house was silent and it seemed to her that her voice was unnaturally loud and sinister. She tried again.

"Kalle, I need you to help me. Do you know why? Because I need to find your grandpa. I also need to find the person who killed that lady in the woods. We want him to be punished for what he did, right?"

Wrong, apparently. Because if Kalle wanted him or her punished, he would have said something by now, and he hadn't.

"Justice," said Hella, because she couldn't just leave it at that, even though she knew full well how pathetic what she was about to say sounded – "justice is the most precious thing on earth. Justice makes the world a better place, for everyone."

"Do you really think so?" asked Father Timo as he strode back into the room, a deep frown creasing his brow. "Is justice more important than forgiveness?"

"There's no forgiveness without justice."

Then, just as the priest was about to say something, she turned back to the boy. "All right, Kalle, do you want to tell Father Timo? Or Irja?"

The child wriggled and bit his lip. If only she knew how to talk to him!

"Kalle, listen to me. Please. It's important. Do you want something from Ivalo? A new toy or a box of chocolates? I can ask my friend who drives the big truck to buy it for you. Or you can ride in the truck with him."

It was still a no, but there was a glint in the boy's eye which made Hella think he might be interested after all. The priest must have noticed it too, because he cut in:

"Kalle, why don't you go and play with Seamus? I think he's waiting for you." And, as Hella started to protest, he added, "No, please, Sergeant, the child is tired. He is under my care. You will question him another day." He practically shoved Kalle out of the living room and closed the door after him.

"What do you think you're doing?" Hella gasped. "This is a murder investigation! I'm the one who decides how it should be conducted."

The nerve of this man! Telling her what she should do, and when! She was seething with anger. This picture-perfect house, straight out of a fairy tale, the beautiful wife, and now him. Not a priest but a male model, with authority thrown in for extra oomph. Of course he'd be popular. Good-looking, earnest, well meaning, well spoken. Religion as the opiate of the masses. Those naive and trusting people probably eating out of his hand.

The priest said: "Kalle won't say anything because he promised Erno he wouldn't, and he's keeping his word. He should be proud of himself."

"You think I don't know that?" screamed Hella, suddenly beside herself with rage at these perfect people and their noble feelings. "I understand that. But a crime needs to be punished. It's the law, and it's right, too, whatever your stupid religion thinks about it!"

Father Timo didn't shout back at her, which only made Hella angrier. Instead, he poured strong black tea into a little cup decorated with forget-me-nots and carried the cup through to his wife's bedroom. Then he returned and took a seat in front of Hella.

"Irja is running a high fever," he explained. "Every two days, which is really unusual. We've consulted Dr Gummerus in Ivalo, but he doesn't know how to explain it. So we've been reduced to home remedies. Tea with raspberry and honey. Would you like some?"

"No, thank you. Did you hear what I just said?"

"I did."

"And you're not reacting?"

"I agree with you. Don't look at me like that. I *do* agree with you. Justice is important, not as much as forgiveness in my view, but the two frequently go together. And Erno is my friend. I want the murderer of that woman punished. But it's not right to force the information you need out of a defenceless child. I don't want Kalle to live forever with the idea that he betrayed his promise. I cannot allow that."

"Oh, you can't?" scowled Hella. "I don't know if you realize it, but Kalle is the one person who can tell us something about what happened here. I have no other witnesses."

"I know that. But what do you make of Kalle's freedom? His freedom of choice, his spark of God. It belongs to every human being. The freedom to follow his conscience. He needs to make that decision himself, and not to be tricked out of his free will by promises of trinkets, like those grown men and women who trade their souls for money, or for prestige."

"Then *you* find a way to convince him without buying him," said Hella, who refused to be thrown by the priest's arguments, even though she recognized their worth.

"I will," replied the priest serenely. "But first I have something to tell you. Maybe you won't need to talk to Kalle after you hear this."

He smiled bravely at her, but Hella could see that he was worried, because his knuckles were white and a vein was pulsing in his temple.

"What is it?" she barked back, which was surely uncalled for but made her feel better.

"Before I start, I need to ask you a question. Did you find a handgun?"

As she looked at him, uncomprehending, he repeated his question slowly, as if he was talking to an obtuse child: "I wanted to know if you found a gun in Erno's house."

Hella was sorely tempted to respond that this was not his business, but if she did, she ran the risk of never finding out what gun he meant in the first place.

"No," she snapped. "I'm still looking. Your gun, right?"

He fell into the trap like a baby. "Correct. I lent it to Erno because he asked me for it a couple of weeks before he disappeared. I'm sorry I didn't tell you about it earlier, but I didn't know what kind of person you were."

She looked at the priest. "Why would Erno Jokinen want to borrow a gun from you? He had his hunting rifle. Two, even."

Father Timo was staring down at his hands, as if he had never seen them until this moment. He, too, was conscious of what this meant. Why would you want to borrow a gun, if not to kill somebody? Then, if things go wrong, you can lay the blame on someone else. Or maybe he just wanted a smaller weapon, something easier to conceal than a rifle.

"He didn't tell me the reason," said the priest slowly. "He knew I had a gun because I told him once, and he asked to borrow it. Karppinen saw us, actually. He's always watching Erno's windows, and when I glanced in the direction of his house after handing the gun to Erno, there he was, armed with his binoculars, staring at us."

"And why do *you* have a gun, Mr Waltari?"

Father Timo paused for a second. *Maybe he's wondering whether he can get away with lying to me*, thought Hella.

"Because I haven't always been a priest. Thirteen years ago, I was a revolutionary, part of a group of radical-minded students."

"Did you kill people while you were at it?"

He looked squarely at her. "I didn't. We had this idea of assassinating a politician, Juho Niukkanen, because he opposed a treaty with Soviet Russia, and I was supposed to be the one to pull the trigger. But when we got to our hiding place, I realized that I couldn't take another man's life. I tried to talk my friends out of it, but it was too late; one of them fired, and fortunately missed."

"Does anybody know about this?"

"My wife does, but not her parents. The patriarch does. Erno does, too, although how he found out about it, I've never known."

"And if the word got around about your past, that would be a problem for you, right?"

"It would. I might lose my parish here. No one wants a criminal priest. But it's not me I'm worried about. I don't want you to think that Erno is dangerous in any way. That's why I didn't say anything at first. I didn't know who they'd send to investigate this case."

Hella felt her pulse quicken while a pounding headache took hold in her brain. Was the man really telling her that he had withheld crucial evidence because he didn't know what sort of person she was? Did he realize that he was only making things worse? Was he telling her about the gun, and about his past, only because he knew she had received the file from Eklund? Had he, or Irja, gone through her things while she'd popped to the bathroom before going to church? She kept her door locked at all times, but they might have a spare key.

"And what kind of person am I, in your opinion, Father?" she hissed. She made "Father" sound like an insult.

"An intelligent, sensitive, caring person. A person who would understand, and not jump to conclusions."

She got up to her feet and grabbed her bag.

"Then you're a poor judge of character, *Father.*"

She slammed the door behind her.

# 25

She had a bar of Fazer Blue chocolate in her bag, for emergencies. The chocolate was hidden under a hand-knitted sweater in bright red wool, which she had made herself during her first year at the police academy. At that time, she'd so missed receiving yet another stupid, ugly, hand-knitted sweater as a Christmas gift from her mother that she'd decided to make one herself. Surprisingly, she had succeeded, in the sense that it was, indeed, ugly, much uglier even than what her mother had ever made. The white snowflakes which, for the sake of simplifying the task, she had sewn onto the sweater instead of weaving them in, were not even level. The first snowflake sat in the middle of her right breast, while the second was way lower, and the third had ended up under her left armpit. Still, she wore the sweater every weekend for three months, until she got tired of the ceaseless comments it provoked. She didn't wear it any more, but she still kept it with her as a reminder of that blessed time when she still believed that things could be mended.

The chocolate that she wolfed down while sitting on the edge of her bed did the trick, as usual. Ten minutes later, Hella's anger subsided, leaving an aftertaste of resentment.

Jokela had been right about her when he'd told her she was too emotional. Their last conversation was still fresh in her memory. One of the worst moments of her life. Not on a par with her family's deaths, of course, but a close second.

She stared at the tiny, brittle snowflakes that the cold northern wind was sweeping before her window. Even now, her hands around a steaming mug she'd brought through from the kitchen, Hella felt a knot in her stomach as she remembered their conversation.

"My dear girl, please take a seat."

Hella cringed but obliged. For all his fatherly manner, Chief Inspector Jon Jokela was not the sort of man one could argue with. She knew already what was coming – maybe not the magnitude of it, but the general idea. And yet the only question that kept reverberating in her brain, like a fly trapped inside a glass jar that keeps banging against the walls until someone lets it out or it dies of exhaustion and stress, was this: *Does he call Inspector Mustonen, his protégé, the poster child of Helsinki's homicide squad, "my dear boy"?*

"You know why I called you in, don't you?"

"Yes, sir," said Hella, while her white-knuckled hands grabbed the edges of her seat.

"Please ..." Jokela chuckled, clapping his hands on his knees and leaning forward as if sharing a confidence. "Don't call me *sir.* Call me Jon, that's what all my friends do."

*Friends.* Not "colleagues". It was worse than she thought.

"Jon," she said in a flat voice. She didn't know what to add, but maybe she wasn't expected to say anything. Maybe it was just a way for him to brace himself for what was coming. No one likes to deliver bad news. Or at least not to twenty-five-year-old girls that the University hospital psychiatrist, who assisted the homicide squad every once in a while, had labelled a depressive and an obsessive personality.

"You must understand, Hella, that I'm not disappointed with *you*, but with myself. What happened is my fault, and I said as much to our chief of staff. I should have known better, but I trusted Colonel Kyander's recommendation. He is a man of valour, a man of sterling reputation, so when he vouched for you ..." Jokela shook his head. "Accepting any woman to the squad was a challenge. But a woman who is almost a child still, who had suffered such a personal tragedy ... It was madness. We should have found you a nice, quiet office job, regular hours, no pressure. You would have had time for a private life. I bet being part of a homicide squad is a sure-fire way to drive away any potential suitors, no?"

"No," mumbled Hella, thinking of Steve, of the increasingly rare moments they spent together. Steve was proud of her and of what she did, she was certain of that.

Pretending not to hear her, Jokela turned to the window, behind which two slow-marching junior officers passed, leading guard dogs.

"All I want to say is, I think you'll be better off elsewhere. You'll be much happier. Chief Inspector Lennart Eklund, head of the newly established Ivalo police station, is looking for an experienced officer. I think you'll be perfect for the job. Eklund is a nice, quiet man, very diligent, very methodical. Lapland is beautiful. That's true Finland for you. Clean air, lots of lakes, mushrooms, wild strawberries and blueberries, if you like that sort of thing."

"I don't," said Hella. "Please let me stay. I'll be less" – she struggled to find the right word, the words that would convince him – "less emotional."

Jokela breathed a long sigh and let his arms drop to his sides. "My dear Hella, you know as well as I do that this isn't possible. Not after what's happened. You just can't go about shooting suspects. And don't tell me it was self-defence. Yes, the man had grabbed a knife, but you were the one who led him into the kitchen in the first place, and at the precise moment Inspector Mustonen went to answer the door. He told me he had expressly instructed you not to go there."

"Mustonen didn't instruct me on anything," Hella said. "And when the suspect grabbed that knife, I thought he would kill us, his mother and me. So I fired first."

"Because you *panicked*," Jokela cried out. "You see, that's *exactly* the problem. And this wasn't just any suspect, was it? It was the man who killed his wife and four of their children, and who was about to walk free because of a procedural error. You were the first officer present at the scene, and you cried. I remember it. I felt bad for you at the time. I still do. You, of all people! Trust me, Hella, that's not the life you want to lead. I'm not doing this for myself. I like challenges. I'm doing it for you."

"No. You're not." She was angry now, rising from her seat like a Fury, her good resolutions forgotten completely. "You're doing it for yourself, because you just don't want to be bothered. You want me off your hands, and you always have. You only hired me because someone in the Ministry decided that the Finnish police were going to be the most progressive in the world and employ women not just as ... as administrative assistants, but as regular officers. You had no choice. Do you think I don't know that? And now at last you've found a pretext to send me away."

Jon Jokela wrinkled his nose, not bothering to conceal his disgust any more. "Calm down, my dear, you're being hysterical. The facts speak for themselves."

"There *are* no facts," screamed Hella at the top of her lungs, and if the whole floor heard her, so much the better. "It's my word against his. You're choosing to believe

Mustonen, that's all. Because you go drinking after work with him, because you go hunting with him at weekends." Her eyes were filling with tears, and she blinked them away. She was not going to let him see her cry.

A silence fell upon the room, troubled only by the scraping of his black and gold fountain pen. At last, he tore a page out of his notebook and pushed it towards her.

"Chief Inspector Lennart Eklund's phone number. He's expecting you in Ivalo in two weeks' time; earlier, if you're ready. The chief of staff will send you the forms to fill in, but you might still want to call Chief Inspector Eklund beforehand. Nothing like human contact to make a good start."

Hella rose to her feet, smoothing her wrinkled uniform skirt. She didn't shake Jokela's hand, nor did she take the paper with her new boss's contact details. Instead, she marched to the door and swung it open.

Dear boy Mustonen was eavesdropping in the lobby. He straightened himself up, but not quickly enough. Hella heard muffled laughter coming from the secretary's office.

"Speak of the Devil," smiled Hella. And then, in the sweetest voice she could muster: "Your brown-noser is here, *Jon*."

# FRIDAY 17 OCTOBER

# 26

"What a lovely sweater!" cried out Irja with a little more enthusiasm than was necessary. It was a lie, too – the red top that Sergeant Mauzer was wearing, full of holes, with three white shapes that resembled crushed spiders on its front, was not lovely at all. But it was touching, in a way. Like an old toy that had been worn to pieces by a child's unrelenting affection.

"Morning," grumbled Sergeant Mauzer. She had dark circles under her eyes, and a pillow crease on her left cheek.

Irja put a large plate full of pancakes in front of her house guest and turned to fetch the jam.

"Do you prefer cloudberry or blueberry? Kalle and I were about to start making *himmeli*, so I've cleared the table, but I'll put everything back now. Would you like to join us for our craft project? Did you enjoy making *himmeli* when you were a child?"

"No, thank you." Sergeant Mauzer pushed the plate away, a sour look on her face. "I don't have time for Christmas ornaments. And I'm not hungry, either. I'll just have some coffee." She seemed to hesitate, then added, reluctantly, "Please."

"As you wish," stumbled Irja, taken aback. She was always uncomfortable when people were rude to her. Not because she was scared, no. She just felt confused, ashamed for the other person, as if it was she, not them, who had done something wrong. And maybe she had, after all. Maybe she had offended the sergeant. She tried again:

"I'm sorry I didn't say goodnight to you yesterday. I was feeling unwell and I've neglected all my responsibilities. Will you forgive me?"

Sergeant Mauzer mumbled something that Irja couldn't understand, and judging by the policewoman's expression, maybe it was better that she didn't. Irja flushed and turned away, busying herself with a stew that was sitting on the stove, ready to go into the oven. Tears swelled in her eyes, but she pressed on her lids with her forefingers and managed to stop the torrent that was threatening to upend her fragile equilibrium. If only Timo was here! If only he didn't have to spend all his time at the church! Behind her back, Sergeant Mauzer's spoon clinked against the porcelain as she stirred in the sugar.

"Your husband said you're quite an artist," said the policewoman all of a sudden.

"I used to be. A long time ago."

"Still, you help him restore the icons."

"Is that important?"

"Could be."

"Why?"

"I need you to go to the shed. Draw the dead woman for me."

"What?"

"You heard me. I need her portrait. A reconstruction, rather. If I had a photographer here I wouldn't ask you, but it looks like I don't have a choice."

Sergeant Mauzer pulled the key to the shed out of her pocket and gave it to Irja. Then she buckled her worn leather shoulder bag and, after one last hostile look at her hostess, she grabbed her parka from the coat rack.

"I'm off to interview witnesses and suspects, your husband first. Will I find him at the church?"

Irja nodded silently.

"I probably won't be back for lunch, so don't wait for me."

Sergeant Mauzer turned away, but the movement was deliberate, designed to make Irja believe she was indeed going, all the better to throw her off guard. Thus she was not surprised when the sergeant paused, her gloved hand on the door handle, the cold wind gushing into the living room, sending goose pimples down Irja's naked forearms.

"When a search party was called to go looking for Erno, did you join the others?" the sergeant asked, attempting to sound casual.

"No."

"Why? You're young, able-bodied, and you could surely leave Kalle alone for short periods. So why didn't you go?"

"My husband preferred that I stay at home."

"Why?"

"He was afraid for me. I've been feeling unwell ever since we came to live in Käärmela. I regularly have bouts of fever, and he is always afraid I'll develop pneumonia, like poor Anna Jokinen."

Sergeant Mauzer acknowledged her answer with a nod. Then she left, for good this time.

Irja grabbed the pot of stew, and dropped it back down immediately. The left handle, which had been touching the oven door, was burning hot. Now a red line was starting to swell across her palm. Irja rushed off to the water bucket and put her hand in it. Then she scooped water from the bucket and splashed it onto her face, letting the drops trickle down her throat.

*Suspects,* Sergeant Mauzer had said. She was off to interview suspects, she was off to interview Timo. All in one sentence. What did she suspect him of? Killing that woman? Killing Erno? That was perfectly ridiculous. What would his motive be?

Last night's conversation between Sergeant Mauzer and Timo, which Irja had overheard from her room, came back to haunt her.

Sergeant Mauzer could not possibly understand. She came from a different place. Almost from a different country. And her last name was German. Neither she nor her ancestors had lived in this land of blurred frontiers, of split allegiances. To her, the world was black and white. Now she was suspecting Timo because he was a former communist, and because he had told her about the gun. And what if she searched the house?

Seamus, who had been loitering at her feet, rubbed his back against her leg. Irja wiped tears from her eyes. She would draw the portrait, but not now.

"Come on, Kalle! Time to start working on our Christmas decorations!"

# 27

In the course of her short career, Hella had already met quite a number of people who only respected sheer force. They were totally immune to rational arguments, and any appeal to their better nature was usually met with an empty stare. But threaten them, bully them, and they turn around completely. Martta Jokinen was one of these people. Even though, during their previous encounter, Hella had taken her prized possessions from her, Martta had opened her door wide and bared those sharp rodent teeth in a welcoming smile when Hella showed up on her doorstep.

The old woman was wearing the same garish red dress she'd had on at the unknown woman's funeral, except that now there were stains all over it. Dark circles under her armpits, with the smell to match, a white stain on one of the sleeves, like maybe she had wiped her nose on it, and brownish stains all over the skirt front. Hella preferred not to think about what *these* spots corresponded to.

Martta Jokinen apparently mistook her scientific interest for admiration.

"Beautiful, isn't it?" she asked playfully, turning her head to admire the big knot that decorated her scrawny behind.

"It's the shoes that impress me most," smiled Hella, pointing at the sort of pumps she thought only flamenco dancers wore and which had replaced the felt boots on Martta Jokinen's feet.

"Oh, those?" With a swing of her skirt, the old woman hid them promptly from view.

Hella congratulated herself. Her first guess had been right. The woman had a club foot, which was not really apparent when she wore boots but was perfectly visible now.

"Would you care for some coffee?" asked her hostess, her long, bony hands flittering in the air. "With or without milk?"

There was a small pot on the stove, made of white metal, stained at the rim as if someone had just tasted its contents. Hella shuddered. The Paula Girl was smirking at her from the side of a coffee can.

"Black, please. You are very kind."

*And if I die of acute food poisoning, I want to be decorated posthumously.*

As her hostess was taking two mismatched cups out of the cupboard, Hella flipped through her notebook.

"So tell me, Miss Jokinen, what kind of a man is your brother? I keep hearing different stories from different people. Some say he's a highly intelligent, almost sophisticated man who relies on nobody and only wishes to do well. Others describe him as a pathetic, unreasonable creature who barely gets by on his own. I don't know who to believe. You seem like a wise woman" – Hella gulped down her coffee, preferring to drink it while it was burning hot and she couldn't make out its smell – "so I'd like your opinion as well."

Martta Jokinen didn't need time to search for an answer. "Erno was unlucky," she said, with the finality of a doomsday soul judge, and sipped her coffee from a saucer. She had a lump of sugar placed between her lips. Esteri drank her coffee like that, too. Maybe all old people did.

"Is he? What do you mean by 'unlucky'? Like when he played games?"

"Games, too. But he was unlucky his whole life. First of all, our parents didn't love him. They only left everything to him because they wanted to even things out. Because I was the one they really loved, so if they left everything to me, too, that would have been plain unfair."

Hella jotted this information down in her notebook, marvelling at the old woman's logic.

"Other examples, Miss Jokinen?"

"Well, he had this daughter of his bring her little bastard home. Not something that would happen in respectable families. Just bad luck. And then she dies on him! Can you imagine? I mean, lots of people died that October, we had an epidemic or something, that's what those doctors said, but still … It could have been the other way around. She could have lived, and her little bastard could have died. That would have been better. But it didn't turn out that way."

Hella had a lump in her throat, thinking of Kalle's sweet, babyish smell, and trusting eyes. Was this woman even human?

Still, Martta Jokinen rattled on. "And now he's gone. Pfuitt! Disappeared. He's dead, but I live."

"You're right," recognized Hella, "that *is* plain unlucky."

As Martta Jokinen creased her brow, trying to make up her mind about the impertinence of this last remark, Hella voiced the question she had wanted to ask from the start:

"Some people I interviewed told me that your brother was concerned with 'evil white things'. Would you know what they were talking about?"

"I don't know," said Martta. "The priest, maybe? His ceremonial clothes are white, aren't they?"

Father Timo. Hella had thought of that too. He had been wearing a white surplice the other day.

"Very interesting observation," Hella encouraged her. "I'll consider it carefully. Just one tiny last question, and I'm gone. What was that thing you borrowed from Erno just before he went missing? I know there was an angel who appeared to you in your sleep, you told me all about it, but I understand there were practical reasons for your visit as well."

The old witch took her time to consider the question. She smoothed her skirt, she stirred the coffee in her cup, she looked out of the window, offering Hella a full view of her dandruffy back. When she finally decided to speak, it was with such gravity that Hella's mind had already raced off imagining all sorts of exciting possibilities: a nuclear warhead, maybe, or a map indicating the exact position of Jesus Christ's grave.

"The Jokinen family album."

Hella's dreams of fame screeched to a halt. "A photograph album?" she asked in disbelief.

"That's right. I've wanted it all my life. Then one day my stupid brother shows up unannounced, asking if I'd like to have it for a while. I suppose he was afraid that that little bastard of his would make paper planes out of all the pictures. Or maybe he felt he was going to die, and wanted to make things right with me. I don't know. So he tells me I can have it, but only the first part, and I'm to bring it back in two days, and that's when I'll get the second volume."

"And did you? Bring it back, I mean?"

"Of course. It was how I found the boy. But I didn't bring it back in two days; I took my time with it. Had every right to do so. Besides, he borrowed something from me, too. A trinket box I dug out from a dump last year." She made a vague gesture towards a shelf jammed with all sorts of objects, most of them old and stained. There was an empty space next to what looked like a pasta machine. "Said he liked it."

Something was wrong here, thought Hella. For what reason would Erno all of a sudden decide to bring the album to his sister? They practically never saw each other. The only explanation Hella could imagine was that the album had just been a ruse to make sure that Martta would come to his house and check on Kalle while he was away. Which meant that he had known there was a risk that he might never come back. But if things had really happened in this manner, it had been a terrible gamble on Erno's part. Martta was not reliable. She had been told to return with the album in two days, and she had waited four more before she had complied with her undertaking. Kalle could have died waiting for her to show up. Why hadn't Erno asked Timo and Irja? she wondered.

"So where is the album now?" Hella asked out loud.

"What do you think? Took it back with me, no point leaving it there. Took the second one, too." Martta Jokinen pointed to two fat, leather-bound volumes that sat on a shelf otherwise crowded with dirty dishes.

"Can I borrow the albums, Miss Jokinen? Until tomorrow?"

Hella thought about the dead woman. The album would certainly contain a picture of the other Jokinen sister. Whether she would be able to match a picture of a child with the disfigured remains of a grown woman was another question.

"No," said Martta, suddenly suspicious. "You can't."

"I'll be very careful," promised Hella. "I'll wear gloves."

Martta Jokinen stared at her. "Write it down. About the gloves."

Hella obediently scribbled a note promising to handle the album with care and to return it promptly, then watched the old woman hide it inside her corsage. Only then were the two albums, fat and bound in pigskin, brought to her. Hella resisted the temptation to look through them straight away; instead, she got up, thanked Martta Jokinen for her hospitality, and, with the albums under her arm, rushed back to the Waltaris'.

When she entered the living room, Kalle was standing with his head cocked to one side in front of a portrait sketched by Irja. Hella suppressed an exclamation. The priest's wife had talent, there was no doubt about that. The unknown woman was staring at her from the page, the jaw resolute, the cheekbones high. But Kalle seemed not to find her to his liking. Just as Irja came into the room, carrying a basket full of clothes, he turned towards her.

"You forgot the little stars she had on her shoulders," he said accusingly.

# 28

Time stopped. Hella felt the little hairs on the back of her neck stand on end. The little stars ... She held her breath. Kalle was staring out of the window now, watching the snowflakes that waltzed towards the ground. How many more days did she have here? Probably one or two. Even if Eklund didn't force her out of the investigation, the snow would.

Then everything snapped back into motion. Not daring to believe what she'd heard, Hella grabbed a pencil. She drew a Red Army star that looked like a capital A, with a bar tied to its extremities.

"This sort of star?"

Kalle nodded.

"How many of them? On each shoulder? Do you remember?"

Kalle counted out dutifully. "Four on each." He showed her his splayed hand, his palms sweaty and pink, the thumb pressed down. "Like this."

A captain. Jesus Christ! Did Irja Waltari understand? Hella didn't dare look at her for fear of betraying her excitement.

"And this woman, she was your grandpa's friend?"

The little boy shook his head. "She wasn't a friend. You asked me already whether Grandpa had a lady friend, and he didn't. Those who say so are lying."

"Who was she, then?"

It emerged from Kalle's long and confused explanation that the woman had come to see Erno the previous spring. She had knocked on their door one evening, and at first Erno hadn't understood who she was, but when he had, finally, he had sent Kalle to bed. The next morning, Erno and the woman had been very angry at each other; apparently, they were not on speaking terms. But the woman was nice, and over breakfast, she had taught Kalle how to make paper planes. Then she was gone, and Kalle hadn't seen her since.

"Do you remember her name, Kalle?" asked Hella.

He didn't. Maybe his grandpa never told him. He didn't remember.

"And did the woman really have those stars on her shoulders?" asked Hella cautiously. She had difficulty believing that a captain in the Soviet army could go wandering across the border wearing her uniform.

No, explained Kalle. She had been wearing a sweater and trousers. But she had showed his grandpa a little book; it had her picture in it, and Kalle had noticed the stars. He thought that the stars were very beautiful. He wanted some on his own clothes when he was old enough.

Hella's thoughts went back to the steel cabinet that occupied the right-hand corner of Eklund's office. The cabinet was screwed to the wall; there was a big lock on it, and inside there was a strongbox. Once, when she had just arrived in Ivalo, Eklund had explained to her that the strongbox contained sensitive files.

"What kind of files?" she asked him. "Criminal investigations? Evidence to be used in court?"

"No. Political files. You can't ignore that our relations with Soviet Russia are tense at the best of times. With Ivalo being located so close to the border, it is our duty to be on the lookout for all sensitive cases. Military intelligence. Diversions."

"Are we expected to cooperate with the SUPO?"

He looked at her in disdain. "Not you. Only officers of my rank can have security clearance."

*Well, good luck to you, Lennart Eklund,* thought Hella. *I'm here, on the spot, security clearance or not. And I'm not giving up on this.*

There was just one more question she needed to ask:

"Was that woman related in some way to what you called the 'evil white things'?"

Immediately, the boy shut up like a clam. He wouldn't meet her eye.

"He doesn't know," ventured Irja. "He's afraid. Can't you see that? He told you all he knows, or what he can tell."

Hella turned abruptly and made for the door.

# 29

*Patience is a virtue,* thought Hella. It was a pity she had so little of it. It was just another admirable character trait that Irja Waltari seemed to possess in bucketfuls and Hella didn't: tolerance, kindness to strangers, generosity, you name it. If it was nice, she had it, and Hella didn't.

She tried again.

"Mr Karppinen! Come on, open up, I know you're home. I can hear you, Mr Karppinen. You're standing just behind the door, and I can hear you breathing."

*This is ridiculous,* decided Hella as she banged on the troll's front door. *This village is populated by old people, and I hate old people.* To her, they were not the sweet, inoffensive creatures everyone imagined them to be. They were egotistic, arrogant, misbehaving brats who believed that their age conferred on them the right to do anything they wanted to. Including murder.

"Mr Karppinen, if you want to be arrested, this is the way to do it!"

What had got into the man? Was he afraid he'd said too much the last time she saw him?

Her patience worn thin, she picked up an axe from a bucket on the porch. *If Eklund ever learns about this* … But she pushed the thought aside.

"Step back, Mr Karppinen."

Just as the axe's blade touched the door, the handle turned.

"What are you, mad? You can't just go around splitting people's doors with an axe!"

"I warned you, Mr Karppinen," sighed Hella. "I told you to open the door, and when you didn't, I told you to step back. Were you hurt?"

But she could see for herself that Jeremias Karppinen was fine. He was seething with rage, but that was *his* problem. And the door wasn't damaged; a mere nick in the wood.

"So may I come in now?"

"You already have."

Still, he stepped to one side, allowing Hella to stomp into the shiny living room. Then he wiped his tiny feet, which was unnecessary given he hadn't been outside, and followed her as she walked casually around the room.

"So what are you hiding from me exactly, Mr Karppinen?" Hella lifted the lid of a huge bin and glanced inside, not that she expected to find anything.

"Ain't hiding anything," intoned Jeremias Karppinen. Hella was under the impression that was what he was going to answer to any question she asked: haven't broken into no house, haven't killed no neighbour, haven't heard of anything untoward. Karppinen made her think of the three proverbial monkeys condensed into one. Not exactly an easy witness.

She decided to change tactic.

Smiling widely, Hella slumped onto the bench next to the window and poured herself some coffee from the small coffee pot. She was not afraid of the germs here. One could trust Mr Karppinen to keep his house nice and clean.

"Good coffee, Mr Karppinen. Nice biscuits. Did you make them yourself?" She fumbled in the box, fishing out a plump cinnamon roll. "I have all the time in the world, Mr Karppinen."

"What do you want?"

"I told you. I want the whole story. One, who was the woman? And I know things about her already, like her rank and where she came from, so the first question is really just to check if you're lying. Two, did Erno have any other visitors? Three, were you the one who searched Erno Jokinen's house? Four, how much do you expect to get for this information if you sell it to the Soviets? No, forget that one. There's no four. You're a law-abiding citizen, a patriot, and you're very eager to make your confession. Free of charge. I'm listening, Mr Karppinen." To drive her point home, Hella picked up another biscuit and started munching it noisily.

*Christ,* she thought, *here I am, a grown woman, an elite police officer, trying to force a witness to cooperate by annihilating his food reserves! I should have begged Jokela to give me another chance in Helsinki. Not that he would have listened; he's not the type to change his mind once a decision is made.*

"I didn't search his house," said Karppinen.

"Martta Jokinen saw you lurking next to her brother's house." She said it very slowly, to make sure the information sank in.

The troll changed his version of events, but still confessed nothing. "Didn't take anything. Went into the house, yes, I did. To check everything was in order."

"Oh yes, I forgot! That was because you thought the house was already yours, right? Given that neither the child nor his guardians would be able to take care of it. So *was* everything in order?"

"No," mumbled the troll in an aggrieved voice. "You saw it yourself."

She started to formulate some threat she knew perfectly well would never be brought to execution, when the little man spoke up again.

"Look, I don't know why you're after me. I haven't done anything. I've seen the woman before, yes, but it was dark. I don't know a thing about her. You're setting me up, most likely. Making me a scapegoat. And you're doing it in cold blood, because you're one of them."

He sat down in front of her and pulled the biscuit tin towards him, slamming the lid shut.

"I'm not setting you up, Mr Karppinen. But I strongly suspect that you know much more about what happened to your neighbour than you've told me."

But Karppinen, possibly feeling that Hella was losing ground, went on in the same high-pitched voice that made her cringe: "You need to pin it on someone, right? Better me than your dear priest and his wife, even though they have a motive and I don't. I know the way the police work. Much easier to pin it on an ordinary citizen."

"Out of curiosity," asked Hella in a scathing voice, "what motive would you credit them with?"

Karppinen smirked.

"What kind of a police officer are you exactly? Even a *polissyster* would have known that by now. Go to the cemetery. Then ask them about Anna Jokinen's death, and what it meant for them. Ask them, and watch them answer."

# 30

It was dark outside. Night had fallen as it always did at this time of the year: creeping in like a crab, hesitating, withdrawing, before finally dosing the sky in indigo and magnifying the stars. Irja had lit all the lamps in her living room, and still dark shadows were lurking in the corners. The table was piled high with food. She had spent the entire afternoon cooking, and now she was wondering who would eat it all. This was something she did when she was worried. She knew it, and yet she couldn't help herself. When her hands were busy, her mind was at rest: no dark shadows there, and no monsters.

Timo was out somewhere. At noon, when he hadn't come home for lunch, she had packed some pierogies and gone to the church, thinking he must be so absorbed in his work that he hadn't noticed the time passing. He was not there. No message from him and no means of finding out where he was or what Sergeant Mauzer had talked to him about. Irja bit her lip. Next to her, Kalle was making paper planes. Their attempt at *himmeli* had fallen flat – the boy just wasn't interested. Ever since Sergeant Mauzer had left them, running out of the door shortly after eleven, Kalle had been making planes out of her drawing paper. There were maybe twenty of them already, but he showed no intention of stopping.

Irja wondered about the portrait she had drawn, and what Kalle's remark meant for all of them. The revelation that Erno's mysterious visitor had been a Soviet army captain had come as a shock. She didn't quite know what to make of it. Was it really possible that Erno was a spy? As far as she knew, he spent his time at home, only going away to hunt for two or three hours at a time. What interest could he possibly represent for a spymaster?

She thought of their last conversation. She hadn't told Sergeant Mauzer about it yet, didn't think it would be useful, but maybe she was wrong. She was always unsure how much Sergeant Mauzer really needed to know. Irja had liked old Erno very much; she now hoped with all her heart that the presence of a Soviet captain at his place had some innocent explanation. Maybe they were family? Erno's sister. A niece of Erno's dead wife, who needed to see him urgently. Something like that.

Kalle's small hands kept working on his paper planes. It was the children who suffered, thought Irja. The innocence, the trust in the world around them, the memories they have – how easy it is to destroy all this. What would Kalle have left, once he learned that his beloved grandpa was a spy who'd betrayed his own country? Would Kalle's memories of him be forever tainted by that knowledge? She hoped she had strength enough to make this child happy again.

# 31

Hella's knee-jerk response to Irja Waltari's welcoming smile was a groan. *And if it was Eklund who was here instead of me?* she wondered. *Or Ranta? Would the woman still be as friendly, as nice?* This gentleness was a façade. When Irja, undeterred, beckoned her to the table, the surface of which was not even visible under the accumulation of plates, saucers and bowls, all brimming with food, Hella pretended she was not hungry. Even though, truth be told, she was ravenous. Karppinen's biscuits were a long-forgotten memory. She had spent the entire afternoon sifting through Erno's belongings. She had opened every book, had looked in every corner, under the benches and on the shelves. She had fumbled inside the stove, dislodging an avalanche of soot. She had paced the front yard, and the back garden, on the lookout for recently disturbed soil while tiny Karppinen in his muskrat hat with earflaps surveyed her every movement from his porch with his stupid binoculars.

She had found some money, but not much, sewn into Erno's mattress. The cache had also contained a lacquered wooden box, surely Palekh. Inside it, there was a wide golden band, well worn, which Hella guessed to be Erno's wife's wedding ring, and Erno's papers: his birth certificate, his passport, his father's will. She had also found Kalle's birth certificate: Father: unknown. No gun. No proof of Erno's involvement in a spy game, either. Could Kalle have dreamed up the stars? Child witnesses *were* notoriously unreliable.

Thus she was back to what Karppinen had insinuated: namely, that she had to take a closer look at the Waltaris. She followed his advice and went to the surprisingly vast cemetery, where she wandered between the tombstones and crosses until she found what she was looking for.

"Are you sure you're not hungry?" called Irja as Hella was heading down the corridor.

Angry with herself, Hella ambled back to the living room. Irja was sitting next to the table, her head in her hands. No sign of the priest. No sign of the boy, either, though it probably didn't mean anything. He could be hiding above the stove, as he usually was.

"Where's your husband?"

The woman smiled a guilty smile. "I don't know. I was hoping you could tell me. He left this morning, and I haven't seen him since. You *did* meet him in the church, didn't you?"

Hella sat down next to Irja and grabbed a pierogi, almost without thinking. The rich, creamy filling, made of potatoes and mushrooms, melted in her mouth. What had they talked about? This morning seemed like centuries ago. "I asked him questions pertaining to his past. To his involvement in the Communist Party."

"Oh," whispered Irja. "That was a long time ago; he was just a boy. He knows now that he was wrong. And he wasn't an active member of the group. Just a supporter."

"My father," said Hella sententiously, "always told me that people don't change, ever. With age, they just grow more like themselves."

Irja thought about it for a moment as Hella devoured another pierogi.

"I'm not sure I agree," she said finally. "People can change. I know *I* have."

"Oh yes, *you* have," confirmed Hella, and coming from her, it didn't sound like a compliment. "Actually, I think that in some ways, you're just like me. The only difference between us is that you *want* to be different. But deep down, you're not. You're in revolt, and angry that this God of yours hasn't helped you, even though you serve Him all day long, just like your husband, and you've prayed, and you've done nothing wrong. And still your God did this to you. So some days you wonder, I bet you do. What if He doesn't even exist? What if it's all a big lie, and your beloved husband is serving that lie?"

She waited for a moment, then delivered the fatal blow:

"So are you going to call him Aleksi?"

Irja froze, her eyes on the copper coffee pot she had just placed on the table.

"What are you talking about?"

"Your new baby. Because you're expecting a new baby, aren't you? So I'm asking if you're going to give him the same name ..." Hella hesitated, but only for a fraction of a second. She was angry at the priest's wife, appalled by her docility, her resignation. How could she live, how could she be normal, let alone nice, when such a terrible thing had happened to her? "I'm asking if you're going to give the new baby the same name you gave his older brother," she repeated in a clear voice. "Aleksi. Is it a family name? Are you going to give him the same clothes? The same toys?"

She had gone too far. Irja drew her breath in sharply, still not looking at her. Then she sat down slowly, smiling through tears.

"Thank you."

"You're mad," replied Hella in a flat voice. "A raving lunatic. No wonder you married a priest. What are you thanking me for?"

"You're the only person I've met who speaks of Aleksi as a real child. Others … They just pretend he didn't exist. They only say, don't you worry, Irja, one day you'll be a mother too. They don't realize that I am already a mother. And this" – she touched her stomach, briefly, and smiled again – "this will be my second child. I'll call him Petar, after Timo's father. And I'll want him to know that he isn't the first, that his brother existed, and still exists in my heart, even though Timo, I and the midwife were the only ones who saw him before he was put in the grave."

Hella could take it no longer. She sprang to her feet and in her haste to get away knocked over a pale blue cup with a gilded rim. The coffee spilled onto the tablecloth. She didn't even pretend to wipe it or set the cup straight again. She just ran away, to her room, to her file and her field notes. To take refuge among things she could understand.

# 32

It was now two hours since Hella had escaped to her room, slamming the door behind her. She had spent those two hours sitting on her bed, in the dark, staring out of the window, not that there was anything to see there, and drinking vodka from a mug. In her head, the conversation continued. At some point, she didn't even know who it was she was talking to, if it was Irja, or her dead mother, or Steve. Or even that other Hella, not the bitchy, ruthless, trigger-happy spinster she had become but the eager, confident medical student with her dimples and ready smile who had died on her doorstep eight and a half years ago.

But though she didn't know who she was talking to, she did know what she was talking *about.* Her conversation was about strength, and weakness, and about how easy it was to mistake one for the other. And she was wondering about herself.

She had always thought of herself as a strong woman. After all, she had survived the death of her entire family and hadn't gone mad. She had even managed to finish her studies – not medical school, she couldn't bear to see blood and human suffering all day long any more – but the *polis-syster* training, and then the course at the police academy.

At the time, it had seemed like a good idea, not only for the feeling of control it bestowed upon her, but also because, in those early years, she had still thought she could catch the bastard who had taken her family's life. Over time, she had amassed a huge load of information, witness statements, weather reports and complicated graphs mapping the deadly truck's trajectory.

In the dark northern sky, the stars were close enough to touch. The lawn in front of her window was dressed in a thin white coverlet. She hadn't noticed it was still snowing. One more day, and she'd have to get out of here. Resume her life in Ivalo. Spend her days writing reports that no one ever read. Go home to her solitary room where no one was waiting for her.

"You're so strong, Hell," Steve used to say. "You're one hell of a woman." Stupid as she was, she had taken it as a compliment, at first. She was strong when she walked through the gloomy Helsinki night alone, dancing her way home after yet another clandestine meeting at Yle Radio headquarters. She was strong when she pretended to be a casual acquaintance when they ran into his mother-in-law on the street. She was strong when they cancelled their evening plans because his daughter had had a nosebleed and his wife was worried.

"You'll be all right, Hell, won't you? You won't start screaming, tearing your hair out or doing other silly things hysterical women do?"

"No," she used to reply with a superior smile. "Of course not. I'm not like your wife."

Elsbeth, Steve's wife of many years, was a housewife. For this reason, she was considered the delicate one. The one to be pitied, because Steve didn't love her any more. He'd told her so himself. The one to be protected, because, in contrast to Hella, she'd never known how to fend for herself.

"You understand, Hell, she's not strong like you, she can't survive on her own. I want to leave her, of course I do, to be with you, but – what kind of man would I be then? You'd be the first to call me a bastard."

Never, not once in three years, did she dare say: *No, I wouldn't. Leave her.*

Which was just an illustration of how stupid twenty-something orphans could be.

"So tell me, what does it feel like to have so much authority?" Steve would ask, propped on his elbow, a lazy finger following the curve of her breast. "Does it feel amazing? To be the one with the gun, to have everyone listen to you?"

"It feels good," Hella would say and smile, even though, to be honest, it didn't always. "It feels like being the master of the universe."

That was what Steve wanted to hear. He was the master of the universe too, in his own way. His deep, husky voice with that mid-Atlantic twang, which was one of the few things, along with the name, that he had inherited from his American father, filled the air every weekday from 3 to 9 p.m. in his popular music and chit-chat show on Yle Radio. When she was still at the police station at nine – as was often the case, not because she wanted to show her dedication to the job, but because Steve's office was around the corner – and waiting for him, she always switched the radio on full blast. She listened intently, because she wanted to be ready to discuss whatever deep thoughts he shared with his audience. Even though, most of the time, he didn't say anything deep, or indeed say anything at all. His dream of being an investigative journalist had not been realized yet; his bosses thought that he was only good for music.

"They don't trust me to do politics yet," Steve had told her once, by way of explanation, all the while unbuttoning his jeans. "They think I'm too frivolous. Why don't you take this in your mouth, Inspector, while you're thinking about how you can help me make my dream come true?"

And she would laugh, pretending to find it funny.

Until one day when, all of a sudden, she couldn't.

"You're a bastard, Steve," Hella said out loud, and toasted his imaginary presence with her half-empty mug. Outside, the stars were no longer visible, and even the moon was struggling to shine through a thick blanket of clouds. "You're a bastard, but I still love you."

Suddenly, it seemed very important that he should know it. She had never really told him, had she? Maybe that was the reason their relationship had gone down the drain. She had never really told him how she felt about him. She had been afraid of coming across as desperate.

Hella struggled across the room and lit a paraffin lamp that sat on a card table by the window. She tore a page out of her notebook and fished out an envelope with IVALO POLICE DEPARTMENT stamped in the right-hand corner.

To Mr Steve Collins,
Yle Radio, Unioninkatu 20, 00160, Helsinki

My dear Steve,

You're a bastard, do you know that? But I love you all the same; I've never stopped loving you, and I never will.

Was that a good way to start her letter? More than likely it would scare him off. Even in her current vodka-induced confusion, she knew that.

She tore off another sheet of paper and wrote:

Dear Steve,

It's been a long time. Don't you miss me? Even a little bit?

That was worse. It was begging for attention, and it lacked panache.

Hella downed the rest of her vodka. Never send a letter unless you've slept on it, her father always said. She'd take his advice. She folded the two drafts carefully and slid them into the envelope, then put the letter under her pillow. *Let's hope I have an erotic dream,* she thought, and wondered if perhaps she should go and fetch more vodka from the kitchen.

The dam had broken, as they always do, first with a little crack that appeared the day she found the bodies of the four children and their mother. She telephoned Steve at his work. She knew she wasn't supposed to, of course she did, but she just couldn't help it. It was not something she could keep to herself.

"Hello, dear, what's up?" He chatted amicably while the person who had called him to the phone stood close by. Then, without warning, he snapped: "What are you, crazy, calling me here? Elsbeth is best friends with our secretary. Do you want her to skin me alive? And what are you talking about? I can't understand you. Stop sniffing and speak clearly."

But Hella couldn't. She couldn't stop crying. She couldn't speak clearly, either. She hung up, and when he picked up the phone and called her three days later, an ominous shadow had fallen over their relationship.

When, just a couple of weeks after that, she was appointed to her current position in Ivalo, his reaction was nothing short of relief.

"It might be good, you know," he said. "For your career. Here, you're just one of many. In Ivalo, you'll shine. And I'm sure the work will be interesting, too. I've heard some weird stories from my sources up north. All sorts of things happen when you live practically on the border with our beastly communist neighbour. Soviet spies, Finnish spies, Western Alliance officials who pretend to go fishing, cameras sticking out of every pocket. Yes, you can learn things there. Promise me that if you hear something of the kind you'll let me know. My audience loves spy stories. Well, who doesn't?"

Hella had promised, fighting back tears. She was a strong woman. She would not let him see her cry.

She hadn't written to Steve from Ivalo, though. Just as she was not going to post her letter now. She was stupid, but not *that* stupid. And pride was important when it was all you had left.

# SATURDAY 18 OCTOBER

# 33

The letter was waiting for Hella, propped against the milk jug. It had been brought at dawn by Kai, who had spent two days doing some business in Ivalo and had been entrusted with the letter by a fat and anxious-looking man called Chief Inspector Lennart Eklund.

Hella expected to read another long missive in standard Eklundesque, full of caveats, assurances and references to official documents, the more obscure the better. A letter that used up a great deal of words while saying nothing of importance.

But what stared at her from the page was a totally different animal.

Mauzer,

When Helsinki forced you on me, they told me you were a reasonable woman. They were mistaken. Any reasonable person, let alone a qualified police officer, would know when to stop and call for help. You cannot do this alone, Mauzer. You do not have medical training. What you took for a bullet wound was probably just a puncture wound made by animal teeth. I fail to comprehend why you insist on treating this like a criminal investigation. Forget it.

> You are required to report to the office ASAP. Your vacation is over and we need you here. Mr Kukoyakka will pick you up on his way back to Ivalo, so wait for him next to the Rajajoosepintie road postbox after 5 p.m. this Sunday. This is an order.
>
> Chief Inspector Lennart Eklund

Hella read the letter twice. She even started to read it for a third time, before admitting to herself that the text was already engraved in her memory.

For God's sake. Whatever had got into the man? Was he afraid she would ruin his statistics, or was he worried about the expenses she'd incurred while working on the case?

One thing was certain. She was not going anywhere tonight. First, she had already organized her day, and she didn't in the least like last-minute changes of plan. Second, there was no way she was going to wait next to the postbox, like a destitute hooker, for Kukoyakka to pick her up. If he wanted to see her, let him come down to the village. Third and most importantly, she had a case to solve, and she was not going to let anyone, least of all Eklund, interfere with her investigation. And the investigation was far from over. She had not one, but three leads now. The Waltaris. The Soviet captain. And Karppinen, too, because if that troll believed he was off the hook, he was very much mistaken.

She pocketed Eklund's letter, everything about her demeanour suggesting that the piece of paper was not important. Then she sat down with the album and a large mug of steaming coffee by her elbow.

The whole Waltari family was gathered in front of her: Irja, who looked radiant that morning, her skin glowing pink, her eyes bright; her husband, who was getting ready for the church, and Kalle with his bosom friend Seamus at his side.

Hella opened the album and immediately met the stern gaze of a slight blond man, dressed in a tailcoat, his face adorned by an impressive handlebar moustache.

"That's Erno's father," explained Irja. "Erno is the youngest son of a timber-factory owner."

Kalle slurped his milk and craned his head to look at the photograph.

"You've seen these already, Kalle, haven't you?" inquired Hella. "Nothing new here, right?"

The boy hesitated, then seemed to recognize that the question didn't constitute a violation of his grandpa's secret. *No,* he mouthed silently. Nothing new.

Hella took the photograph out of the album and scanned the back for clues. But the ink was faded, the words barely visible, and, in any case, unsensational: name, date and place of birth and death. She put it back. She flipped the pages and more photographs followed: a pale woman, pretty in a very conventional way, her almost white hair dressed in an elaborate construction that obscured her tiny, birdlike face.

Irja provided an unnecessary explanation: "Erno's mother", but Hella had already guessed as much herself because of the full page the photograph occupied, and because Mrs Jokinen and her children had the same mouth: small and resolute.

The next double page was dedicated to the children: there was Erno as a young boy, dressed in a sailor suit. Another little boy standing next to him: you could see in his face that this one was not going to survive the rigours of Finnish country life. An older girl, who would have been beautiful if not for the huge scar that ran across half her face. Finally, Martta, the youngest child, with her rodent smile and her peculiar, calculating gaze.

No clues here either. She flipped forward a few pages which contained pencil sketches of the house and the furniture, with the price written next to each object. Hella dutifully took out each photograph, each drawing, to inspect it, but there was nothing whatsoever of interest. Just a plain, old family album, useful to a historian, not so to a police officer who was about to violate her chief's direct orders.

The last page contained only three photographs: a portrait of a stern young woman in a checked dress, her hair tied in a bun – probably Erno's wife – occupied half of the page, the space next to it empty. One picture at least must have been taken out of the album, and Hella believed she knew which one it was – the photograph of Anna that Kalle had been carrying around.

Then there was Kalle himself, smiling. *He has a beautiful smile,* thought Hella, but she'd never seen it, and given the turn that her investigation was taking, she doubted she ever would. Next to him was a recent picture of Erno, staring grimly at the camera. Was Jokinen defying her to uncover his secret, or was he hoping that the secret had died with him? It was a strange case, full of contradictions and hidden motives, and, not for the first time, she wondered if she would ever manage to solve it.

She closed the album with a soft thud, with the Waltaris still watching. OK, so the album was not important in itself. It was just a tactic Erno had used to make sure someone would come and check on Kalle. Because he was afraid he might not be coming back. But why hadn't he asked the Waltaris to check on the boy? Was he afraid they would ask too many questions? Still, he could have thought of something, invented a plausible lie. So there must have been a different reason. Had it been because of his argument with Father Timo? Or was his mission perhaps somehow related to the priest and his wife? Once again, Hella made a mental list of the questions that remained unanswered: the unlocked door, the presence of the Soviet officer, and now this. Not to mention the "evil white things", and something Karppinen had mentioned and that she had only realized now. Digging. He said Erno had spent his time digging. Didn't make sense, any of it.

Hella, who for a short moment had allowed herself to join in the domestic bliss, lapsed back into her professional self:

"So, Mr Waltari, why don't you tell me again the exact words you exchanged with Erno Jokinen when you saw him last?"

Father Timo looked at her thoughtfully. "I don't remember the exact words. I suppose I must have mentioned Kalle's enthusiasm in helping me out in the church – his ambition was to become an altar boy. I knew Erno was a non-believer, but he was also a friend, so when Kalle told me his grandpa had agreed to let him attend, I believed him. It was a shock to me when I realized Erno knew nothing about it."

"So he became angry?"

"Angry is an understatement. He was seething with rage. I think, for him, it was a betrayal on my side, and I didn't manage to convey to him that it was just a misunderstanding. So I apologized, took my chessboard, and left."

"And that's all?"

"It is. I wanted to talk to Kalle, to explain to him that his grandpa had his reasons for not allowing him to come to the church, but Erno wouldn't let me."

"He didn't mention his intention of going anywhere?"

"Not to me."

"And you haven't seen him since?"

"No."

Hella had already asked these last few questions before, when she had gone to interview Father Timo in the church, and he had given her the exact same answers. Answers that led her nowhere. She was about to close her notebook when Irja, who had remained silent throughout their conversation, spoke up suddenly.

"I saw him. I've been meaning to tell you this, though it's probably not significant. Erno came here the day after the dispute. He said he wanted to talk about Timo, but now I'm wondering if that wasn't just an excuse."

# 34

Irja remembered the scene in all its vivid detail.

She was standing next to the table, peeling beetroots, when Erno knocked on the window. Unlike the other villagers, Erno never came in uninvited, so Irja wiped her hands on a kitchen towel and went to open the door. He stood on her doorstep, his grey *ushanka* in his hands, and she suddenly remembered Timo's words: *Erno is a natural gentleman.* He hadn't needed an expensive formal education to become one.

She beckoned him in. She was happy to see Erno, because she knew about the dispute from her husband, and she looked forward to their reconciliation.

"Would you like some coffee? I have Swedish cinnamon buns straight from the oven."

Erno nodded, but she could see that his mind was elsewhere. Still, she poured him a huge mug of strong, very hot coffee, and placed a basket full of buns at his side. She also packed another basket for him to take home to Kalle.

"Timo isn't back yet," she ventured, while her guest remained silent. "Have you tried the church? Sometimes he works with only one candle, so the windows look dark from the outside —" She bit her tongue. Church was maybe not a good subject.

But Erno looked at her absent-mindedly, and shook his head.

*He's trying to make up his mind about something,* thought Irja. *And he's not sure I'm the right person to talk to.*

To put him at ease, she picked up her beetroot again.

"Would you mind if I continue peeling it?"

Sometimes it was easier for people to talk to you when you didn't look at them. It occurred to her that that was what they'd had in mind when they had invented confessionals.

Erno sipped his coffee in silence. Then, just as she was about to ask him a question about Kalle, he spoke up.

"Do you remember when you first moved here? A year ago, right?"

"Of course I do. It was early October, and the village was so lovely, all gold and red. It was very warm for the season."

"It was. The soil wasn't even frozen, and I had no trouble digging Anna's grave. You came because old Father Nikolai died."

Irja nodded. Father Nikolai's passing away had been unexpected, and the church had stayed empty for three weeks while the authorities had frantically searched for a replacement. They had wanted to find someone quickly, because there were quite a number of funerals to conduct.

"Yes, old people dropped dead in droves that year," confirmed Erno quietly.

Irja poured him some more coffee, but for once she didn't avert her eyes, which were full of tears. Erno knew she had lost her son that very October. Just a couple of weeks after he had lost his daughter.

"Do you remember Anna?" he asked her. "You took care of her during her last days, didn't you? You see, I don't remember how it was, exactly, and who was there. When I try to think back to those days, I just get glimpses of this and that … but the big picture is blurred."

"Yes, of course I remember her."

Although, come to think of it, did she really? For Irja too, those days spent at the bedside of a dying woman had become a blur, annihilated by her own, private grief. She remembered a blotched face, hollow eyes and spidery hands. She had wondered, at the time, how this emaciated, barely-there woman that nothing seemed to interest any longer could have given birth to such a big, healthy, lively boy. She remembered wondering about Kalle's father, whom Anna had not even mentioned once. As if he'd never existed.

"I was very grateful when you came over to help me," said Erno finally, breaking the spell. "But I was afraid that you'd fall ill too. Catch the flu from Anna. And you did fall ill, didn't you? Then, because of that, you lost your own child. This entire time, I haven't been able to forgive myself."

Irja forced the tremor out of her voice. "That's nonsense, Erno. I could have caught it from just about anyone. The entire village was ill. Why do you think they sent a whole team of doctors here? Because the situation was so serious."

Erno shook his head and looked away. "Didn't stay long enough, did they? They were already gone by the time Anna and you fell ill."

Irja waited, thinking he wanted to add something, but he just sneered at Seamus, who had surreptitiously crawled next to him.

"Did you want to ask me something about Anna's last days?" She tried to meet Erno's gaze, but he kept looking away. What was he hiding from her?

"You're expecting again, aren't you?" he asked.

"Yes," she smiled, a little concerned that he had guessed so easily. Still, he was one of the very few people she wanted to share her good news with. But if she expected him to offer his congratulations and the reassurance that this time all would be well, she was mistaken.

"I don't feel guilty any more about you catching that fever from Anna. That's what I came to tell you. I shouldn't have felt guilty in the first place. And as for your husband … I suppose he means well. But he serves a God I neither like nor trust."

Erno got up and carried his cup to the washbasin.

"Please don't tell him I came round. He doesn't need to know. Yet."

# 35

Sometimes, what is *not* there is more important than what is. And what was not in the album was the photograph of Anna Jokinen that Kalle kept carrying around with him. Hella saw it, of course; she saw it every day. Propped against a coffee pot while Kalle ate his breakfast. Between the pages of Kalle's picture book. Peeking out from under his pillow. She saw it, but she had never looked at it, not really, just because it had been under her nose the whole time. She picked it up now.

Kalle had inherited his features from his father, there was no doubt about that. And yet he looked uncannily like Anna Jokinen – the same anxiety in his eyes, the same pursing of the lips. Even the same cowlick in the hair. She turned the photograph and read the half-erased caption: ANNA JOKINEN, BORN 2 JUNE 1927 IN KÄÄRMELA, DIED 18 OCTOBER 1952.

*Were you in any way involved?* asked Hella silently. *Did baby Aleksi die because of you?* She thought about Irja's last conversation with Erno again. She couldn't shake off the feeling that Erno's last visit had been meaningful, but failed to see in what way.

As a more immediate concern, there was her answer to Eklund to think about. Even though she had no intention of going back to Ivalo yet, she couldn't afford to antagonize her boss at this point in her career. If you could call her miserable position at the Ivalo police station a career. She decided that she would devote herself to the task immediately. Then, after she had unleashed her inner Scheherazade on him, she would be free to pursue more constructive occupations. Like searching Erno's house all over again. Finishing the job. She might have missed something. Must have. If Erno was a spy, there must be proof of his trade. Maps. Cameras. Caches full of money. And then there was also the matter of Father Timo's missing gun. Of course, there was a possibility that Erno's mysterious assailant had taken all the compromising materials, and the gun as well, from him as he or she had shot the old man in the forest, but Hella didn't believe it. In her experience, there was always something that a person, however careful, left behind.

She scribbled a quick answer to Eklund, explaining to him why it was of paramount importance that she stayed a couple more days, then she slid her feet into her short felt boots and pulled the furred hood of her parka over her head.

Outside, the temperature had dropped overnight. It was still dark. They'd be lucky if they got six hours of daylight. Hella swore between her teeth and turned back to the house. It would be prudent to get some matches and a paraffin lamp. She wasn't sure that whatever remained in Erno's house was still in working order.

She hurried across the streets, empty except for a few stray cats which were more daring than Seamus the Siamese aristocrat. People were already at church, even Martta Jokinen, whose door Hella knocked on in passing. No answer. She pushed the door: closed. She would have to drop in after she was done with her search.

The dirt road that led to Erno's house was sprinkled with fresh, gleaming, soft snow. It lay in a thin layer over the black soil, lending it an eerie beauty, making it look like the Milky Way. And it hadn't melted. Winter had come, finally. Another dreary, freezing, interminable winter, and she would be stuck in Ivalo, dutifully typing reports.

Hella's heart started racing as soon as she got near the house, she had so convinced herself that it held the key to the whole affair. Once inside, she lit the paraffin lamp and squatted down on the floor. When searching an unfamiliar place, one had to be methodical. Floor to ceiling, or left to right, you had to find your vantage point, otherwise you ran the risk of missing something.

The floor was dirty, but no more so than on her last visit. She went over each floorboard, pressing down, sliding her knife in between the planks, expecting each second to uncover some secret hiding place. But no. Just one of Kalle's paper planes that had crash-landed under the table. She picked it up.

Still on her knees, which were starting to hurt, Hella scanned the room, her eyes resting in turn on the big bucket next to the stove, the two-pronged cast-iron stick, the benches that surrounded the table. The stove's black mouth gaped at her. She had searched it before, of course she had, but she hadn't climbed inside, afraid of getting her face and clothes full of soot.

Thinking of what Irja Waltari would do if *she* was the one who had to play chimney sweep, Hella picked up a towel and tied it around her hair. Then, she took off her parka and felt boots, placed the lamp on a chair next to the stove and resolutely climbed inside.

A piece of soot, dislodged by her clumsy movements, fell on top of her head. She had barely had time to close her eyes. Hella sneezed, brushed the soot aside and started to painstakingly inspect the great cavity. Nothing. Still nothing. *There!* But it was only a piece of mirrored glass, and it left a small but painful cut on her palm. Her hands moving above her head like spiders, she explored the lining of the chimney, stretching her arms to go as far up as was humanly possible. She kept thinking about the traces of soot she had found on the stove when she first came. Someone had searched the chimney, but neither Martta, nor Karppinen, nor the Waltaris had admitted to it. For what she had to do, her narrow body, a boy's body, was an advantage. Erno was slightly built, too. And then there was Kalle. He could probably stand upright inside the chimney quite comfortably. She wondered for a moment if she could convince the Waltaris to bring Kalle back here. But they would never agree, she knew that. Stubborn as donkeys, those people were, and the fact that all the clues pointed in their direction didn't make the slightest difference to them.

She was now in a half-crouch, her legs bent at forty-five degrees, her back hurting with the strain of the effort. Slowly, she pushed her left arm down and extended her right arm still further above her head. *If I get stuck here, I'll die,* she thought. If not of hunger, or cold, then of humiliation. She could just about imagine the running joke she would become, from here all the way up to Norway. Our police are so stupid, they stick their heads inside chimneys and then they need firefighters to save them. But then her fingers closed on something that seemed different to the touch. A piece of metal. A brick had been dislodged and replaced with a tin box. Her spine tingling with excitement, Hella slowly pulled it from its cache in the wall and lowered it to eye level. The dim light of the paraffin lamp was not nearly enough; still, it allowed her to make out a potato-shaped head and the long lashes of Snorkmaiden. What she had in her hands was a tin box that had originally contained a selection of Fazer Blue chocolate. What was inside the box, however, was an entirely different matter. Hella scrambled out of her uncomfortable abode and, almost forgetting to breathe, slammed the tin box down on the kitchen table.

# 36

Her hands trembled so much, she had to start over twice to count the stars. She'd counted eight, but one of them had fallen from her hand and rolled under the table. Hella lowered the lamp to look for it, but it was nowhere to be seen. She upturned the tin box on the table, noticing as she did so that its shiny blue lid was bent as if a metal claw had seized it, and spread out its contents before her. It was all the proof anyone could want, and then some. The little stars, removed for some unfathomable reason from the dark green shoulder straps. The straps themselves, their red piping ripped off. A manila envelope, stuffed with what looked like a detailed map of Lapland. A small pouch containing three roubles, and an identity card bearing the name Daria Mikhailovna Makarova, Captain, Senior Army Surgeon, Murmansk Military District. The photograph on the card, that of a middle-aged, plump woman with protruding eyes, wearing a stiff white collar under her khaki jacket and an army cap perched on top of her head, stared back at her. *So here you are,* thought Hella. Captain Makarova. She had tried to imagine what the woman could have looked like, and, without knowing a thing about her, she had not been far off the mark. Had Jokinen killed her? Why? Because she was his spymaster and things had turned sour between them? Or was it connected with the fact that the woman had been an army surgeon? No, her listed occupation was almost certainly just a cover.

The paraffin lamp threw a soft halo of light over the polished surface of the table. Hella hesitated, suddenly conscious that sitting as she was, with the curtains open, she was plainly visible from outside. Karppinen would be able to see her easily, and given what she knew about the little man, he was surely doing just that: following her every move. If anyone was posted in the shadow of the big pines at the forest edge, they would be able to see her too. She got to her feet and drew the curtains. The little cut on her palm hurt like hell.

She took the map out of the envelope, uncovering as she did so a fat pile of markka stacked beneath it. The map was old, pre-war, printed in Turku by a publisher named Frenckell Printing Works Ltd. It had obviously been used a lot. The paper was fraying at the edges, and some parts of the map were discoloured.

Hella spread out the map before her. Her eyes rested on the maze of streams, creeks, fjords and tiny islands that characterized the local topography. Käärmela was circled in ink. So was a spot to the north of it, almost on the border with Norway, that bore a handwritten annotation, a single initial: R. From that spot, a jotted line ran down until it crossed what Hella believed was the Rajajoosepintie road. There was another spot marked on the map just north of Käärmela. Was it a cross? Hella bent closer. They had walked along the Uusoppijoki River when they went to recover Captain Makarova's body. It seemed to her that the cross on the map was not far from there, just a little bit to the north of the spot where they had found the head.

The map made no sense. The reference to R, for instance. Hella supposed it meant 'radar', as in, I am a big country up north, part of the Western Alliance, and I will make sure that the actions of my huge and angry bear of a neighbour do not go unnoticed. The Soviets had built a huge base on Kola, only sixty miles away from their enemies. Which, in geopolitical terms, meant under their very noses. What were they doing there?

She remembered her school history lessons all right. The Northern Fleet had been established by the Soviets from the remains of the imperial Arctic Sea Flotilla in order to safeguard Allied transportation routes through the Barents Sea from German naval forces. At first consisting only of patrol boats, the force had grown rapidly to include submarines and destroyers. Airfields and artillery had quickly followed, so that, when the Winter War had broken out in 1939, the Soviet base had been fully operational.

And the Finns had not been all too happy about that.

She cast her mind back to the newspaper headlines from those troubled times:

DESTROYER FROM KOLA BASE
IN FINNISH TERRITORIAL WATERS

YOUR NEIGHBOUR IS NOT YOUR FRIEND

FISHING FOR INFORMATION

This last one had been accompanied by a grainy photograph of a peasant tying up his small fishing boat next to a huge military ship. A pair of binoculars, the sort birdwatchers use, was protruding from the pocket of his jacket. These were indeed wartime classics, those stories about ordinary, unthreatening folk who turned out to be Soviet spies. Your neighbour, who raised his head from his fishing nets just long enough to snap a picture of a military base. Your long-lost uncle from some godforsaken village who turned up on your doorstep one day, claiming blood ties while discreetly questioning you about the work you did at the explosives factory. They took many forms, those newspaper spies. What they had in common, though, was a shared bonhomie, depicted in their posture, hands extended, faces grinning, in stark contrast to their small, shrewd eyes and probing gazes. Until now, Hella had always believed those spies existed solely in the reporters' feverish imaginations. But maybe she had been wrong.

So, contrary to what she had imagined so far, Erno *was* a spy. She had proof of that now. Erno was a man who had grown up here, on the Russian border, under Russian imperial rule. He was not ethnically Russian, but his late wife had been, and he spoke the language fluently. He was an educated man. He lived in relative austerity, but what if he hadn't been spying for money? He could have been swept up by communist ideas. A world of equality, of progress, of idealistic moral values that lay just the other side of a narrow divide ... Older folks like him went across the border to buy groceries in the dead of winter out of convenience, or habit. How easy would it be to approach one of those people, strike up a conversation? A younger woman, a doctor, anything but threatening. She asks you something, and you have no reason not to answer, because it's no secret, it's common knowledge, and her smile is so nice, and her eyes twinkle when she looks at you ... Then, next thing you know, you're putting your skis on and going on an errand for her. Maybe not even spying yourself, just transmitting the information. Yes, it was possible.

Her last conversation with Steve sprang to mind. *I've heard some weird stories from my sources up north. Soviet spies,*

*Finnish spies, Western Alliance officials who pretend to go fishing, cameras sticking out of every pocket.* In her two years in Ivalo, she hadn't come across any espionage cases, but it didn't mean they didn't exist – it was more likely that Eklund took care of the sensitive stuff all by himself.

Suddenly, she was overcome by an urge to see Steve again. To check how he was doing. What if he had indeed got divorced, as he had promised he would, but had been too proud to let her know? As soon as this case was over, she would take a couple of days off and travel to Helsinki. See old friends. *What old friends*? screamed the nasty little voice inside her head, but she silenced it. Nothing pathetic, just a chance meeting with an old friend. Nothing to it.

She drew back the curtain and peered cautiously outside. The air was tinged with blue. It was one of those days at the onset of the polar night when the last of the daylight they were to see for months to come was haemorrhaging down the line of the horizon, and, by some curious optical phenomenon, everything seemed blue. Some people loved it, even travelled to Lapland in the winter to see it. Hella shuddered.

So what next? The discovery of the tin box was the high point of her investigation. She could go on searching the house, but somehow she was certain she had already found all there was. She sat for a moment, considering her options. She hated the polar nights, she hated Ivalo, and she hated the idea of going into the forest again. But there was no other choice. She had to go and check for herself.

Gloomily, Hella made her way towards the barn, where Anna's skis were stored. She should be able to get to the place marked on the map in a little under two hours – if she didn't get lost, that was, or eaten by a bear desperate to add to its winter fat reserves before it went into hibernation.

*Christ Almighty*, she thought as she fitted the bindings of the dead woman's skis around her boots. *Why am I doing this? Why don't I just go back to Ivalo with my dear suitor Kukoyakka and tell Ranta to get his fat backside over here and do some work for a change*? But she knew that she would never hand this case over to Ranta, not in a million years. Too much was at stake. Not only for herself, but also for these people she now cared about.

# 37

Erno Jokinen had not been the only one to believe in evil spirits that lived in the forests. Hella believed in them too, even though she would rather die than admit it. When she had been a child, she had hated those family outings when, at their mother's insistence, they would go off to picnic in the woods, grilling sausages over the campfire. Christina would jump for joy, always the one to take comfort in nature, to rake the fallen leaves, to eat raspberries from the bushes, to hunt for wild mushrooms. Hella, who was two years younger, would sit by the fire, next to her father, making it crystal clear to everyone just how bored she was. *She* was a city girl. *She* was a good student, excelling in maths and literature, at home in concert halls and museums. Nature was unruly, untidy; it was something beyond her comprehension, and that scared her. Sitting before that campfire, her hands wrapped tightly around her knees, she would vow she'd never ever set foot in the forest again once she was old enough to decide for herself. If Christina could see her now, a solitary and clumsy skier slaloming between the pines, she'd make fun of her. But Christina's milky ghost had long ago dissolved into the clouds; or else it was busy playing with Matti's ghost, catching stardust and giggling.

As she skied, Hella talked to her father. Not a silent conversation in her mind, no; she was speaking out loud, even if it meant she began to get out of breath. She was explaining the case – or what she knew about the case – to him.

"It looks like the man was a spy after all," she panted. "Can you believe it?" She cocked her head to one side. "Yes, I know. I find it hard to believe myself. But there's *evidence.* I still don't know where he is, though. Was he the one who killed Captain Makarova? In that case, I'll probably never find him."

A squirrel … Hella wiped the thin veil of perspiration off her forehead and checked her map. She was still going in the right direction, or so it seemed.

"I'm afraid, too," she whispered. "But not for the same reasons. I'm afraid I'll never know for sure, and Kalle will grow up like I did. Not knowing. Blaming himself for not stopping his grandfather."

It seemed to her that she could hear her father's voice coming from the stream. She looked down at the half-frozen water and, feeling completely stupid, explained herself:

"Yes, I know I have nothing to blame myself for. If I hadn't been so ill that day in January, I would have died like the rest of you. I couldn't have saved you. It's the not knowing that gets me. Not knowing whether you were all just victims of a senseless accident, or if you and Mom and Christina and Matti were killed" – she stared into the wilderness, fighting back tears – "on purpose. In cold blood. Because of your work."

Hella fumbled in her pocket for a handkerchief and, in doing so, dislodged Kalle's paper plane, which fell into the snow. She must have put it in her pocket without thinking. Hella hurried to pick it up – the boy would be devastated if she damaged it in any way – before carefully wiping the narrow wings and putting it in her pocket again. She was about to pull on her gloves again when she noticed an ink stain on her index finger.

The paper plane.

She fished it out again, looking at the back where the pale purple ink had run from the contact between the snow and her warm fingers. She noticed for the first time – *what kind of police officer are you, Hella Mauzer?* – that there was text on the other side, almost impossible to read. She peered at it. POSITIVE. 19/19. An ink stain. She cursed the dimming light and brought the paper up to her nose. …ININE, she read. …QUINE.

What was it?

Slowly, she willed her aching legs to start moving again. If she was not mistaken, she still had about an hour to go until she reached her destination. The writing on the paper plane was probably nothing; otherwise Erno would never have allowed the boy to play with it. Still, it was something to think about. That, and the other inconsistencies of the case. She would have time for it all in the evening. Cuddled up in her big ornate bed, under the faded pink quilt. She hadn't thought about it until now, but the Waltaris' house had started to feel like home to her. Maybe she should surrender to the temptation, wait one day too many and remain stuck in the village for the whole of winter. Surely Eklund could not fire her for that? But in her heart she knew that he could, and he would, and that he'd be all too happy about it. Whoever had had the deranged idea that a highly strung girl eager to sort out all of the world's injustices, and a pale, limp, malevolent bureaucrat, whose only passions in life were his exotic wife and the proper use of the filing system, could work together as a team had, unsurprisingly, been proved wrong. They didn't get on and they never would, even if she, out of boredom or ambition, developed a sudden passion for filing and he pretended to be interested in the cases they had to solve. It was as hopeless as teaming together a sea lion and a pointer and hoping that they'd work out a way to enjoy each other's company.

Another glance at the map, another check of the compass. She was almost there. The bed of the stream was narrow now, becoming a sort of gorge, and the eerie silence of the forest gave way to the low humming of the waterfall. She'd take a look around, and then she'd turn back. She felt depressed all of a sudden, wondering how Erno could have betrayed his own country. But who was to say he'd even felt Finnish in the first place? He had spent most of his life under Russian rule. Maybe he saw himself as Russian, and providing the Soviets with information was a natural thing for him rather than a betrayal. Her heart went out to Kalle. The boy was suffering already; she didn't need to add to his plight. But how could she avoid disclosing that Erno was a spy? And how would she ever find out what had happened to him? She didn't even know if Erno's activities were the reason for his disappearance; they could be two separate matters. Karppinen was not off the hook yet.

She tried to imagine what the Waltari family were doing now. They were surely back from church, and they had probably finished their lunch, too. Irja would be washing dishes, Timo reading to Kalle. She had been wrong to lash out at them like she did. They really were nice, honest, kindly people. She could be friends with them. The thought stopped her in her tracks. She felt for the first time that she had glimpsed the underlying cause of her anger. The Waltaris were the closest she had got to making friends since Christina had died. As far as Hella could remember, anyway: she had never had a friend other than her sister. Not before

Christina's death, and not after. Steve had not been a friend, he had been a lover. She had come to see herself as a person who didn't need friends. A loner. A lone wolf. But maybe she had been denying herself other people's friendships out of loyalty to Christina. Maybe it was time she changed.

She was approaching the waterfall. The trees were now spaced wide apart, and they were lower, bent at sharp angles. She glanced in passing at the place where they had found the woman's body, but there was nothing to see – no suspicious traces, no broken shrubs. She struggled up the steep bank, panting, her skin moist with exertion, and followed the stream north.

She would need to make sure that the Waltaris didn't become scapegoats in this story because Chief Inspector Eklund wished them to be just that. She'd need to prepare a rational, the-facts-speak-for-themselves argument to counteract Eklund's theories. Most important of all, she would have to abstain from mentioning her gut feeling, her instincts, to her boss, for Hella had by now learned the unwritten rule: hunches, certitudes based on nothing more than instinct, were good for men only. In women, they were just whims or emotions, both of which were dirty words in Eklund's mouth. She would be called hysterical and unprofessional if she ventured forth any idea not based on solid facts. And so she wouldn't.

Hella was steaming now from the effort of going upstream. She took her woollen cap off, briefly wondering what her hair now looked like. Probably not great, but who cared. It was then that, out of the corner of her eye, she caught sight of something in the water. She had to look twice, because at first she believed it was just the glint of the sun on the ripples.

She blinked and stopped in her tracks. Her heart stopped too, missed a beat, and then started thumping furiously.

She edged closer to the dark, foaming stream. There it was, black and shapeless, a lump protruding from the ice that had formed on the shore. A dead bird, thought Hella, but deep down she knew already that it was much worse than that. An eye was staring at her from under the ice, and she could make out the shape of a nose, a dark patch of hair. The collar of a white shirt. The rest of the body, which was lying on its back, had disappeared under the ice.

She bent in two, suddenly nauseous yet unable to tear her eyes away from the dead body, from the eye that seemed fashioned out of frosted glass. Her crime scene course instructor's words sprung to her mind: *first of all, you need to make sure that the crime scene perimeter is secured, and that your working conditions are good.* Hella laughed mirthlessly. Working conditions! Did the pure blue ice qualify as good working conditions?

Something snapped behind her and Hella sprung to the side, her right hand tearing her gun out of its holster. No one. Tree branches giving way under the weight of snow, because it was snowing again. She hadn't even noticed, absorbed as she was in the contemplation of that eye. *All right, pull yourself together, Hella Mauzer. Think.* This was not the first violent crime scene she'd seen. *No,* corrected the nasty little voice inside her head. It was the third. Captain Daria Makarova had been the second. *The first one was that family, and you got yourself fired from the homicide squad for the way you handled it.* But it was different now. No one would see her even if she cried. No one had to know that she had panicked.

Moving slowly, as if in a dream, Hella picked up a fallen branch and started raking through the snow for clues. What she expected to find, she didn't know. The dead man's backpack, maybe? But she didn't find his backpack, nor any other belongings, even though she had been very thorough in her search, very meticulous. The snow wasn't lying like a fluffy blanket on the ground any longer; it was a sodden mess. Slowly, she sank down onto the shore, just above the dead man, her entire body shaking from stress and exhaustion. She prodded the ice with the branch. It was not really set yet, the edges transparent and crumbly. Maybe with some luck she could pull the body onto the riverbank, but then what? She wasn't strong enough to carry it back into the village all by herself. And she was afraid that if she pulled the body ashore, she would destroy vital evidence. Now that she was closer, she could clearly see that the man had been shot, a wound gaping in his left temple. Better leave it there as it was; she'd go back to the village and call for help. But still she lingered, filled with unease yet unable to put her finger on what exactly was troubling her. The snow was blowing in her face in a horizontal blur, and the gloom enveloped her like a shroud. And then she realized. That glint in the river she had noticed before seeing the body. It hadn't been the sun playing on the ripples. There was no sun.

Hella's eyes narrowed and she drew in her breath sharply. She rolled her sleeve up to the elbow, grabbed the branch. The stream was very shallow, its bed raised in the middle. There was something in there, in the water, but she couldn't get at it with the branch. She bit her lip, took off her shoes and socks and rolled her trousers above her ankles. The freezing water took her breath away. She bent over, grabbed the object. A pistol. Hella rushed back to shore, wiped her feet with her scarf and put her shoes and socks back on again. When her pulse stopped thudding and the blood returned to her feet, she picked up the gun to inspect it. An M1921 Bolo Mauser. Still four bullets in the magazine, so two must have been fired. The initials T. W. were engraved on the side. She dropped the gun in the snow, feeling dizzy. It was worse than she had imagined. The bullets were the same type as the one she had extracted from the woman's skull. She had her murder weapon at last. But who had used it?

She stood very still, her eyes on the whirling water of the stream, her mind focused.

So Timo Waltari had lied to her when he said Erno Jokinen had borrowed the gun from him. He was the one who'd killed Captain Makarova and Jokinen. Killed them both in cold blood. Executed them. The white evil: it was him.

But then how could she have found Captain Makarova's papers in Erno's chimney? There must be another explanation.

Jokinen had borrowed Timo Waltari's gun to kill Captain Makarova, for reasons Hella could only guess at. If ever the body was found, Timo would be accused of murder, not him. That was why Erno hadn't taken his own rifle. She had thought at first that Erno had borrowed the gun because he wanted a weapon he could conceal easily, but the truth was much simpler. If the captain's body was found and Erno was questioned, he would have denied ever seeing the gun. He knew Timo Waltari's past. It would be his word, the word of a respectable, older citizen, against that of a young man with a troubled past, a newcomer to the village, a would-be murderer already. There was no doubt as to which one of them would be believed in court.

So Erno Jokinen kills the Soviet captain, hides her things inside his chimney, then has a fight with Timo Waltari. The priest is younger, stronger. He overpowers the older man, snatches his gun and kills him. Throws the murder weapon into the stream, confident it will never be found. He already knows where Captain Makarova's body is buried, and this is where he leads his fellow villagers so that they can discover her body by accident. Even when the skull is found, with its bullet wound, he is not afraid. He says Erno borrowed the gun from him, and he has a witness, Karppinen.

She sighed and closed her eyes for a second, trying to regain her composure, to lapse back into her professional self, confident, sharp. The priest had been lying to her from the start. She had been sleeping under a murderer's roof. But why? Because he had discovered that Erno was a spy? Because of Kalle? Or because he held Erno Jokinen responsible for the death of his firstborn son? It could be vengeance, pathetic, ineffective, ill-guided vengeance, but people were not always logical.

Hella sighed. Eklund was right about her, and Jokela had been right, too, when they said she was too emotional to be a good investigator. Once again, she had let her feelings get in the way. But she had so wanted Erno and Timo to be innocent. For the sake of Kalle. For her own sake.

She took the slightly moist woollen cap out of her pocket and wrapped the gun in it before placing it in her back-pack. Her feet hurt; she hoped she was not going to lose any toes. She felt like some ancient creature, half-woman, half-demon, as she turned her skis downhill and started to gain speed. *I don't have to be afraid of the evil spirits any longer,* she thought grimly. *I'm one of them now.* Filled with hatred, ready to lash out.

# 38

As Irja placed her hand on Kalle's forehead, the boy felt stone cold to her touch. He shook her hand off vigorously, flashed a smile at her, and ran to the bedroom to play with Seamus.

"Are you sure you're all right, Irja?" Timo paused in the doorway, his arms full of wood he was bringing in to dry. "You look flushed."

"I'm fine," smiled Irja, because she was determined to be fine. If she started falling to pieces now, what would become of them? "I'm fine," she repeated again, and this time she almost believed it. "Are you hungry?"

Timo put the logs down and shook his head. "Let's wait for Sergeant Mauzer. I suppose she'll be back soon enough. Kai saw her heading towards the forest, so I guess she went back to the place where we found the woman's remains."

Irja froze. "Alone?"

"Yes," nodded Timo. "Alone. But she's that kind of woman – if Kai or someone else had proposed to accompany her, she wouldn't have appreciated it. She would have thought we considered her not capable enough, or not strong enough, or not professional enough."

"She's not a meek creature like your wife, then?" Irja tried to say it lightly, but it didn't come out that way.

"You're not meek. You're ..." He hesitated, not sure the word was right. "Gentle, but strong. True, you come across as sweet, quiet, so people might think that's all there is to you, but I, your husband, know better. Your soul is rock solid." Timo paused and looked at her pensively. "Sergeant Mauzer is the other way around. She looks tough, she looks angry, but deep down she's brittle. Frail. Something must have happened to her. Something sad. She's fighting as hard as she can not to let that thing destroy her life."

"Do you think she suspects us?" whispered Irja.

"Well, I suppose she must. Everything seems to point towards us, doesn't it? But she is an intelligent woman, and she's still working on the case. I wouldn't worry too much."

"I'm not," Irja said.

"Aren't you?" Timo glanced at his watch. "I'm sorry, I need to be going. Jeremias Karppinen asked to see me. I'm already late."

Irja slumped into a seat, suddenly drained of all energy. She now regretted having called the police to investigate. With the best of intentions, Sergeant Mauzer could still do more harm than good. What would Kalle think of his grandfather as he grew older? Even if no one ever formally proved that Erno had been a spy, the shadow of doubt would hang over every memory people had of him.

"Timo, maybe after you're done with Karppinen, you should go to ..." She let her sentence trail off, not sure how her husband would take it.

"I should what?"

"Go to look in Erno's house again. Or in the garden. Kalle saw Erno digging there some weeks ago. I told Sergeant Mauzer, but she said it was nothing. Said it was such a long time ago it wasn't significant. And Kalle wasn't sure of the exact place. So I thought maybe ..."

Suddenly, it seemed to her that that was the only reasonable thing to do. Go and look for clues by themselves. She briefly wondered if what she really wanted to do was to *destroy* any evidence of Erno's involvement with the enemy, but she brushed the thought aside.

"No," said her husband. "It wouldn't be wise. What reason would we give her if she asked me what I was doing there?"

"Then *I'll* go."

But then she slumped back again, suddenly afraid of her childish outburst. "I'm sorry. Of course I won't go. It's just that I feel we're completely in the dark. I can't believe" – she lowered her voice, casting a worried glance towards the bedroom – "I'll never believe Erno was a Soviet spy. Never. But if we can't prove it …"

Timo remained silent for a few seconds, no doubt weighing the pros and cons. In the end, he sighed. "All right, I'll go and look. After I'm done with Karppinen. But what if I find something that incriminates Erno? Do I destroy it?"

"No," she whispered. "Of course not."

Now that the thought had crossed her mind, she would not stop thinking about it until Timo came back home. She so wanted to protect Kalle. To clear his name, and the memory he had of his grandfather.

The front door creaked. Must be Timo coming back for something. She rose to her feet, smiling. Her husband was an organized man when he tended to his church, but at home it was a different story. He kept forgetting his things. She was already scanning the coat rack to see if his *ushanka* was there.

"Mrs Waltari?"

She turned, startled. It was not Timo. It was that big man with the dirty shoes, the one who had lied about being Sergeant Mauzer's fiancé.

"May I come in?"

# 39

Hella stood on the porch of the Waltaris' house, her heart thumping. What was Kukoyakka doing here? He was supposed to pass by the postbox on the Rajajoosepintie road, and, not seeing her, go on minding his own business. Had Eklund insisted that he bring her back to Ivalo, no matter what? Or was Kukoyakka acting on his own initiative? In that case, he had done well. It would avoid her tramping through the snow for hours on end.

On her way back from the forest, she had thought things over and decided that her initial intention, that of arresting Timo Waltari for the murders of Erno Jokinen and Captain Daria Makarova and taking him back to Ivalo with her, at gunpoint if need be, was not right. She was not ready yet. There was Kalle to think of. She couldn't very well arrest his guardian and leave the boy with the killer's wife. No, she needed to contact social services, so that they could come and take care of him. That would take several days, but so what? There was no rush. Timo Waltari didn't have to know she had found Erno Jokinen's body and the gun.

Hella unlocked the door of the shed, placed Captain Makarova's ribcage, arm and skull into the same canvas sack they had been brought in, and carried her ghastly package to

Kukoyakka's truck. She didn't know how things would play out once she was in the house, whether she would be able to control herself, and so she decided to take care of the vital evidence before going inside. She decided she could rely on the biting cold, and the darkness, to dissuade the villagers from taking a closer look.

Now, shivering from the cold or maybe the stress, she hurried back to the Waltaris' house. She was suddenly eager to pack her things and leave that place. She couldn't bear to think of how only a few hours earlier she had been telling herself that these people were her friends. An idiot, that's what she was! A sentimental fool! They were all laughing. For one wild, mortifying moment, Hella imagined they were making fun of her. But no. It seemed that Kukoyakka had been telling funny war stories, if such a thing existed. Something about spy-grade radio equipment and his colonel who was making a fool of himself trying to make it work.

She pushed the door ajar, but only a little. She wanted to see them before they saw her. She wanted to know if Father Timo was there. Kukoyakka was sitting with his large back to her; he had a pierogi in his right hand. The table was piled high with food. Hella's stomach gurgled, and Kukoyakka stopped mid-sentence and turned to her. Now Hella saw Irja, who was sitting opposite Kukoyakka at the dining table. There was no one else in the room.

"There you are, beautiful," roared Kukoyakka and winked at Irja. "I was getting desperate. Come and sit with us, have a shot to warm yourself up, and then you can go and pack."

At any other time, Hella would have met this declaration of familiarity with a glare, but now, when this rude, unfeeling Cyclops was her only ally, she just shrugged and, taking off her parka, slumped on the bench beside him. Jabs of pain shot through her feet, but as she wriggled her toes inside her felt boots she comforted herself by thinking she hadn't lost the feeling in them.

"What happened to you?" exclaimed Irja. "What's that stain on your sweater?"

It was soot from the chimney, but Hella didn't feel like going into the details. "I fell," she said curtly.

Kukoyakka was pushing a small glass filled to the brim with vodka towards her. Hella downed it without a word.

"There you go!" cried Kukoyakka, his eye twinkling.

She had to stay on her guard. If she went on drinking, he'd try to take advantage of her. She refused a second shot, although the first one was not nearly enough to warm her up.

Irja Waltari was looking at her steadily. "Did you find what you were looking for?"

"No." The lies came easily to her now that the trust she had in these people had been shattered. "I just spent close to four hours running around in the forest, didn't find a damn thing."

"Nothing in the house either?"

Maybe the wife *was* an accomplice, after all. She would have to think about it when her head cleared.

Hella shook her head and, to prevent any more questions, got to her feet. "I'm off to my room. I need to start packing."

Irja's eyes opened wide in her flustered face. "So it's true that you're leaving? I … We thought you might want to stay for a while longer; that you weren't *done* yet."

"I'm not," lied Hella. "But I need to get back to Ivalo to start on a different assignment. I'll be back when I can. In a couple of weeks, if the roads are still passable. Or next spring. Or I'll ask Inspector Ranta to step in for me."

Kukoyakka was looking at her with a big smile on his face. Did he expect their relationship, or courtship, or whatever he called it, to move to a different level now that she was going to be back in town?

"But," stuttered Irja, "I asked Timo to go and dig in Erno's back garden to help you out. Maybe he'll find something!"

"Just write to me if he does."

Hella turned abruptly and marched to her room, passing Kalle along the way. As usual, the boy stared at her with his huge eyes but said nothing. Maybe it would be a good idea to ask Ranta to come over here, arrest the priest, deal with the boy. He'd be the one to get all the credit for the case, but as far as Hella was concerned, that was all right. It was not like she had any chance of being transferred back to Helsinki, no matter what she did. Asking Ranta to step in for her would stop her from having to look into those eyes again.

Packing was easy when all you had was a worn-out sweater with three sloppy snowflakes sewn on it, and a few case notes. She stuffed everything into her backpack in no particular order. One last look at the violets, and the dark Finnish night that lay beyond, and she slammed the door behind her.

In the living room, no one was laughing any more. Irja was busying herself at the stove, which was her usual way of dealing with unsettling news. Kalle was nowhere in sight.

Kukoyakka shoved a last buttery, crumbly piece of pierogi into his mouth, ready to go.

"Goodbye, then," said Hella awkwardly. "Give my regards to your husband."

Irja nodded, not looking at her.

"Thank you for your hospitality. It has been much appreciated."

"Good pierogi, too," added Kukoyakka. "Very tasty."

They turned towards the door in unison, like the old married couple they would never become.

"Goodbye, then," said Hella again, but Irja didn't answer. The door shut behind them, and they were out in the cold.

# 40

"It's very considerate of you to worry about my dinner," said Kukoyakka, "but I'm not hungry at the moment. Give it to the dogs."

"Ha ha," glowered Hella. "Very funny."

But she had to give Kukoyakka credit – the mangled remains sitting on the truck's step didn't impress him much. He deposited them in the cabin then patted the seat next to him, ogling her as if he had nothing better to do.

"Sit down, pretty. It seems to me you've put on some weight in that place. Did you good. I like it when a woman has … you know —"

"No, I don't. And I'd appreciate it if you could abstain from giving me anatomy lessons. I've had more than my share of body parts for the day."

"As you wish," cooed Kukoyakka, his voice mellowed by Irja's vodka; the truck crunched into gear. A thick halo ringed the moon. Hella wondered how on earth they were going to make it to Ivalo, what with Kukoyakka's one eye and the vodka and the ice-glazed road.

"Don't you worry, beautiful." He must have noticed her anguished look. "Now, did you solve the crime?"

"No." There was no way she was going to tell him anything.

He would talk to Kai, and Kai would hurry to the Waltaris and warn them.

"Just as well," he said, as the truck trundled out of the village. "We still have two days left before the dance. You need to take care of your looks, not sit in the office writing reports. I'm sure Lennart will understand that."

The dance. Hella had forgotten all about it, but apparently her cyclopean dance partner hadn't. She could barely believe it: the man really had the hots for her. She stole a suspicious glance at him. Maybe he meant it as a joke?

"So what did Lennart Eklund tell you, exactly? How did he convince you to come all the way over here?"

"He told me that a damsel in distress needed saving from the bad influence of this place. Said you couldn't think clearly when you were out here, and that you weren't listening to what he told you, either. A neat little case like that, served to you on a platter, and you were still trying to think up complications. So the poor man practically begged me on his knees to fetch you as soon as I could." Kukoyakka chuckled. "And here I am."

Hella looked out of the window, not that there was anything to see. The sweeping headlights of the truck caught glimpses of tall pine trees, and it seemed like at any moment the truck would go crashing into them, but either they were lucky, or Kukoyakka was experienced, because each time they managed to swerve past.

*I don't trust evidence that leaps out at me,* thought Hella suddenly. This was exactly what was bothering her, the fact that it had all worked out so neatly. She was like a hunter who could sense a set-up, foul play, prey that had been positioned so he couldn't miss his shot. And she didn't like it.

Still, just because the evidence was neat, was it necessarily wrong? If one man is dead, and the other one is standing over him with a gun in his hand, that man is the killer, right? That's what Eklund, and Jokela, and just about everyone else would think. In ninety-nine per cent of cases they would be right. In some cases they would be wrong, just like they'd been wrong about her. But did Father Timo qualify for that meagre one per cent?

Kukoyakka's hairy hand was again in close proximity to her thigh. "So what will you be wearing to the dance? Do you want me to drive you over to Sodankylä to get yourself a new dress? I have a late shift tomorrow. And I like pink, if you're wondering. That's what suits a young girl best."

Hella sighed. "Seppo" – it felt funny to call him that; to her, he would always be Kukoyakka, but she couldn't very well say that to his face – "Seppo, I'm not a young girl any more. I'm getting close to middle age."

Suddenly, she felt awfully sorry for herself. Here she was, a middle-aged but still junior police officer, friendless, childless, an orphan. The best she could hope for in life was to keep her dreadful job and maybe, one day, get married. Not to Kukoyakka, no, she would never dream of marrying him, but to someone else. Someone who could never be as interesting, as attractive, as Steve. And by that time it would be too late for her to have children. Maybe she should adopt Kalle. She'd have someone to love, someone to care about and who would love her back. Who would be happy to see her when she got home in the evenings. *Get yourself a cat then, Mauzer,* chided the small but nasty voice that was always somewhere at the back of her head, raking through her brain for dirt. *Get a cat, and you'll be the perfect spinster. Don't drag an innocent child into it too.*

"You're still all right," said Kukoyakka, and his hand briefly touched her thigh.

"Yes, I am," snapped Hella. "I'm also still carrying a gun. So both hands on the steering wheel, please. Concentrate on the road. I have no intention whatsoever of ending up smashing into a tree."

But if she hoped that this last remark would put an end to their conversation, she was wrong. Instead of shutting up, Kukoyakka told her that he was possibly the best person in the whole of Finland with whom to crash into a tree in the dead of night.

"How so?" inquired Hella grudgingly, because he clearly expected her to and because he had put his right hand on the steering wheel.

"Do you know what I did in the war?"

Here he was again, trying to bowl her over with tales of his bravery.

"No." She sighed with exasperation. "What did you do during the war?"

She could well imagine him doing unheroic work like driving an army supply truck, helping himself to food and cigarette parcels when an opportunity arose.

The single eye gleamed with pride.

"I was in the radio transmission forces. State-of-the-art technology. They trusted no one but me to take care of it. Do you know how the radio works?"

Hella glanced at him sideways. Was it true what he was saying? *Radio*, of all things? It was so out of character, she didn't know what to say. He took her silence for an admission of her ignorance.

"Electromagnetic waves! They're all around us, but we can't see them! Amazing, I know. This great Italian guy, Guglielmo Marconi, he found a way. He built the first radio, and he was just a kid at the time. I'll give his name to my firstborn son. What do you think?"

The prospective mother of Guglielmo Kukoyakka gurgled something appropriately laudatory, but her suitor didn't really need encouragement. He continued:

"You might not know it, being a civilian and a woman, but information is what does it. Not bombs, not troops, not even tactical alliances. Information! And radio is at the heart of information. I used to fine-tune listening devices. The wires, they called them. You can wire anything you want, an office for instance. Then you listen. I have one here, if you want to take a look." He motioned towards a small wooden box that sat behind the driver's seat.

But Hella didn't want to look. She was dumbfounded by the turn her life had taken. Kukoyakka, a radio man! Her humiliation was complete. Just as the Ivalo posting was a miserable substitute for her high-profile position on the Helsinki homicide squad, so was her relationship – if you could call it that – with Kukoyakka a distortion-mirror reflection of her affair with Steve. Somehow, the fact that her one-eyed suitor was passionate about the same things as her sophisticated ex-lover made matters much worse.

Next to her, the man was still talking.

"So do you know what makes me the best person to be stuck on the road with?"

"What?"

"I have a portable transmitter. A miniature version. Here, in the box. I can always call for help. Aren't you impressed?"

She was. Much more than he could ever imagine.

# MONDAY 20 OCTOBER

# 41

It was Monday morning, and, true to her word, Hella was back in the poky little office she occupied at the Ivalo police station. Nothing had changed in her absence, except for a salty, pungent smell that hung in the air. She looked around, but couldn't identify its source. Her friend the aspidistra in its clay pot by the radiator was still dying, its yellowish leaves hanging limply; dying, but not quite dead yet. Hella watered it with a guilty conscience. She had promised herself she would ask her landlady, Mrs Tiramaki, how to care for the plant. Mrs Tiramaki had a way with plants. She pruned them, whispered to them, fertilized them with tea leaves and (Hella suspected) her own urine, and the plants loved her back. They thrived. Some days, Hella had the impression that she was living in a jungle. Mrs Tiramaki would know what she should do with the aspidistra. Maybe Hella had watered it too much. She knelt to observe a whitish mould that seemed to be growing on the soil.

"What are you doing, Mauzer? Praying?"

Ranta was leaning against the doorway, the usual crooked grin playing on his face. She hadn't heard him open the door, and he certainly hadn't knocked. Hella sprung back to her feet, but it was too late. His nasal baritone filled the room.

"I was right to tell Lennart that sending you away to stay with a priest was a bad idea. They screw with your brain in no time, those people do, and the next thing you know, you're saying a prayer before every meal and you're only fucking to procreate. You know what the Soviets say? Religion is the opiate of the masses."

Hella marched towards the door, stopping only when she was just a step away from him. "So happy to see you, Inspector Ranta," she muttered, hoping he would catch the sarcasm. "Your wise observations are what I missed most while working on the case."

If Ranta noticed the sarcasm, he didn't show it. "Any time, Mauzer! Any time!"

His breath stank as usual – a mixture of decaying teeth, vodka and the cured fish he nibbled on, even at eight in the morning. Instinctively, Hella recoiled.

Ranta smiled, knowing full well that he had won this round. Hella suspected him of cultivating his bad breath and using it deliberately as a weapon.

"I'll see you later, then. If you're looking for Lennart, he's just arrived. Oh, and by the way, thank you for the gherkins."

Hella turned around. The glass jars that Esteri had sent her were not on the windowsill any longer. Ranta must have taken them while she was away. The bastard.

She straightened her skirt and hurried down the corridor to where Lennart Eklund's office was. Her heart was beating a bit too fast, even though she tried to convince herself she had no reason to be worried.

Eklund must have spent his days eating while she was away. He looked much fatter now. The striped white and navy shirt he was wearing was stretched like a goatskin on a drum over his meaty back. He was taking paper files out of his briefcase, arranging them in neat columns strictly perpendicular to the edge of his desk. Not for the first time, she wondered what Esmeralda really thought of him. But of course that was their problem. She had her own.

"Chief," said Hella, trying out a smile when she was certain he had finished with his briefcase and was ready to start his working day. "I'm back, as promised."

He turned, startled, and stared as if he'd seen the Nazi invaders returning. Hella smiled again, as ingratiating a smile as she could manage. She didn't quite know what to say now that she'd stated the obvious.

"Well, well, well, here you are," Eklund said at last, when it became clear that his stray subordinate was just going to keep standing there with that foolish grin on her face. "And not a moment too soon. Did you get my letters?"

"Two. I've filed them."

Surely that would impress him. Why was he so weird about the whole thing? She was back on time, after all. She hadn't done anything rash. She hadn't caused any turmoil whatsoever. He must be pissed off for a different reason, decided Hella. Esmeralda, most likely. It was usually what it boiled down to.

"Did you finish your report?" he barked at her.

"Me? No, I've started it, but I have no typewriter at home, so it's just my case notes —"

"Type it up. Then come and see me. Once you're through with it, I have two more files waiting for you. Vandalism. Disruption of public order." He beckoned to the white filing cabinet, the one containing "local affairs", as he called them. Two pristine paper files, attached with an elastic band, were waiting for her on top.

Hella snorted. "The beggar again?"

"Yes." He glared at her. "Dr Gummerus is an esteemed member of our local community, and as such, he deserves justice."

Hella opened her mouth to comment – everyone deserves justice, every member of the community, no matter how respected or not – but then thought better of it. This was what Eklund was expecting her to say. It was a trap, another one of them. No way. He would not have the pleasure of scolding her again.

Realizing he'd get no answer, Eklund squeezed his wobbly body into his office chair and opened a file marked CIVIC EDUCATION OF POLICE FORCES in front of him, to show her just how busy he was.

Hella snorted again, picked up the files and retraced her steps back to her little office. Welcome back, she thought. Welcome back, Hella Mauzer, to the world of missing cats, stolen sausages and Lahti, who liked to wreak havoc by urinating on the doctor's doorstep.

For once, her office door was closed, but as she walked in she thought she caught a whiff of Ranta's stench. She really needed to find a way to stop him from sneaking in, going through her things. Not that she minded the gherkin theft all that much, but she didn't want him to find her letters to Steve, the ones she had written but never sent. She kept these in her locked drawer – as far removed as possible from the prying eyes of her landlady, who had a key to her room – in a file marked PRIVATE AND CONFIDENTIAL. But what if Ranta was capable of picking her lock?

All right, the report. Hella inserted a sheet of typing paper into her shiny typewriter. The introduction was easy. Who, where, when. Done. It filled half a page. But what now? The certainty she'd felt the day before was floundering, much like her aspidistra. The nagging feeling that she had first experienced in Kukoyakka's truck as it struggled along the ice-covered Rajajoosepintie road came back to haunt her. The case was just too neat. It worked on paper, true, but somehow it didn't feel right. And yes, she was a poor judge of character, her relationship with Steve proved it amply, but still ...

She was getting nowhere.

She got to her feet and peered out of the window. The smell was stronger here. The gherkins! That's what it was. As he rummaged around, Ranta must have dropped one of the jars and broken it. There was a sliver of glass lying on her windowsill. She stared at it, biting her lips. The glass ... With shaking hands, she searched in her shoulder bag. There it was! She took out the slivers and held them to the light. The letters were plainly visible. LOROQ. But it was only part of a word; the rest of the glass vial had been shattered. Suddenly, she thought about Kalle's paper plane. Hadn't she seen the letter Q there as well? She wrote it down. Loroq-quine. Loroquine. It meant nothing to her. POSITIVE. 19/19. She had a ghost of an idea, but how could she be certain?

Hella picked up one of the two files she'd taken from Eklund's office. Inside was a typewritten statement by Dr Gummerus. The crime, as he called it, had been committed on Friday, and before his very eyes. The repeat offender Lahti had ventured to his front door, extracted his organ – *his organ!* Hella chuckled; for a doctor, Gummerus was uncharacteristically prudish – and urinated against his front door, staining the doormat, destroying his property and offending the women of the household. This was the sixth time that Lahti had done this, and this state of affairs could not be tolerated any longer. Measures had to be taken. Public order needed to be restored.

Hella folded the statement in two, imagining how Eklund would cringe if he saw her doing that, and put it in her shoulder bag. Then she picked up her parka. She'd go and check on the doctor, tell him the police were taking his concerns seriously and that measures would be taken. Oh yes.

As she left her office, Ranta was loitering outside her room. Hella flashed him a smile. "Come for more gherkins?"

"I've come to warn the pariah that her boss is in a foul mood today."

"Thanks. I've already noticed."

Ranta edged closer and Hella held her breath.

"There's trouble between him and the Carmencita. Heard from the grocer she ran off with her dancing partner. She'll be back, just like the last time, but in the meantime ..."

So she'd guessed right. But it was not like she could delay this inquiry until the storm blew over. She needed to act now. Aloud, she asked, "Do you know if Anita keeps records of all the lunatics who come in to report crimes that don't even exist?"

Ranta chuckled, and the stench of his breath almost made Hella faint. "Of course she does. Has to, doesn't she? The ledger is in the reception area, second shelf from the top. Anita will show you."

When Hella had arrived that morning, Anita was not in yet, but now she could hear the clinking of a coffee pot.

"Thanks, but there's no urgency. I'll ask her later."

Or not. Ranta's cousin had many virtues, but discretion was not one of them. Hella glanced at her watch. Almost ten o'clock. Anita would be out for her lunch break between 11 a.m. and noon. She could go out now and come back when the coast was clear.

Hella sped up when crossing the reception area, waving a hand at Anita.

"Hello there! Got to rush, the boss asked me to deal with Dr Gummerus' complaint. If he's looking for me, that's where I'll be."

She didn't wait for an answer. Outside, the bleak October morning was cold and wet. Hella could see almost nothing beyond the circle of yellow cast by the street light at the corner of the police station. She rushed along the empty street, not because she was that eager to see Dr Gummerus again, but because of the damp that was creeping up her sleeves, freezing her to the bone.

# 42

Dr Gummerus lived on Kaamospolku, in what Ivalo townsfolk called a mansion, even though in reality it was just a big old house that was now in dire need of repair. The doctor answered the door himself. He must have been sitting next to it, in his flower-patterned easy chair, ready to defend his property from the beggar. Contrary to what Hella had expected, the doctor didn't seem too happy to see her. The reason for this lack of enthusiasm became apparent as soon as he opened his mouth.

"Couldn't they have sent a man to deal with this … issue? I cannot very well see what *you* can do about Lahti and his organ."

"Probably nothing," said Hella, shivering at the door. "But someone still needs to investigate before we assign the serious part of the job to a man who is able to deal with the suspect."

The doctor stared at her for a moment, trying to make sense of her words. Finally, he nodded. "Let's go to my study, and I'll answer your questions, even though I fail to see why I need to be interrogated. It's the house he's targeting, because to him this house is an embodiment of the establishment. Of something he aspired to when he was younger, and that he now rejects out of spite. Don't you agree?"

Hella didn't, actually, but she abstained from saying anything that might antagonize the old man. She followed him to his study, an aggressively masculine room decorated with the heads of boars presumably shot by the doctor himself. A fire blazed in the hearth. Hella flipped open her notebook. She went through the doctor's statement again, asking for specifics on this and opinions on that and dutifully jotting down the answers. Then, when she felt she had done enough, and the doctor started losing patience, she got to her feet. She wanted her question to appear unremarkable, almost an afterthought.

"Oh, by the way, I came across a strange character recently, a deranged man. His obsession was with medications, in particular a drug called loroquine, but I don't know what it is, nor what it is used for."

The doctor stared quizzically at her. "Loroquine, you said? Chloroquine, more likely. It must be the same man."

"Excuse me?"

"The same man. He came here. Twice. The first time, it must have been a year ago, he brought me his daughter to be examined. But the second time … He is medium height, slightly built, probably in his late fifties – are we talking about the same man? He was practically foaming at the mouth." The doctor's own mouth twisted with disgust at the recollection. "What was the expression you used? A deranged man? I would say a raving lunatic."

Hella held her breath. She knew that Erno had come, he must have done, like the good citizen that he was, but she hadn't dared hope that the doctor would remember him. But on the other hand, why wouldn't he? Although the doctor was a pompous ass, he had nothing to feel guilty about.

"When was this?"

"The second visit? In March. The twentieth. I remember because it was my late wife's birthday." He glanced ostentatiously at his watch. "If you have no more questions, Sergeant —"

"Just one last question. What is chloroquine used for? I haven't had any medical training" – a lie, but what did it matter? – "so I don't know."

The doctor frowned at her.

"Chloroquine is a new drug. I only heard about it two years ago myself. It's used as a cure for a tropical disease called malaria, which is a fever spread by mosquitoes. Not exactly something you can get in our part of the world. These aren't the same mosquitoes we have here." The doctor hesitated. "I've read in some medical publications that chloroquine can also be used to treat lupus erythematosus, but I don't know whether anyone has used it for that purpose yet. Maybe that's what your man was after?"

"And would you know where one could find" – she glanced at him, her pen raised above her notepad – "chloroquine?"

"In Helsinki, I suppose. At the army pharmacy, most likely. They have all kinds of medicines, just in case. But your man couldn't just go into the pharmacy and ask for this drug. He'd need a prescription."

Hella nodded. "Thank you, doctor."

His tall, stooping figure stood in the doorway as she ran down the steps to the street. Then, with a sigh, the old man pushed closed his front door. She heard the grating of the chair's legs against the wooden floor. Dr Gummerus had resumed his vigil.

# 43

As Hella had expected, Anita was out when she returned to the police station. Hella scraped the soles of her boots clean of snow then tiptoed across the room and sneaked a look at Eklund's door: closed. She didn't have to worry about Ranta, who always left at 11.15 sharp and never returned before 1 p.m.

Anita's dainty porcelain coffee pot and matching cup stood, perfectly clean and dry, in the exact centre of her desk. Hella set them aside and climbed onto Anita's chair to reach the second shelf from the top. Ranta was right. The shelf was crammed with notebooks bound in dark green fabric, the cover inscribed with the year. The notebooks went as far back as 1944, but Hella was only interested in recent history. She pulled YEAR 1952/1HALF out and placed it on the table. If Eklund surprised her, she could always say she'd just had a visitor, a peasant from up north who had come to complain about the wolves that attacked his reindeer herd, and that she was comparing similar occurrences.

She leafed through the notebook, raging against Anita's clumsy handwriting, her weird annotations – what did "dressed in the prettiest pale pink beret" have to do with any crime? – and her ability to cover a whole page and still not say anything. A 23 June entry caught her eye – a certain Irja Waltari, dressed in a grey dress ("of cheap fabric") and a shawl, had come in to complain about a wife beater in her village. She had been received by Ranta. No reason to take measures. *Poor thing,* thought Hella. It was little wonder that Irja felt distrustful of the police after that.

There was only one entry per page. During some weeks, the whole region seemed to storm the police station, complaining of everything and anything: neighbours, dogs, the state of the roads, food rationing (which was always blamed on the hunchback who ran the grocery store, whatever his name was). And then there were periods of quiet, of maybe one visit a week. March had been that sort of month. People had been busy repairing the damage that the heavy snow had inflicted on their houses. One entry on 3 March – a woman accusing her husband of cheating. One entry on 26 March – a dispute between neighbours. Nothing in between. Hella leaned in closer, her heart thumping against her ribcage. There was nothing between 3 and 26 March because a page had been cut out. Not torn out. Excised with a razor blade, neatly, meticulously. Hella knew of only one person who would do this instead of just yanking the pages out.

But she couldn't be sure, could she? He might have had a perfectly ordinary reason for that – maybe Anita had spilled some coffee on the page and stained it. Or it could have been someone else after all. Someone she didn't know. Someone who'd sneaked into the station like she had done, maybe during Anita's lunch break, and extracted the page. But that brought her back to her starting point. Back to the question of why. Slowly, Hella replaced the notebook on the shelf and positioned Anita's cup and coffee pot at the exact centre of the desk.

Her head was swimming with confusion. She had more questions now than she had answers. Chloroquine was used to treat lupus erythematosus or malaria. It must have been terribly important, otherwise why would the woman have kept it in her mouth? Perhaps she'd done it to keep the medicine from freezing because she intended to use it. There was also Father Timo's gun, and the bullet wounds. Erno's cache inside the stove, with Captain Makarova's identity card inside it. And baby Aleksi, and Anna – they were involved too, indirectly, she could feel it. What happened in that forest? What chain of events led back here, to the Ivalo police station? Was Eklund involved? Did it explain his attitude?

There were two things she could do. First, she could confront Eklund head-on. Ask him if he had seen Erno Jokinen before. Ask him if he knew more about the case than he was willing to tell. Gauge his reaction. But that would probably not be a very smart thing to do, because even if he was innocent, he still wouldn't like it. He was in a foul mood already. The second option was to wait an hour until Anita was back, and ask her. Anita liked nothing better than a little chat, and she had a good memory.

Hella slid towards the door, opened it and slammed it shut behind her. It felt childish, but if Eklund was paying attention, he would expect her to act in that manner. She marched towards her office, took off her parka and boots, and started typing. It felt easier now that she knew what she was doing, and why. She briefly summarized her actions over the last few days, resisting the temptation to interpret the facts. In the end, she listed the questions she still had. It was not the neat closing her boss had hoped for, but she didn't have anything else to offer.

When she was done, she glanced at her watch. The report didn't take as long as she had expected – still fifteen minutes to go until the ever-punctual Anita materialized at her desk. Suddenly ravenous, Hella crept out of her office and in the direction of the larder. There was always some stale bread left over, and cured fish.

In retrospect, it was a mistake. The larder was accessible through a narrow door that opened behind Anita's desk. You never knew if anyone was in there unless you opened the door, or unless Anita told you, but Anita was not back yet. So Hella swung the door open, and there he was. Lennart Eklund. His left arm was circled around a huge jar of strawberry jam, his right tightly clutching a big chunk of stale bread. Hella cursed under her breath. If there was one thing her boss hated even more than improper filing of official documents, it was losing face. And nothing screams more that you are a cuckolded and abandoned husband than a chunk of stale bread and jam for lunch. Now he would pester her just to make her forget what she'd seen.

Eklund's eyes narrowed. "I presume you've finished your report on the Käärmela case?"

Hella attempted a smile. "Yes, I have. I wanted to discuss it with you. After lunch."

He glared at her. "I'm done with lunch. Esmeralda keeps feeding me those pork meat pierogies of hers, and I can't take it any longer. I told her to take a break from cooking for a while. So I'll see you in my office now."

It was not a suggestion but an order.

"I'm coming," sighed Hella. This was going to be even more difficult than she had imagined. Abandoning all thoughts of lunch, she hurried back to her office and picked up her typewritten report.

Eklund waited for her behind his desk, his big body slumped in the swivel chair with his elbows up in the air and his fingers interlaced behind his neck. He didn't bother with a smile or any other niceties, just snatched the report from her hands.

While he read, Hella, who'd taken a seat without having been invited to, stared at his fat, hairy fingers and thought about Esmeralda. Granted, the girl was a birdbrain, but still … How could she have married him? How could she continue to be married to him? Or was he different when he was at home? Was an obsessively neat husband an asset, or a nuisance?

"Is this some sort of a practical joke, Mauzer?" Eklund's eyes seemed to bore into her. "You write here that you're not convinced that the priest, this Waltari, is guilty. Not convinced! What kind of proof do you need to be convinced? The man is a communist, a former terrorist, practically an assassin."

"He is," recognized Hella. "Even though 'assassin' is probably too strong a word. After all, he didn't actually kill anyone."

"Just because he got scared at the very last moment." Eklund waved a dismissive hand at her. "Now listen. He acknowledged that he had quarrelled with Jokinen."

Hella nodded.

"Good. He had a key to the dead man's house. He went into that house to search it before you arrived."

"He went in to get the boy's clothes."

"That's what *he* says. Didn't they teach you at the police academy not to trust anything your suspect says?" Eklund sighed deeply to show her, if there was still any need, just how stupid, how un-police-like her attitude was.

Hella dug her nails deep into the soft tissue of her palms and managed to say nothing.

Eklund went on in a condescending, hectoring voice: "Now, he also had a gun, an M1921 Bolo Mauser, which went missing after the murder. Didn't he? Didn't he?"

"He told me about it himself."

"Because he knew you'd find out about it sooner or later. So he had a semi-automatic pistol, and the old man was shot at point-blank range with a pistol, not with a rifle. Which for Lapland is unusual, to say the least. You, Sergeant Mauzer, you found that gun, with two bullets missing, in the stream, not far from the dead man's body. It's written here, so I'm assuming you were the one who wrote it. I'm not inventing anything, am I?"

If she opened her mouth now, she would just end up screaming at him. So she kept it shut.

"Did the gun have fingerprints on it?" asked Eklund ominously.

"No. And neither did the tin box that I found inside Erno Jokinen's stove. I cannot explain it."

"Can't you, Mauzer? This is Finland, for Christ's sake. It's cold. People wear gloves. Yes, indoors, too, I wouldn't be surprised. The old man came in from outside and hid the damning evidence inside the stove without taking his gloves off."

Hella stared at him.

When Eklund spoke again, his voice was two octaves lower. It sent a chill down Hella's spine. Here was her career, or what was left of it, going down the drain.

"I rather thought that an experienced police officer like yourself would have reached a logical conclusion. Your priest killed that Soviet woman and Jokinen. Everything points to him. Motive, means, opportunity: you have it all. Now you need to write it down."

"It's just that it doesn't make sense. Means, opportunity, yes. But I'm not sure about the motive. It was Erno Jokinen who was angry at Timo Waltari, not the other way around. Why would he kill him?"

"Maybe he discovered that the old man was a spy? Or maybe he killed Jokinen to steal the money that the woman was paying him for his spying activities. Whatever." Eklund turned to her, his eyes narrow slits in his fat and blotchy face. "Does it make sense what I'm saying, yes or no?"

"It does," acknowledged Hella. It was all the more difficult to argue with Eklund because she'd had exactly the same theory just the previous day. "But ... some things don't fit."

"Like what?"

"Well, if the priest had discovered that Erno was a spy, why didn't he just turn the old man over to us? We, or rather the SUPO, could have dealt with it. Also, I have a hard time believing that Erno Jokinen could be a spy. There's nothing to spy on around here. Unless there's something I don't know."

The chief inspector's eyes involuntarily darted to the grey metal filing cabinet in the corner. *Here we are*, thought Hella. So the SUPO *were* involved. Eklund didn't say anything, just picked up a little tin that held an assortment of paper clips and started turning it round in his big fat fingers.

"There are things that you're ignoring, Mauzer," he said at last. "Of all people, I'd have expected you to be quicker on the uptake. Given your parentage and everything. The SUPO are involved. They have to be. The man is a spy. There. Now you know."

*Is a spy?* thought Hella. *Not* was *a spy?* Did he mean Timo? What was this nonsense?

Eklund's malevolent gaze was on her.

"I was wondering," she said, in as innocent a voice as she could muster, "I was wondering if it'd be possible for me to meet with our local SUPO representative. To ask them for details. I still don't fully understand —"

The tin rotated anticlockwise, the paper clips crashing against the lid. He'd flatten it out if he continued to twist it like that. Still, better that thing than her.

Eklund stared at her without speaking for a full minute. Then, having made up his mind, he let go of the unfortunate tin, got to his feet and went to open the metal cupboard. His bulging back hid the combination as he dialled.

"You are the most obnoxious employee I've ever had," he said in a low voice. "But if you really insist, here is your proof."

He pulled a thin paper file from the top shelf.

The typewritten text on the cover read: THE KÄÄRMELA CRIMINAL RING.

Eklund handed it to her. "Read it. And then we'll talk."

# 44

She read it. It was the most extraordinary assemblage of unverified information, far-fetched assertions and fiction masquerading as fact that she had ever come across in her life. Did the SUPO really work like that? Were they prone to giving in to flights of fancy?

According to them, Käärmela – the aptly named 'Snake's Nest' – was riddled with spies. Erno Jokinen was a spy, and Father Timo was a spy, and even Irja was a spy, too. What they were spying on, what interest they could possibly represent for their Soviet spymasters, was anything but clear. There was talk of a mine that the Finnish military-industrial complex was considering building in the region, of Norwegian radars set 130 miles to the north, but it all remained very vague. Less vague were the accusations of treason. Daria Makarova was mentioned, too – according to the file, she was no doctor. She was one of the most cunning spymasters in the entire Soviet Union.

Hella put the file down. Was she expected to believe this? Apparently Eklund did. He believed everything that came from above, and there was no greater god in his mind than the SUPO. And Hella had to recognize that at least part of the information contained in the file was true. Daria

Makarova's name, for instance. She hadn't expected the SUPO to know it, but they did. Just as they knew that the woman was an army surgeon. Did they have their own agents in Svetly? How had the whole scheme been uncovered? No source had been mentioned in the file.

Hella wondered what this new piece of information would mean for the Waltaris, and for Kalle. Nothing good, certainly. If both the Waltaris were arrested, she would adopt Kalle. She'd probably never be a good mother, or even a good substitute for a mother, but she would do the best she could.

She went to see Anita at reception, but Anita had a phone pressed against her ear. Hella waited for a while, trying to guess who she was talking to – there was mention of car tyres – but in the end gave up and went to see Eklund again.

She had the impression that Eklund hadn't moved since she had left him, almost an hour before. He sat slumped in his chair, and he was still fiddling with the tin, which by now was almost flattened.

"I don't believe it," Hella said quietly.

"You don't believe what part exactly?"

"Any of it."

He laughed: "That's because you're in love. Smitten."

"With the priest or his wife?"

He glowered at her. "You're a smart alec, Mauzer. Do you know that?"

The tin snapped between his fingers. Hella stared at it, the image flashing in her head. The Fazer Blue tin! Her mind's eye saw the shiny lid, and the dent where it had been forced into the cache. The Fazer tin had not been hidden long before she found it, certainly not long enough to have been darkened by smoke from the stove. Was it just a red herring? Had those who'd hidden it expected it to be found? And then, suddenly, the pieces of the puzzle fell into place.

The chloroquine vial in the doctor's mouth, and Kalle's paper plane, and baby Aleksi. The white shirt Erno had been wearing, the execution-style killings. Until he had seen his own gun pointed at him, Jokinen had probably thought he'd be able to explain. *You're one of them,* Karppinen had told her. *One of them.*

Eklund's fury abated as suddenly as it had flared. He even smiled at her, but it was a smile that didn't in any way reach his eyes. Hella forced herself to listen to him. At first, she had trouble understanding what he was saying.

"I must tell you that you're a lucky smart alec. I have a surprise for you. Personnel telephoned and told me that they think you'll be happier in Helsinki. That's what they said, *happier.* As if police work has anything to do with *happiness.*" He paused, picked up the remains of the tin, and threw them in the waste bin. His voice was curiously expressionless when he spoke again. "So I told them that, much as I appreciate having you as one of my officers, I'll let you go. As soon as you finish writing your report." He looked her in the eye. "So get back to it."

Hella stared at him, dumbfounded. Was it true what he was saying? The tight-lipped officers in Personnel had stooped that low and called Eklund to announce that she was welcome again? Or maybe they had only meant —

"Did they say what position they're offering?" croaked Hella, her mouth dry.

"Excuse me? Oh. Didn't I say? Homicide. They feel like they were a little bit too harsh on you. They'd like to offer you a second chance."

Hella's mind was suddenly flooded with visions of her former life. The river view from her apartment. The park where she took long, solitary walks. The embankment. The Parisian bakery. Steve. No, not Steve. Her work. Back in

Helsinki, back on the homicide squad, she wouldn't spend her days writing reports no one read. She would have real crimes to solve. She was being offered an opportunity to do something that mattered again.

"When?" she asked.

"As soon as you've written a well-thought-out report on the Käärmela case."

"No, when did they call?"

"On Friday."

Which meant – if he wasn't lying – that they weren't taking any chances. Who *they* were, she didn't know yet. The SUPO, most likely. Almost in spite of herself, she was impressed by their foresight. Before she had even had a chance to give her opinion on the case, they had already built up a line of defence, written their own file and accused everyone involved of treason. They could have stopped at that, but no. Because they were prudent, they'd also pulled some strings in Helsinki and arranged for this marvellous carrot to dangle before her eyes, to be used as a last resort. This must have reached all the way to the top of the police hierarchy too, because Jokela took orders from no one but the big boss himself. She tried to imagine the discussion they'd had, Jokela and the big boss. Did they even tell her former supervisor the reason she was being forced back on him? Probably not. They wouldn't want a thing like that to get around.

"All right," she heard herself saying. "I'll go and rewrite that report."

Eklund nodded. He hadn't expected anything different from her. After all, she had just been offered an opportunity that no one in their right mind would refuse.

Once Hella was back in her office, she set about typing furiously. For once, she felt free not to worry about punctuation, margins or other such drivel. They'd edit it if they felt like it. She didn't have the time.

When she was done, she glanced at her watch. It was only quarter to one. She made for the door, then turned back, unlocked her desk drawer and took the yellow toy bus out. She stuffed it into her shoulder bag.

In the reception area, Anita was hanging up the phone. The young girl flashed a smile at her.

"Just back in time for the ball, then? Did you decide what you're going to wear?"

"Not yet," said Hella. "If Eklund asks after me, I'm going out to get some lunch." Before Anita had the time to say anything else, or offer her food out of her bountiful reserves, Hella smiled and was gone.

# 45

It was stiflingly hot in the house, but Timo kept telling her that it wasn't, that it was only she who felt it, and refused to open the windows. Instead, he went outside, broke off some icicles which were hanging from the roof and crushed them into a bowl. Irja pressed the ice to her face.

"I think we need a doctor," he said. "You're running a fever. I'll borrow a horse and go to Ivalo. They have a doctor there. I'll bring him back to examine you."

"I'll be fine."

Timo's proposal was madness, and they both knew it. Even if he managed to get to Ivalo somehow, plodding with his horse across the great expanse of snow, he'd never convince the doctor to come back with him. And she was not in a position to travel that far by horse. The baby was not due yet, she still had two or three months to go, but she already felt strained in her movements and out of breath if she had to walk for more than ten minutes. No, she had to get better on her own. Just like last time. But last time was not something she was keen to mention. Last time she'd been pregnant, she'd made it, but their son hadn't.

"Irja?" Her husband was kneeling beside her. "I know you don't believe in God any longer. You haven't really believed since Aleksi's death. But I'm praying for you, and for the baby. I'll do whatever it takes to help you. I'll kidnap that doctor if I have to, and bring him here."

"You don't have your gun any more," smiled Irja feebly.

"I'll think of something."

"No. Please don't go. I'm better already. See?" She pressed his hand against her cheek. "The fever is abating. I'll be fine. Not like" – she glanced at the top of the cupboard, where the vials were – "not like the last time."

Timo was looking at the top of the cupboard too. "I shouldn't have bothered digging those out. The case is closed, in any case. It doesn't look like Sergeant Mauzer is coming back."

"We can write to her. Tell her what you found in Erno's back garden."

"I don't think it would make any difference. She's made up her mind about this case. If anything, she suspects me. And we don't even know what these vials are, and why Erno had hidden them. We don't know what Ysteria is."

# 46

As she skidded across the slippery road, Hella wondered if she, too, would be accused of treason. It was the logical next step, and one that they would not hesitate to take. She tried to imagine the headlines: DAUGHTER OF CELEBRATED FINNISH AGENT BETRAYS HER COUNTRY. THE APPLE FALLS FAR FROM THE TREE. What photographs would they choose to illustrate the publication? An image of Hella Mauzer as a young, eager medical student? Or that of a bereaved, hollow-cheeked police academy graduate? Would they find out about Steve? Would they interview her landlady in Ivalo? Ask Eklund how he felt, now that he knew he had been harbouring a venomous snake in his vast and manly bosom?

She laughed out loud, but there was no one in the streets to hear her. One – if not the only – advantage of the Finnish polar night was that there were no witnesses around. No one to tell Eklund that his subordinate had been in that part of the city.

The little house stood at the end of a narrow lane. The curtains were drawn, but that didn't mean anything. She could hear the radio blaring in one of the back rooms. Hella banged on the door, dislodging as she did so a mini-avalanche of soft white snow. After a couple of minutes, she heard a shuffling of feet.

"It's me," she cried. "Hella. I need to see you."

The door opened with a squeak.

The first thing she noticed was his toenails, black-rimmed and gnarly. The vision almost made her turn back. What if he expected her to ...? But it was too late to back off now.

"Hello, beautiful!" whispered Kukoyakka, while a stupid smile spread across his face. "Come to cook me dinner?"

"I've come to take you shopping." She smiled enticingly. "You offered to, remember? You said you only needed to go to the logging camp in the evening. I want a lovely, pink dress with a floral print, and I know just the place. Shall we go?"

The tiny entry hall was bare except for Kukoyakka's parka, which hung on a rusted nail. He picked it up and slid his feet into a pair of felt boots he grabbed from behind the door.

"All right, I'm ready. Where are we going?"

"I'll tell you later."

They walked side by side towards the timber factory. Kukoyakka was humming; his only eye gleamed in the darkness.

"You seem eager," he chuckled.

Hurrying along for fear that Eklund would surprise them and put an end to the whole enterprise, Hella nodded. Let him think whatever he wanted. In less than ten minutes, they were standing in front of the great wooden doors of the timber factory.

"Wait here," ordered Kukoyakka.

Hella stood in the shadows cast by the wall. After a few minutes, the great doors were pulled open, and she heard the roar of Kukoyakka's truck.

"Climb in!"

He didn't have to ask twice. She was already in the cabin, smiling. So far, so good.

"So where are we going?"

"Käärmela."

"Käärmela?" He stared at her in disbelief, and the truck swerved. "There are no shops there."

"Irja Waltari is a fabulous seamstress. I want her to make my dress."

"That's a three-hour drive! For a bloody dress. Are you mad?"

"Please," she said. "Please, Seppo. This dress is so important to me. It will be our first … our first evening together. I want everything to be perfect. I want you to be proud of me."

He shook his head, but shifted the truck into gear and turned the wheel to the left. She seized his hand and held it.

"Thank you, Seppo."

But Kukoyakka was still not convinced. "Does Lennart know that you're going back to Käärmela?"

"Relax," smiled Hella. "Of course he does. Do you think I'd risk my career on a whim? He gave me the afternoon off. He knows how much the dance means to me, and he also knows why it's important." She waited, but Kukoyakka said nothing. Maybe he hadn't got the hint. She tried a more direct approach. "The dance is important because of you."

*And don't stop driving,* she thought. By now, Eklund must have realized that she hadn't just gone out for lunch. He'd go into her office, not find the report, and grow restless. How long before he called the SUPO to inform them that she had fled? That they hadn't managed to buy her off with that irresistible offer they'd cooked up? He'd probably wait until tomorrow. He wouldn't want to pass for a complete fool in their eyes. She shivered, remembering Eklund's fishy stare.

Ten minutes later, the last of Ivalo's houses were behind them, and Hella relaxed a little. For the first time, she started thinking about what she would say to the Waltaris. And, most importantly, what she would do next. She hadn't the ghost of an idea.

"Can you turn on the radio?" asked Kukoyakka. "I love listening to the radio. You'll have to get used to it."

*That's probably the only thing we have in common,* she thought grimly, but what she said out loud was, "I like the radio too. Especially music." She was tempted to mention that *Steve's Music Hour* was her favourite programme, but didn't dare to for fear of betraying herself.

She fumbled in the wooden crate behind the driver's seat, pulling out all sorts of cables until she finally managed to locate the Grundig radio. She switched it on.

"I'm not sure we'll be able to get good reception in the middle of the woods," she ventured, turning the knobs and catching discordant noises but no music. "What kind of music do you like?"

"Perry Como. People tell me I look like him. If only I had my other eye ..."

*You what?* thought Hella. *You wouldn't be taking me to the dance, but some other, prettier girl? Someone like Anita?* But it was not the place nor the time to start an argument, and in any case, contrary to what he believed, they were not going to any dance. Still, the conversation brought up the question she had wanted to ask for a long time.

"How did you lose your eye, Seppo? Were you wounded during the war?"

"Sort of ..."

Hella settled back into her seat, abandoning the radio. Outside, the massive sea of tall pine trees reached up to the black-blue sky.

"Tell me."

"All right. But it's not a good story."

No, Hella supposed it wasn't. Kukoyakka surely had some redeeming qualities, but somehow she couldn't imagine him as a war hero. He was too complacent for that, and too self-absorbed. Still, they had nothing better to do, so she might as well listen to him.

"It was during the Continuation War," he said finally. "I didn't have a job at the time, so when they offered me a spot in the army, I didn't say no. I hate the Soviets, so it seemed like a good idea. All I had to do was help them with radio transmissions and show them around; they weren't familiar with the marshes ... Anyway, we were part of the Petrozavodsk offensive and one day we came upon this village, Polovina, and of course it was empty. They usually were; the villagers must have developed some sort of sixth sense, because they always managed to disappear right before we turned up. You could still see stoves burning, food cooking and some handiwork abandoned, but no people. The guy who led our detachment, Colonel Koch, was angry – he would have liked to surprise those stupid villagers at least once. So here we all were, standing in a circle on the main street, the colonel drawing a map on the ground with the sawback bayonet mounted on his rifle – and all of a sudden we heard a child singing. I don't know what that song was about – it went something like *babushka, dedushka* – but I turned my head and I saw him. A small boy, dark-haired, dressed in a sweater too big for him and short trousers, and there he was, coming towards us and singing. The colonel froze. We all did. And the child saw us, of course he did, but he didn't stop or run away, because he was too small to know who we were and what it meant. And as he was singing, he was waving his arms above his head and skipping a little. I looked at the colonel, and he was smiling, and that was when I knew it wasn't going to end well. The boy was just a few steps away from us, and the colonel joined in the refrain, singing *babushka, babushka,* and then he lurched forward and thrust the bayonet into the child's belly. He ..."

Kukoyakka tightened his grip on the steering wheel. When he spoke again, the tremor was gone from his voice. If anything, he sounded matter-of-fact.

"They put the boy's body in the larder of the house Colonel Koch occupied. I don't know why. I suppose it was indecent just to leave him outside, but no one wanted to bother digging a grave. I was given a bed in the house next door, in a room I shared with three Nazi soldiers. In the middle of the night, I had to go out to relieve myself. That's when I saw a shadow slipping into the colonel's house. I went after it, for no reason. That colonel, after what he did to the child – I didn't even want to look at him any longer."

He paused, his gaze on the road, his big hairy hands trembling slightly.

"Anyway, I went in. The colonel and his men must have stayed up late, because the coals in the stove were still red hot. That's how I saw that the intruder was a woman. She was wearing a long black skirt, and her hair was tied up in a headscarf. She was frightfully thin. 'Stop it,' I said, in Finnish because I don't know any Russian. 'Get out of here.' I don't know if she understood. I don't think so, because she whispered something and shook her head.

"I wanted to take her by the shoulders and lead her out of the house. I guessed she was the boy's mother, or sister maybe, and she wanted to retrieve his body. Or maybe avenge him, I don't know. But when I made a step towards her, she scooped up the burning coals with her bare hands and threw them into my eyes."

He paused and sighed.

"I think they killed her after that. I'm only telling you this because it still keeps me up at night. That nightmare."

But whether the nightmares were about the little boy or the burning coals, he didn't say.

# 47

Neither of them uttered a single word during the rest of the trip. Even when the dim lights of Käärmela appeared in the distance, they remained silent. Hella was thinking about the little boy and the Nazi colonel who'd killed him. Colonel Koch. She'd remember that. How many of them were still out there, child murderers who had gone unpunished, authorized killers who now hid behind the masks of respectable citizens? She also thought about those who, like Kukoyakka, had contributed to the Nazis' inexorable progression through Europe because they had been swept off their feet by propaganda, or simply because they had nothing better to do, and who had realized too late the horrors that lay behind the façade.

She almost wished she hadn't asked Kukoyakka about his eye. Now she saw him differently, as a human being, a man who had made a terrible mistake and had paid for it, not just a truck driver who had designs on her. It would be difficult to put her plan into execution without compromising him. She'd need to think about it when the time came.

The truck's brakes screeched as it pulled up next to the church. Hella laid her hand on Kukoyakka's arm. "Could you please come back for me this evening? I promise you it'll be …" She stumbled, unsure of herself. Hella Mauzer, a would-be seductress! But there was no way back now. "Unforgettable."

He nodded, ogling her, his eye suddenly alight and fiery, and she jumped out of the truck and ran towards the Waltaris' house. How should she play it? Tell them she still had a couple of questions left?

It was Kalle who opened the front door. "I saw you coming," he said accusingly. "Why are you here?"

He had the bearing of the man of the house. Not a frightened little thing any longer, thought Hella. He had found his place.

"I need to talk to you, Kalle. And I want you to tell me the truth. Did someone come to the house while you were all alone waiting for your grandpa to come back?"

The boy nodded, looking away. "But I didn't see them. They came at night. I only heard them when they were leaving."

"And the next morning, was the stove all smeared? Is that why you're sleeping on the stove now? To guard it?"

He nodded: yes.

Hella looked at the tiny warrior who stood before her, his eyes downcast, his mouth resolute. So she had been right. This realization didn't make her feel any better, though. If anything, she felt worse.

"Irja's ill," said Kalle suddenly. "Timo went out to look for a horse. He wants to take her to Ivalo. I told him it was no use, but he wouldn't listen."

Hella, who was now inside the house, stopped in her tracks. "Why is it no use, Kalle? Surely the doctor can help?"

The boy shook his head. "Not the old doctor in Ivalo. He doesn't understand a thing. That's what Grandpa said."

Hella knelt beside him. "When did he say that?"

Kalle looked away. "I don't know. A long time ago."

He was shutting up like a clam. She would get nothing more out of him. Not like this.

"Let's go and see Irja," she proposed.

She took Kalle's hand, and together they passed through the narrow corridor into the living room. As soon as she saw the priest's wife, Hella realized she would have to change her plans. Irja's eyes were too big for her face and her breathing came fast and shallow. Jesus! No wonder Timo had gone to look for a horse. This was not labour, though. It was something different and altogether more sinister.

"Please make yourself comfortable," whispered Irja. She was sitting on the bench, her head in her hands. "I am afraid I can't help you much. I'm a little under the weather today."

"No problem." Hella seized the coffee pot and poured a cup for her hostess. "You need to drink. You also need a doctor. Although young Kalle here thinks Dr Gummerus is not a good bet and, having seen the specimen in person, I would have to agree with him. At least Dr Makarova was interested in what his grandpa had to tell her."

She turned towards the boy. "Dr Makarova, the Soviet doctor, examined your mother, didn't she? She drew her blood. She asked all sorts of questions. She examined you as well, even though you weren't ill like your mother. Is that what happened?"

Kalle cocked his head to one side, probably remembering the scene. A year is an eternity when you are seven. Had he forgotten it? Had he forced the painful memory out of his mind?

"The Soviet doctor was nice," he said finally. "She gave me chocolate. Not Fazer Blue, hers had a ballerina on the wrapper, but it was very good." He brightened all of a sudden.

"Was she the same woman who came to see Grandpa again last spring? She taught me how to make paper planes."

"I know," said Hella. "I found one in your old house. Is that what you did, while you waited for your grandpa to come back? You made paper planes. So I suppose you were happy when Dr Makarova came to see you last spring? Your grandpa must have been very surprised!"

Kalle hesitated.

"He was. But then he was angry, not at her, but about something. After she left, he told me I couldn't go to the forest with him any more. That there were evil things in the forest, and even in the village, too. But he, he was away all the time."

"I think he was looking for something," said Hella slowly. "Something he was afraid of finding. Proof of what Dr Makarova had told him." Her eyes rested on the steel container that was sitting on top of the cupboard. "I think, in the end, he found it."

# 48

The Waltaris didn't believe her at first.

"Malaria!" exclaimed Father Timo, incredulous, when he finally returned home, leading two nags he had borrowed from someone in the village. "Isn't that some tropical disease?"

"It is," said Hella, forcing him to sit down next to his wife and listen to her. "It's endemic in sub-Saharan Africa, India and parts of Latin America. That was precisely the reason they chose it. To see how a mosquito-borne tropical disease would adapt to local conditions. I guess they had this idea to use it as a biological weapon of sorts. Or else they were afraid someone else – the Soviets, probably – would use it as a biological weapon on Finland, and they wanted to see how it would spread in a cold climate."

"And they tested it on us? Knowing full well that some people would die from it? Who would do a thing like that?"

"It could be our local authorities, as my boss Chief Inspector Eklund lovingly calls them. That's his term for the SUPO. But I think it was probably the Western Alliance. Because Eklund didn't know anything about it at first. Otherwise, he wouldn't have authorized me to come here. He would have just classified the case, or else he'd have assigned it to Ranta to put a stamp on it. It was only once I was already here that he realized what I had stumbled across. That's why he made such a fuss about getting me back."

Irja's face was ashen. "But if what you're saying is true, it means that they set out to poison us – in cold blood – like lab animals?"

Hella shrugged. "Well, it does sound melodramatic when you put it like that, but it's not unheard of. There are precedents. And they did take precautions. Remember you told me that a team of doctors came up to the village to treat a flu epidemic? Those doctors, where did they come from? No one knows. My guess is that they weren't doctors at all, or at least not all of them. They were scientists studying the spread of malaria in local conditions. When people started falling ill in droves, they arrived with a cover story – a flu epidemic, because the symptoms are apparently similar – and they had their chloroquine, this new anti-malarial drug, ready. They just didn't anticipate that their experiment would work so well, that some of the mosquitoes would indeed survive at the end of the summer and continue infecting people. The experiment was supposed to come to an end, naturally, when the temperatures dropped. But last October was uncharacteristically warm, and some of the malaria-infested mosquitoes survived. That's how both you" – she pointed at Irja – "and Anna, who had only just arrived in the village, became infected. And as the experiment was officially over, and the 'doctors' had left, you didn't get the medical help you needed."

Father Timo was staring down at his hands with a puzzled expression. "Do you think they ran their tests here, of all places, because the locals are second-rate citizens to them? Because this land has been changing hands so often, its inhabitants are – well, they don't belong anywhere, do they?

They're refugees, even if they don't wander from place to place any longer."

"Maybe. I don't know. It's possible, of course."

But Father Timo was already pursuing a different line of thought.

"Erno couldn't have possibly realized all this," he objected. "Erno was educated, yes, but he wasn't a scientist. If what you're saying is true, he was the only person around who figured it out. How could he have done?"

"He didn't figure it out all at once. He just knew that his daughter had fallen seriously ill, just like many other people in the village had fallen ill before her. But by that time, the so-called doctors had already left, and Anna, who was fragile, was getting worse by the day. So Erno did a perfectly normal, logical thing. He borrowed a horse and took his daughter and his grandson, because he didn't know who to leave him with, to Ivalo, to see the doctor there. That visit wasn't a success. Dr Gummerus barely examined Anna. He diagnosed her with the flu and sent them away. Erno was desperate. He could see that his only daughter was dying. So he made a decision. If the local doctor couldn't find what was wrong with her, he'd take his daughter across the border, to Svetly. And why not? He went to Svetly for his groceries, he spoke pretty good Russian, it was worth a try."

"The Soviet doctor, Daria Makarova, was different. She became interested in Anna's case. She must have noticed that Anna's fever was peaking every other day – you noticed that too, Irja, by the way, you told me so yourself – and she found it strange. Also, Anna's spleen was enlarged. It didn't look like the regular flu. Still, Dr Makarova didn't know what it was exactly, so she drew Anna's blood and sent it somewhere, to Murmansk probably, or even to Moscow, for a test. I don't think they have a lab in Svetly, the town is too small."

"She wanted to keep Mama with her," confirmed Kalle all of a sudden. "She wanted to send her to a local hospital, but Mama refused. She didn't want to leave me. So Grandpa brought us back."

"I think," added Hella, "that another thing that probably puzzled Dr Makarova was that neither Erno nor Kalle was sick. Erno was a strong, grown man, so maybe he was more resistant than others, but Kalle? He was just a child. How come he didn't catch the virus from his mother? Because it was not a virus. Malaria is transmitted by a parasite. It lives in the body, but it doesn't spread from one person to another. Except" – she forced herself to look Irja in the eye – "from a mother to her unborn child. It's not your fault Aleksi died. And you didn't catch the disease from Anna. You mentioned once that you'd been devoured by mosquitoes when you arrived in the village. That's how you got infected."

"When did Erno know for sure?" asked Timo, addressing the polished surface of the table.

"I suppose the blood tests must have taken a long time," explained Hella. "The Soviets must have been so stupefied with the results that they ran the tests over and over again, until they were a hundred per cent sure. When they were, in March of this year, Dr Makarova crossed the border to find Erno and explain to him what had happened to his daughter. It was a big risk to take, but she was a doctor, a real one. She wanted to shed light on what had happened. Quite possibly, she had a personal motive too. A scoop like this! It could have advanced her career no end. She could have got out of Svetly with a promotion."

Irja's burning gaze was fixed on Hella. "You mentioned that the woman had slivers of glass in her mouth. Was it ...?"

"Yes," confirmed Hella. "She was bringing you chloroquine, because Erno had asked her to. He was feeling guilty about you losing baby Aleksi, and when he realized you were expecting again, and that your illness could be cured, he must have contacted Dr Makarova – I don't know how – and told her that he'd provide the Soviets with proof of malaria testing in exchange for chloroquine. I'm only guessing, of course, but I think that's what must have happened. It explains why both of them were killed when they met for the exchange. I imagine their killers destroyed the evidence that Erno had gathered. Luckily for us, he put a few of the vials aside. He —"

Irja cut in, her voice terse. "How did they know? Erno's killers, who told them that the exchange was to take place?"

"I don't know," admitted Hella. "Maybe there's a mole in Svetly selling Russian secrets to the Western Alliance."

Timo gasped, but Irja was not listening any longer. Her eyes were closed, and beads of perspiration had appeared on her forehead. Her husband cast an anguished glance at the door. She was running a high fever. They needed to find her a doctor, and quick. All the rest – the political motives, the responsibilities, the killers – could wait. First things first.

"Dr Gummerus won't help you," Hella told them. "I saw him just this morning. He is old, and he's not very bright. He'll never believe us if we tell him you're suffering from malaria, and in any case, he hasn't got the medicine we need. He said chloroquine would only be available in Helsinki, at the central army pharmacy."

Timo Waltari frowned. "Do you really think the officers there will agree to give Irja the drug? Just like that? Won't they be tempted to decide that we're all hysterical villagers who have no medical background and no idea what they are talking about? Or it could be even worse. Because it was either the SUPO or the Western Alliance who killed Erno and Dr Makarova. So that this thing doesn't get out."

"It's possible," said Hella. "Even likely. But I know someone – Colonel Kyander. He's an old friend of my father's, and he's part of the SUPO, one of its most senior officers – I think he can help us. My father trusted him."

She paused, wondering if she hadn't promised more than she could deliver. After all, how could she be sure? People change. And Colonel Kyander might not even be there. Still, it was worth a try.

But Timo had a different idea. "It will take ages to get to Helsinki. A horse to Ivalo, then we would need to find a car … and then go and explain the entire story to your friend …" He drew a deep breath. "The Soviets will believe us. I expect they'll be ready to help us if we tell them we're going to expose the whole thing. That will give them a card to play. 'Western Alliance poisons capitalist world', that sort of thing. Just imagine *Pravda*'s headlines!" He looked around, his eyes resting finally on the icons that adorned the wall opposite him. "If we leave now, we can be in Svetly in four hours."

Irja opened her eyes at last, turned to her husband. "I absolutely forbid you to go across the border. You must be out of your mind. You are a priest, remember? The enemy of the people. The Soviets destroyed all of Käärmela's icons. The fact that you used to be a communist won't make the slightest difference. There's a place for people like you and me in the Soviet Union. A place called the Gulag."

# 49

While Irja changed into her travel clothes, Hella stood by the window, absent-mindedly gazing at the pair of brown horses that Father Timo had tied to a post. She couldn't shake the feeling that something was very wrong. Was it Kyander she was worried about? She glanced at the steel container at her feet, with its three vials labelled YSTERIA. It had taken her a long time to guess that the metal jar Erno had borrowed from his sister had been thrown away by the so-called doctors and that Martta had picked it up, as she picked up every trinket she saw. Now, Hella had her proof. The typewritten report, with dates and names and places, was in her bag. What then? They still had three hours before Kukoyakka was due back in the village. She'd persuade him to drive them to Helsinki. She'd promise him … whatever. Kukoyakka was in a good mood. And if he didn't want to drive them all the way to Helsinki, she'd just ask him to drop them off at the Ivalo bus station. They could easily catch a bus.

She froze in apprehension. Easy. That was the word.

It was too easy.

She had got away from Eklund without the slightest difficulty. She had persuaded Kukoyakka to drive her back to Käärmela. And he had agreed to come back for her.

At the time it had felt like a miracle. But now Hella had to recognize that, for better or worse, she was long past believing in fairy tales and good luck.

What had he been doing at home when she'd gone over there, in the middle of the day? Just hanging around doing nothing, waiting for her to drop in? He had said while he was driving her back from Käärmela on Sunday that he only needed to go to the logging camp on Monday afternoon. To do what? He'd never told her, and she'd never asked. And even if he really had a reason to go to the logging camp in the middle of the afternoon, how come he'd agreed so easily to drive her all the way to Käärmela? Was he so smitten with her that he would indulge her every whim? Were her womanly charms reason enough?

She glanced at her reflection in the mirror. She had dark circles under her eyes, and her hair hung limply around her face. Some beauty queen!

Still, Hella tried to reason with herself. Why not, after all? Maybe he did find her beautiful. Maybe he was in love with her. Otherwise, why would he have told her that awful story about the little Soviet boy, if not to explain his nightmares to her? Because he expected to soon be sleeping by her side. There was no need to worry.

But the nagging feeling just wouldn't go away.

Was Lennart Eklund just a dim-witted bureaucrat, as she had always thought, or was there more to him than met the eye?

"Hurry up, Irja, please. We don't have much time."

Irja looked at her, frowning, stopping in mid-movement. "What is it? You sound worried. I thought we were waiting for your friend Mr Kukoyakka to drive us to Ivalo?"

"I'm fine," snapped Hella. "Just hurry up."

"You don't have to do this, you know. I'd just be a nuisance to you. Think about what it would mean for your career."

"I don't have a career, but it's not because of you. Hurry!"

"There's something I need to give you," murmured Irja, reaching inside her pocket. "Something you forgot —"

"Wait!" Hella paused, her hand on the door handle. She heard a floorboard creak in the corridor outside the room. "Who is it?"

"Kalle."

She opened the door and the little boy ducked in. Irja, who was tying her scarf, leaned over and kissed him on the forehead.

Hella glared at her. "Hurry!"

With Irja moving again, Hella pulled a travel bag out of the wardrobe and started throwing warm clothes into it. Outside, the horses stirred, dancing on their hoofs. Were those voices she could hear?

"Kalle, do we have a visitor? Who's there? Go and look." But before he stepped out of the room, she laid a hand on his shoulder. "Like a cat, Kalle, all right? Like Seamus. Just glance in the living room, but make sure no one sees you. Then come straight back."

She held her breath while she waited for the boy to reappear. As soon as she saw him, she knew.

"Three policemen, they came to talk with Father Timo. One big and fat, one small and dirty. The third has a red moustache. Do you know them?"

"Oh yes," said Hella. "I think I do. Two of them, at least. Hurry!"

She glanced out of the window. The road was clear.

No, it wasn't. The man with the red moustache – someone from the SUPO, surely – emerged from around the corner and took up position next to the horses. They were not leaving anything to chance.

The sound of voices from the living room grew louder. What should she do? Did she have a fighting chance against the sentinel? Was she ready to use her service weapon against another officer?

More shouting from the living room. The red-headed sentinel had heard it too. He hesitated, glanced at the house, then, his right hand thrust under his parka, ran towards the door, ready to lend a helping hand to Eklund and Ranta.

Hella thrust the window open and almost pushed Irja out, then jumped after her. Kalle climbed onto the windowsill. He didn't have his coat on, but they'd figure something out.

"All right, come with us."

She felt rather than heard movement behind her back.

"Hello, pariah!"

Ranta! He must have been sent outside to replace the red-headed man, to guard the horses. Now he stood before her, clad in a dirty parka with a muskrat-fur collar that he wore in all seasons, an unlit cigarette between his chapped lips.

"Listen," said Hella, panting. She realized she didn't even know Ranta's first name. "I don't know what Eklund told you —"

But to her astonishment, Ranta winked at her and turned away.

"Live your life, pariah," he said. "I've always enjoyed good drama … and there's not nearly enough of that in Ivalo."

Hella didn't kiss him; but it was only because she didn't have the time. She and Irja mounted the horses, Hella taking Kalle with her. She grabbed the bridle of Irja's horse, and, gaining speed, headed for the forest. They had to take Kukoyakka by surprise. There was no other way.

# 50

It was a big affair, the logging camp. Hella hadn't expected it to be so huge. It spread for more than three hundred yards along the river. To one side, there were wooden barracks for the workers, and a sauna. Opposite the barracks, separated by parking spaces, stood a big, square house made of logs. It had two porches. One side was an office, the other a kitchen. Hella, who had left Irja and Kalle with the horses hidden away in the forest, peered through the kitchen's tiny mullioned windows and was immediately rewarded with the sight of Kukoyakka slumped over a bowl of soup, smack in the middle of the dining area. *Waiting to be found*, screamed her inner voice. She hesitated, casting an anguished glance over her shoulder, towards the parking lot. Kukoyakka's Sisu was there, instantly recognizable with its eagle drawings and its crooked bumper. Could he have left his keys in the ignition? Trying to act nonchalant, Hella sauntered towards the truck and climbed the ladder to the cabin. If anyone asked her, she would say she was looking for her lost book. A pathetic fallback plan, but it would do. After all, she didn't suspect the whole camp of being in cahoots with Eklund and his clique.

It was cold, and dark. There was no sign of the keys. Hella hesitated, unsure of what to do next. Appealing to Kukoyakka's better nature was too risky, and as such, not an option. The story of the Soviet boy and Colonel Koch made her realize that, at a crossroads of his conscience, Kukoyakka would always choose the side of authority. The safe side. Also, even if she was mistaken about him, even if for some unfathomable reason he agreed to help them, she didn't really want him involved because that would make him her accomplice. It wasn't fair to the man.

How could she recover the keys, then? She didn't have many choices. Out of the blue, her dead sister's image floated into her mind. Christina would have found this fun. She would have known how to seduce a middle-aged Cyclops and steal his keys from him. She would have let loose her curly blonde hair, painted her lips crimson and mesmerized her victim in no time. But Christina and Hella were not from the same mould. Also, she had no lipstick with her.

*OK, here goes.* Hella rubbed her cheeks to make the blood flow to her face, bit her lips and pulled her shoulders back. *Like a queen,* Christina's teasing voice sang into her ear. *Like a queen! You can do it.*

If Kukoyakka sensed her presence, he didn't show it, only lifting his head from his bowl of soup when Hella was a couple of steps away from him.

"Seppo!" she cried out loud, too loud. "Here you are! The priest's wife was as boring as hell, and when she realized what I needed the dress for – Sin, with a capital S – she refused to make it. So I came here, to spare you the drive back to the village."

To say that Kukoyakka was happy to see her was surely to overstate it. If anything, he recoiled.

"How?"

"How what, Seppo?" she cooed.

"How did you get here? On skis?"

"That's right," she said. "Borrowed an old pair of skis from the priest, but the right one broke in half while I was still in the forest, so I left them there and finished on foot."

*Don't say too much,* warned Christina's voice inside her head. *Ask him how he is.*

"What have you been doing, Seppo? Were you thinking about me?"

Kukoyakka hesitated, then nodded cautiously.

Hella blundered on, smiling at him. "It was so nice of you to drive me to Käärmela. So sweet. You know, I really appreciate it. I think we'll make a great couple at that dance. If I ever manage to find a nice enough dress, that is."

He smiled back at her, a stupid smile. She thought she could hear the wheels turning in his head. *Trying to figure out what to make of me, aren't you?*

She drew in closer and laid a hand on his arm, then withdrew it quickly, noticing too late that her nails were bitten to the quick.

"I was thinking, Seppo dear, do you have a room here? I'd like to visit it. To see how my man's settled when he's away from home." She smiled from ear to ear and grabbed hold of his arm, dragging him to his feet. "Come on!"

He rose reluctantly. "It's over there" – he made a vague gesture towards the barracks – "but there's nothing to see, really. Just a steel-framed bed and a locker."

Still, he let himself be dragged towards the barracks. The cook, an overweight Sami with a greasy apron, shook his head when he saw them pass.

The rooms in the barracks were set on both sides of a long and dark corridor; Kukoyakka had the fifth room to the right. Hella, who had unbuttoned her parka as they walked, threw it on top of the locker.

He had been looking at her with the dead eye of a fish until that moment, but now she believed she could see a spark of interest. Well, she'd kiss him if she really had to. Poor man, he had done so much for her already.

Hella reached out to him and stroked his cheek, trying to avoid staring into that blazing eye of his. Where did he keep the keys? She ran her hands over his body and felt something sharp in his back pocket. Afraid he would recognize her interest for what it was, she hastily pulled her hands away, pretending to be shy. Kukoyakka was leaning forward to kiss her. She smiled enticingly. His hard, blistered lips pressed down on hers as she contorted herself to try and get hold of the keys.

Kukoyakka groaned, stiffened, and then suddenly gripped her wrists. "You're not going to get away with just a bit of kissing," he hissed at her. "It won't do. You want to play a dangerous game, you pay with your body."

Hella wriggled, but his grip was too tight. Terrified, she tried to make light of it. "Next time, Seppo dear, all right? When we know each other better."

"What do you think I am, an idiot?" She could see now that he was furious. He shook her until her teeth chattered. "Do you think Lennart didn't warn me that you'd come running to my door and ask me to drive you to Käärmela?"

If only he'd let go of her wrists, she could grab her gun from its holster, but Kukoyakka was expecting her to do that. He brought her right arm behind her back and twisted it. With the left, he got hold of her gun and tossed it into the corner. This done, he unbuttoned her trousers and lowered them to her ankles. Then he turned her around to face the door.

"Now, beautiful," he stated matter-of-factly, and, twisting her arm still further, brought her to her knees at the foot of his bed and expertly gagged her with her own scarf. Her face was down on the floor. "This is a small price to pay for all that driving I did for you." He ripped her panties off. "Oh, and if you haven't realized yet, I'm going to use the back door. No kids that way. No liabilities. In any case, you look like a boy. You shouldn't expect anyone to take you like a woman."

If only she had a handful of burning coals! She kicked and writhed, trying to bite him, but he was stronger and kept twisting her arm until she almost fainted. She felt rather than heard him fumbling behind her back. She knew he must be unbuttoning his trousers. She stopped kicking and, with a deep sigh, hung limply to signal her submission.

The man chuckled. "Good girl. Now you're being reasonable. If you stop squirming, it won't hurt all that much."

She was gathering her strength. There was a small rusted nail, barely half an inch long, in a heap of dust at the foot of the bed. She'd use it as a weapon. She waited until he lowered his underpants and his penis touched her body. He kept holding her arm, but she felt his grip loosen. She was not fighting any more; he thought he had won. Then, just for a split second, he let go of her arm. She spun round and struck him with the nail. She planted it in Kukoyakka's bare thigh and it went all the way in. The man howled and rolled backwards, his penis fully erect. The image of the murdered boy's mother flashed before her eyes. She struck him again, with her feet, and this time she aimed for the groin. When he'd passed out from the pain, she pulled her scarf out of her mouth and tied his hands behind his back with it. She used her ripped-off panties as a gag. Trembling with disgust, she put her clothes back on. Then she pulled the truck keys out of his pocket and made for the door.

There was no one in the corridor and no one outside. Hella climbed into the truck's cabin and shifted it into gear. She forced herself to breathe slowly and drive carefully. As the Sisu rumbled out of the yard, she saw the round face of the Sami cook, who was following her progress from behind the kitchen's mullioned window.

# 51

"If ever I'm hit by a bus ..." Her father had laughed to show her how remote, how utterly improbable that possibility was. "If ever I'm hit by a bus, you need to promise me, Hella. You don't talk to anyone. You take my notebooks – you're the only person who knows where they are hidden; even your mother pretends not to – and you bring them straight to Colonel Kyander. He's the only person in this country I trust. Apart from you, obviously. You give my notebook to Kyander, and then you forget about the whole thing. Promise?"

Hella promised.

She would never have admitted it, but she was terribly proud to be the only one her father trusted. Not Christina, even though she was older. Not her mother. Her. She had always known she was the favourite.

"Now, that's settled," her father had said. He was not really worried. No spy worth his salt worried about such things. Having survived the war, an interrogation by the Gestapo and a plane crash, he firmly believed that after over two dozen years in the field setting up spy networks, he was all set to enjoy a peaceful retirement. The image he had of his retirement years was always the same. He and

Kyander – "the best man I've ever met, Hella" – fishing trout together on Kemijoki. It was this image that had led the whole family to get up so early that Saturday morning; a cabin next to the river had come up for sale, and they wanted to be the first there. Hella, who had spent the night being sick, had been forced to stay behind.

They never got to see the cabin. The role of the proverbial bus had been taken by an ancient Sisu truck that had skidded on the icy road, careering towards the four of them at a crazy speed, only stopping a hundred yards further on. They had all been killed instantly, except for Hella's mother, who had passed away as the paramedics lifted her onto a stretcher.

"At least they didn't suffer," Kyander said when Hella brought him the notebooks. "They still haven't identified the driver, by the way. Probably some village idiot who just wanted to have some fun. You must believe me when I tell you that your family's death was a tragic accident. It is absolutely not related" – Kyander paused, peering at her through his spectacles – "to your father's activities."

"How can you be so sure?" asked Hella in a hoarse voice. She had spent many sleepless nights agonizing over that very question.

"Because even our enemies aren't so cruel as to kill off our whole families. Not like this." Kyander patted her arm awkwardly. He clearly didn't know what else to say. "At least they didn't suffer," he repeated dutifully, and cast a soulful glance at the door. Hella took the hint.

"Thank you for everything," she muttered, like the good girl she had always been, even though she would have been hard-pressed to say what she was thanking him for.

"If you ever need anything …" said Kyander. "Anything at all. Just call me." He fumbled around in his pocket and gave her a card which had no name on it, only a telephone number scribbled in black ink.

"Thank you," Hella replied. "I will."

And now she was bloody well going to.

Driving Kukoyakka's truck turned out to be much easier than she had expected. There were only two gears, and while the steering wheel was huge, it didn't take much force to turn it. And the engine was powerful, calibrated for a heavy load of logs that Hella was no longer carrying. She had uncoupled the truck's trailer as soon as she'd exited the logging camp's yard, with the idea of staving off any pursuit.

Hella glanced at the speedometer: thirty miles per hour. If they could keep up this speed, they should be able to get to Helsinki in about thirteen hours. But as she made her calculations, she realized that her thinking was flawed: there was no way they could keep the truck. They needed to find a different vehicle, and that might take some time. Still, it was probably not urgent. She doubted very much that Eklund and Ranta were already back from their expedition to Käärmela. Which meant she still had a fair chance of driving through Ivalo without being intercepted.

She put her foot down, and the big truck leaped forward. Kalle mumbled something. The initial excitement had worn off, and the boy, who was bundled in one of Irja's bulky cardigans, was sleepy. Irja patted his head, then turned to look at Hella. "Do you think they arrested Timo?" she mouthed.

Hella didn't dare look at her. "Maybe," she replied. "I don't know." She was afraid to admit that not only was she certain that Timo had been arrested, she knew it was her fault too. If she hadn't come barging in, the missing persons case would have died off by itself. When the SUPO had shot

Dr Makarova with their service weapons, then later murdered Erno to cover their tracks, they hadn't really expected anyone to investigate the case. After all, who would bother to open a case for an old man going missing in the wilderness? As for Dr Makarova, it should have been easier still. Hella supposed the Soviets knew what had happened to her but couldn't do anything about it. She had been beyond the Soviet border, and she'd had no legal justification for doing what she had done. So the Soviets had kept their mouths shut. Hella bit her lip. Because she had been bored to tears in Ivalo, she had wreaked havoc in people's lives. And she hadn't even got justice for old Erno.

If only her enemy was a man! Nothing had prepared her to battle the faceless monster she had been taught to obey. But maybe this was the ultimate test that destiny held in store for her; her moment to stand up and be counted. To face the system and win, or to perish.

The straight and narrow road, packed with dirty snow and only illuminated by the truck's headlights, stretched endlessly before her. A sea of ice. It was going to be a long, long journey, and she didn't even know if it would end well. As she drove, she went over the arguments she would present to Kyander. He was a good man; he must be. One didn't get to such a position of responsibility without being equanimous, rational and ... yes, moral. Everything depended on him now. She'd invoke her father's memory. She'd explain the suffering endured by the villagers, Anna's death, baby Aleksi's death, Erno. Dr Makarova. She was not one of their own, but she was as much a victim as the others. Somebody's daughter, sister, niece. A mother, maybe. Hella hoped not.

"I'm hungry, Aunt Hella." Irja had dozed off, but Kalle was awake now. He looked at her from his seat, a little ghost, his eyes huge and scared.

"There's chocolate in my shoulder bag," said Hella. "Fazer Blue, your favourite. You can have it. And I have a gift for you, too. I forgot all about it."

She wondered what the future held for Kalle, and for herself. She had briefly thought about adopting the boy, but that was before she had broken the law. Now he'd be better off with Irja. Maybe the priest's wife could go and live with her parents. Unless the SUPO somehow managed to prove that she was a traitor too, Hella didn't think Irja would end up in prison.

Kalle, whom she could hear rummaging around in her shoulder bag, stifled an exclamation. So he'd found it. She looked at the boy in the rear-view mirror. He had a smile on his face, the sort of smile that lights up young children's faces on Christmas mornings. She had already decided to give the bus to him – she had held on to it for too long, and it was just an object, after all – but somehow seeing Kalle smile made her decision a hundred times easier. In her mind's eye, Matti's face came sharply into focus. Just one month before his death, he had been unwrapping his gifts, sitting in a pool of light in the middle of her parents' living room. The toy bear she had given him had been tossed aside – "What am I, a baby? I'm five already, five and a half!" – but the bus! He hadn't torn the wrapping paper off all at once. He had peeled strips off it, like an archaeologist uncovering a precious Egyptian mummy. A bumper had come into view, then a chrome-plated wheel. "Is it really mine?" Matti had whispered, dumbstruck by so much happiness. "Of course it is!" Hella's father had bellowed. "These women here ..." He made a large sweeping gesture to include them all. "Your mother, your aunt, and above all your grandmother ... they're afraid of buses. Heaven knows why.

Well, now you're the bus master, and there's nothing to be afraid of. Show me!"

Matti had roared with delight, finally stripping the gleaming yellow bus of its wrappings and brandishing it above his head, a huge smile on his face.

"You can have it, Kalle," whispered Hella. Next to her, Irja shifted in her sleep and smiled. "It used to belong to my nephew, but he doesn't play with it any more. It's yours if you want it."

# TUESDAY 21 OCTOBER

# 52

"Have you ever been in love?" asked Irja.

They had passed Ivalo without a snag. No one on the road, no one following them. Kalle was sound asleep, snoring, his chocolate-covered mouth drooping, his hands still clutching the bus. Irja was sitting bolt upright; and for the last hour, she hadn't stopped talking. *Maybe she's talking to keep me awake,* thought Hella, and suppressed a yawn.

"I don't know," she replied finally. She never liked discussing her private life. Maybe that was why she didn't have any friends. "Perhaps I was," she said as Irja remained silent. "Once. A long time ago. Nothing came of it. Does that shock you?"

"Why should it?" asked Irja. "I don't expect you to be a saint."

Hella laughed bitterly. "So if I told you that I had an affair with a married man, and that some nights the only thing I long for in life is to touch him again, you'd just give me your blessing."

"I'm not in the business of giving blessings. But I won't judge you. Did he love you too?"

"I don't know really. He said he did, and at that time I believed him. Even when he listed all the reasons for not leaving his wife and child – did I tell you he had a child, too? – I still believed him. Which is just another indication of how stupid I am."

"You were in love," said Irja. "When we're in love, we see everything in a different light."

"Oh, spare me!" cried Hella, who couldn't take it any longer. "I don't need your understanding. I don't need your commiseration. I'm fine as I am."

*Or not,* she thought wearily, but refrained from saying it out loud.

She turned towards Irja.

"Now, you tell me. How does a girl end up being married to an Orthodox priest? And why are your priests allowed to get married in the first place?"

Irja stretched, smiling, her hands on her belly. In that cold and narrow cabin, she looked comfortable, almost snug, her shawl (*of cheap fabric,* Anita would say) draped around her shoulders.

"That's because they're supposed to set an example. To be given a parish, a priest needs to be married. This way, he can show his parishioners how they should live. I guess you could say that Timo and I have failed at it spectacularly, at least on the most basic of terms – no children of our own, and now this suspicion of treason. Not exactly what the patriarch was looking for when he sent Timo to Käärmela."

Hella nodded, her gaze still on the road. It was four in the morning, and the soft snow that was falling through the night gleamed like stardust in the truck's headlights.

"I met Timo in 1939," continued Irja in a dreamy voice. "In Turku; that's where my family lived before my father's porcelain-manufacturing business went bankrupt. I was just a child at that time. A child of fourteen. My ambition in those days was to become a nurse. Even then I had never seriously considered that painting could be more than just another hobby. That year, there was a lot of unrest." She laughed. "I don't know why I'm telling you this, you probably know it better than I do. Anyway, after school, I was wandering around the streets with a bag full of bandages and disinfectant, looking for someone to save. One day, I heard shooting. I later learned that an unknown group of terrorists had attempted to kill Defence Minister Juho Niukkanen, who was strongly opposed to exchanging territories with the Soviets. Timo was supposed to be their hit man, but at the last moment he realized he couldn't do it. He had tried to talk the others out of it, but no one would listen. They were just a group of overexcited children, and they had already gone too far. One of his friends picked up the gun, shot and missed. I think he missed on purpose. Timo cried with relief. After the shot was fired, the police showed up almost at once. The other boys dragged Timo along, and as they turned into a side street, they ran into me. Timo was deathly white. He was shaking and his right hand was grazed from falling. The other boys were all too happy to leave him with me. While he sobbed, I bandaged his hand. I told him to calm down, not to talk, but he told me anyway. So we both went to the church and he confessed. He felt better instantly. That's what a confession does to you, it lifts your spirit. The next time I saw him, I was three years older. He had just been released from prison, and he came to thank me."

"Was he still a communist at that time?"

"No. In prison, he had time to read and think. After he was released, the church accepted him into the seminary. So I had to wait three more years. I would have preferred him not to have been a priest – I could have painted then – but that's who he is."

There was a note of bitterness in her voice that made Hella realize that loving a priest was not the easiest thing in the world. You had to love his cause too, and never waver.

Hella stared straight ahead, suddenly exhausted. The horizon was still dark, but in three hours they would reach the outskirts of Helsinki. She had Kyander's telephone number engraved in her mind. She would call him from a public phone when they got to Helsinki and insist on seeing him straight away. She would not mention Irja or Project Ysteria – she would just tell him that she needed to see him immediately, and that it was a personal matter. He couldn't refuse her that. Hella wondered if, during the night, the news of her escape had seeped over the radio. If she was news. She briefly imagined Steve's bewilderment.

"There's a radio in the box behind the driver's seat," she said. "Could you switch it on? I'd like to know if we've become famous overnight."

Irja dutifully obliged and started fumbling in the big box full of cables. "Is it the eavesdropping device that Mr Kukoyakka told me about when he last visited?" she asked. "He was very funny about it." Hella kept silent; she hadn't told Irja what Kukoyakka had done to her. "Here, I found the radio." Snatches of classical music and fragments of conversation from far away burst into the cabin as Irja pushed the buttons, trying to find Yle Radio. When at last she found the frequency, they sat in tense silence for ten minutes listening to local and international news, but there was nothing about them. Hella sighed with relief.

At five in the morning, they abandoned the logging truck in Jyväskylä, and Hella rented a battered little car for an exorbitant price. The owner, a small man clad in so many layers of clothing that he was as round as a ball, looked at them suspiciously but kept his thoughts to himself. Hella could hardly refrain from smiling. She had been afraid Eklund and the SUPO had transmitted her description all around Finland, but either they hadn't launched a nationwide search for her or the news had not spread yet. She felt full of hope. Maybe Ysteria was a local operation that had got out of control. Maybe in Helsinki they would listen to her.

The little car, its boot stuffed with Kukoyakka's radio equipment, lurched forward. In the back seat, Kalle started polishing off what remained of the chocolate. Irja smiled at him; her fever had abated. *One happy family on a weekend outing*, thought Hella. *If only we all get out of this alive.*

# 53

Helsinki is a sprawling city. Built by the Swedish king Gustaf Vasa in the middle of the sixteenth century as a merchant town, its territory stretches between the tip of a peninsula and some three hundred islands. There is water everywhere. The Daughter of the Baltic, as the city is sometimes called, revels in it, because water is its only permanent element. Partly destroyed by the great fire of 1808, rebuilt by the Russians to resemble St Petersburg, it was now changing again – and not for the better, as people who didn't appreciate the modernist style of the architects who had brought the city up to date for the Olympic Games would say. They drove into the city shortly after eight; Hella stopped the car near the first public phone she saw. Leaving her wide-eyed passengers behind, she clambered out of the car and stretched, extending her stiffened limbs.

The telephone booth was empty. Hella fished a handful of coins out of her bag and glanced at her watch. It was 8.18 a.m. She hesitated. Was it too early? What would she do if no one answered? She dialled, and the phone was picked up almost before it had rung. As if someone was standing next to it, waiting.

A woman's voice, cracked and loud. "Listening!"

"Good day. My name is Hella Mauzer. I am the daughter of Colonel Mauzer. I would like to speak with Colonel Kyander. Is he home?"

She held her breath. There was some shuffling at the other end of the line. She had a feeling that the woman was wiping her greasy hands on her apron. Was it breakfast time? Did Kyander have a family? She had never thought about him in these terms – as a man who had a life outside his Secret Service work – but that didn't mean he lived alone.

After more shuffling, the woman finally made up her mind. "I'll get him."

Hella waited, her heart thumping against her ribcage. A full minute passed before the phone was picked up again.

"Kyander."

"Colonel, this is Hella Mauzer. You once gave me your card and said I could call you any time I needed help. I need help now."

Kyander's voice was curiously flat. He didn't even pause before speaking. "Of course. A man keeps his word, always. Where are you, Hella? In Helsinki? Would you like me to meet you somewhere, or would you prefer to come over?"

"I'd rather come over," she said gladly.

He gave her his address on Luotsikatu. Hella jotted it down in her notebook, even though she was perfectly capable of remembering it; Kyander's house was within walking distance of Steve's radio station.

"I'll be there in about ten minutes," she said. "Thank you so much!"

She cast a triumphant glance at Irja. All was going according to plan. Hella eased herself into the driver's seat and put the car into gear.

"I'm going to meet with the colonel," she explained. "He lives in Katajanokka. We can park there, and while

I talk to him you can visit the Uspensky Cathedral. Are you OK?"

But she could see that Irja was not OK. She just sat there panting, the discarded shawl in a heap on her lap, one of her hands on her belly and the other clutching the small silver cross she had pulled out from under her clothes.

"I'll be quick," said Hella as she parked the car. "I promise. Then, after I've explained the situation to Kyander, we'll get you to the military hospital and put you on chloroquine. It's all going to be all right. Do you believe me?"

Irja nodded, trying out a smile, not looking at her. Her cheeks were crimson and her breathing was rapid.

Kyander lived in a rather grand house, a mansion even, built in an art nouveau style and painted a watery yellow. There seemed to be a small formal garden, too, but at this time of the year it was buried under fresh snow. Hella noticed with relief that the snow lay undisturbed. She rang the bell. A matronly woman of indeterminate age opened the front door, peering at her with suspicion, but when Hella started to introduce herself the woman stopped her with a wave of the hand.

"The colonel is expecting you. He's in the breakfast room."

Hella followed the woman across the marble floor of the hall, her footsteps echoing in the eerie silence of the house. A breakfast room! She had never heard of anyone who had one. Was this the same man her father had expected to share a lakeside cabin with?

"My dear girl! So, so happy to see you! Why haven't you kept in touch?"

Colonel Kyander smelled of cinnamon and freshly brewed coffee. His bald head glistened, reflecting the light from a chandelier, and his small, unnaturally red mouth was moist under a bushy moustache. Hella smiled back, not knowing what to say – had he been expecting a Christmas card or something? – and looked around. The breakfast room was yellow too. Ancestors' portraits in heavy gilded frames covered the walls; the napkins were damask and the cups made of bone china. A state-of-the-art percolator took centre stage on the breakfast table.

"Care for some coffee? Straight from Colombia, best quality ever, not what you'd get from a grocers' on a rationing ticket."

"Yes please," said Hella gladly. "I'd love to. Good coffee is hard to come by in Lapland."

She unbuttoned her parka and sat on the edge of a gilded reproduction chair, waiting while Kyander poured her a cup.

"So how have you been doing, my dear child? Not married yet, are you? It will come, it will come. No doubt about it."

"I'm fine," said Hella, doing her best not to look offended by this allusion to her unmarried status. "Or at least, I was until about a week ago. Then, I uncovered" – she paused, wondering what words to use: a great injustice? A state-ordered crime? – "I discovered that a series of crimes had been committed. To make it worse, an innocent man has been wrongly accused. I need your help to put things right. So I'm afraid this isn't a social visit."

Kyander leaned back in his chair, joining his fingertips over his protruding paunch. The lowest button on his crisp white shirt was close to giving way.

"I'm listening very attentively," he assured her.

# 54

"A little over two weeks ago, a man went missing in Lapland. His name was Erno Jokinen."

Kyander nodded. "Go on."

"I went to investigate. I discovered not one, but two bodies. Both had been shot in the head. The second victim was a Soviet woman. A doctor."

Kyander's eyebrows shot all the way up. "How can you be sure the woman was Soviet?"

"I found her identity card," Hella said. "She and the old man had stumbled across a case of biological weapons testing. Erno Jokinen's daughter was one of the victims."

"Of this biological weapon?"

"Exactly."

"What kind of agent was it? Anthrax? Plague?"

"Malaria."

Kyander's eyes narrowed. "I've never heard of malaria cases in the northern hemisphere."

"They were testing," explained Hella. "They wanted to see whether it could work in our climate."

"They? Who are *they*?"

"I don't know," admitted Hella. "I think it might have been a project run by the Western Alliance, because, according to the villagers, a couple of the doctors who went out there spoke with heavy foreign accents. But I know that the SUPO is also involved, at least locally."

"The SUPO would never do a thing like that!" snapped Kyander. "Poisoning our own people! Is that what you're accusing them of?"

"In a way. Put like that. I suppose so. Yes. I'm not saying they did it on purpose," muttered Hella, suddenly afraid of her own allegations and Kyander's ice-cold stare. "I'm saying that these scientists – whoever they were – put everything in place to avoid casualties. They had sent doctors out to the village, they had enough medicine, everything was planned, but what they had not anticipated was the weather. It was a very warm autumn. Against the odds, the mosquitoes were still active in October, and some people fell ill after the doctors had already left. And when that old man, Erno Jokinen, realized what had happened, they had him silenced. They also killed the Soviet army doctor he had consulted."

"There's one thing I don't understand," said Kyander slowly. "Even imagining that the rest of your story is true, which I doubt, why would an honest Finnish citizen unlawfully cross the border to consult a Soviet doctor? Don't you have a doctor in Ivalo?"

"We have one," said Hella. "Dr Gummerus. But he's worse than useless."

"Then your old man could have gone to a bigger city. To Sodankylä, for instance."

"He could have," sighed Hella. "But Svetly was closer, and at the time he went to see that Soviet doctor he wasn't expecting to uncover anything suspect. He thought his daughter had the flu. But he could tell that she was dying and that it was urgent."

"All right," said Kyander. "Unusual, but why not? So you suspect that your man Jokinen uncovered something damaging and unwittingly shared this information with the Soviets. Which is why my colleagues in the SUPO did him in. Is that it?"

"More or less," confirmed Hella. "They killed the Soviet doctor, too."

"Ah, yes, the Soviet doctor. An army surgeon, wasn't she? What did you say her name was?"

"Captain Daria Makarova. Daria Mikhailovna Makarova."

Kyander pulled a small spiral notebook from his pocket and jotted the name down. "Did you go across the border?" he inquired.

"Me? Heavens, no. Of course not. Her body was on Finnish soil."

Kyander raised his eyebrows again. "Do you mean to tell me that the Soviet military has invaded our country and we don't know it?"

Hella sighed. This was proving even more difficult than she had expected.

"It was not an invasion. I think that woman – Dr Makarova – crossed the border to give Erno chloroquine in exchange for proof of the bioweapons testing."

"She acted alone in this?"

"Yes, I believe …" Hella paused, flushing. "I know it sounds silly, but I think she just wanted to uncover the truth."

"Or she was using this information to mount an espionage operation with the full knowledge of her superiors. But it's true that this is something we can only guess. More coffee? Did you try the cinnamon rolls? Home-made."

Feeling jittery, Hella declined both.

"Now then," said Kyander. "You have also stated that an innocent man is being accused. Who is he?"

"An Orthodox priest. A friend of Erno Jokinen."

"A good-looking man?" smiled Kyander. "Orthodox priests can marry, can't they?"

Hella dug her nails deep into the palms of her hands.

"They can, and he is. Married. And now it looks like the SUPO will prosecute him for a murder he didn't commit just because he makes a good suspect. His unborn child will have no father when he comes into the world. This is" – she hesitated, then said it, for lack of a better word, even though it made her sound childish – "unjust. This whole situation."

"It's up to the law to decide what is just and what is not," said Kyander pensively. "And the law decides based on the facts, not conjectures. You people are amazing. You want a state that protects you, but when it does, you're still not happy. Someone – a philosopher – said once that, to avoid the war of every man against every man, people need order, represented by the state. That order cannot be twisted on a whim. I hope you understand that."

"I do. And I have proof of the priest's innocence – or rather, of the SUPO's guilt – that I'm ready to present in court."

"Hmm," said Kyander. "I'm not at all convinced. So what do you want from me?"

"I need you to call your local office in Lapland and tell them that the police officer in charge of the investigation – me – has come to the conclusion that Father Timo Waltari is innocent. That whatever Chief Inspector Lennart Eklund told them is a lie, because in a case like this, it's easier to tell a lie than the truth. That's the first thing. And second, I need your help in immediately referring Mrs Waltari, the priest's wife, to an army doctor who can provide her with chloroquine. She is suffering from malaria, and it's possible that the baby she's carrying will die, just like his older brother did. After my father died, you told me that I could come to you whenever I needed help. I've never asked you for anything, because everything that happened to me, however bad, I could deal with on my own. But this is different, and without your help, I can't manage."

Kyander remained silent for a moment, delicately rotating the little gilded coffee cup between his beefy fingers. When he spoke, his voice had a finality that sent a chill down Hella's spine.

"Well, if you want my humble opinion, this Erno fellow is the one to blame. He betrayed his country. Of course he did. He went across the border to give sensitive information to the Soviets." He looked squarely at her. "My dear child, you have a trusting nature. I recognize your father, who was my dearest comrade in arms, in you. You believed those people when they told you the old man's daughter had suffered from malaria. But how do you know that for sure? You're not a doctor, are you? You didn't take the dead woman's blood sample. So how do you know she didn't simply die of the flu? Come to think of it, how can you be sure that the corpse you found was that of Captain Daria Makarova? Was her face easy to recognize? Or was it beyond identification, half-eaten by animals? Was she wearing her uniform or was she clad in civilian clothes, a sweater maybe? She could just have been some poor soul who died of natural causes. You don't have any tangible proof of what you're suggesting, do you?"

Hella shook her head while her throat contracted painfully; she was having difficulty breathing. *I'm drowning*, she thought. Drowning in a sea of lies, of half-truths, of hypocrisy. Kyander's hectoring voice seemed far away, as if coming through water. "I totally understand that you're worried about your friends, but if this priest is innocent, my colleagues will set him free. The SUPO isn't in the habit of condemning people without serious proof." He paused, looking at her with what he imagined to be pity. "As for the priest's better half, what she needs is a good midwife. Pregnant women are subject to all sorts of delirious thoughts. You wouldn't want her going around accusing the Finnish state or our trusted allies of being cold-blooded murderers. That wouldn't do. Could be bad for your career, too. Did you think of that?"

Hella rose slowly from her seat. There was still some coffee left in her cup, and she drank it before cautiously replacing the cup on the table.

"I'd better be going, then," she said in a matter-of-fact voice. "Get back to work. Sorry I took up so much of your time." She tried out a smile, but it came out more like a grimace. "It was good to see you. I'll send you a card at Christmas, if you don't mind."

She breathed slowly, trying to not let her anger overwhelm her. It would have been the easiest, the most natural response to call the man a liar to his face and ask him who exactly had told him about the sweater Captain Makarova had been wearing at the time of her death. It had been a mistake coming here. She should have known. As soon as she had seen the house and heard about the breakfast room she should have bolted. Too late.

Kyander was holding up her parka for her.

"Would you like to stay here and rest? I can put you in the guest bedroom. Draw the blinds. You can get some proper sleep. You'll feel better afterwards." The red mouth quivered. The beady eyes were looking up at her with a mixture of contempt and worry.

"No thank you. I'm perfectly fine. I thought that maybe while I was here, I'd go and see my former colleagues. My new colleagues, I should say. Apparently Jon Jokela wants me back on the homicide squad."

"And that is very good, very good indeed. Jon is an excellent man, one of the best. When you're back, we should get together one day, all three of us. Talk about the good old days."

*What good old days would those be, exactly?* wondered Hella, but said nothing for fear of betraying herself. Her intellect put a lid on her emotions; or rather it chose one emotion and decided to stick with it, however much effort it would cost her. She picked up her shoulder bag from the floor and tried to open it to extract something, maybe her gloves, but the buckle stuck. When it finally gave way, after much pulling, all of its contents spilled onto the parquet floor. Kyander crouched down immediately to collect her miserable belongings. Her keys, her badge, a wrinkled apple she had been meaning to eat for some weeks now. A handkerchief. Discarded Fazer Blue wrappers. Her gloves. Finally, her blue notebook and a small leather pouch which he held in his hands a split second longer than necessary.

"Are you certain you don't want to stay? You look so pale."

"It's a polar night tan," she quipped. "When I'm back in Helsinki for good, I'll thrive."

# 55

She had never felt so lonely, not even after her parents had died – she'd had neighbours then, who had come over to console her at all hours. And even her separation from Steve, and her exclusion from the homicide squad ... well, that was life. But what was coming at her now, like a giant wave ready to swallow everything in its way, was death. The death of that unborn but already loved baby. The death of Irja, his mother, who would not survive a second tiny coffin. The death of the Hella Mauzer she knew, not of her body – that was the least of her worries – but of everything that made her life worth living.

As she was descending the stairs, gripping the banister in order not to slip on the icy steps, she thought about her options. She had none. Her defeat was utterly, hopelessly complete. No chloroquine for her. And no truth. She wondered how on earth she would be able to explain the situation to Irja. By the time she reached the gate, she even thought for a moment about turning back and starting over again: her reasoning, the arguments, the proof. But it would do no good. Kyander wouldn't listen to her. He was surely already summoning his fellow spies to get rid of her.

She realized that she was wrong as soon as she saw her car. Kyander must have called his colleagues before she'd come to see him. Otherwise, how could she explain the fact that the driver's door had been forced open and Irja's belongings lay scattered on the floor of the car? Searching for evidence, thought Hella. She tightened her grip on her shoulder bag. At least she had saved something. Her trade-off for Irja's medicine.

"Did he refuse to help?" Irja was suddenly standing next to her. Hella hadn't heard her arrive. A little further down the road, Kalle was playing with his bus in the snow.

"He did," said Hella. "He already knew about it; he'd clearly been warned by his colleagues. They've searched the car as well. It's a good thing we have a plan B." She smiled with more confidence than she really felt.

"What's plan B?"

"We'll go to the Western Alliance. They have an office next to the American embassy. We'll ask them for chloroquine. They must have it; they were the ones who ran the tests. We'll trade the vials for chloroquine, get you healthy and agree to forget about the whole thing."

Irja frowned, thinking it over. When she spoke at last, her voice was firm, but her eyes held all the anger, sorrow and pain of the recent months.

"That won't do. The truth is important. Truth and justice for the dead. I'm not trading that."

"I'm a police officer," said Hella. "Justice is the only thing I believe in, but I'm willing to let that go to save your child. Do you realize what the risks are if you don't get chloroquine? For you. For the baby."

"I do."

"And you still think the truth is more important?"

Irja nodded, her eyes brimming with tears. "What

becomes of our freedom if we sign a pact with the Devil? I want my child to be born a free man."

*I'll never be a good police officer,* thought Hella. *Jokela was right about that. I favour the particular over the general good. A victim's life over some intangible, bigger truth. But I am what I am. There's no changing me now.*

"Truth is meaningless," she said out loud. "It's a ripple on the water. It'll soon be forgotten. But your child … he could live. Isn't that more important? Isn't it?" She wanted to shake Irja, to slap her, to make her understand. "Your child's life is more important than truth, more important than loyalty to the dead, more important than anything. And you might not want me to" – she touched Irja's stomach, driving the point home – "but I'm going to save him."

She paused, looking at Kalle but thinking of her nephew. She could no longer remember his face.

When she spoke again her voice was soft, barely a whisper. "You cannot save the world. Not you, not your husband. The world – what I know of it – is unsaveable. Irredeemable. There's too much at stake, too many superpowers vying for control, for dominance. But I respect your feelings. I'll need to leave you alone for a while. Will you be all right? You can wait in the park. No, not the park. Another public space. There's a restaurant on Unioninkatu. Wait for me there, and don't move."

Hella got into the car without waiting for an answer and drove off, her hands white-knuckled on the steering wheel. She headed straight for the railway station in Kluuvi. Once or twice she glanced into the rear-view mirror, and it seemed to her that the dark grey Volvo in the left lane had already crossed her path earlier that day, but she couldn't be sure.

In Kluuvi, Hella stopped the car two hundred yards from the granite arches of the station, on the far side of

Elielplatsen. The clock tower, partly destroyed in a fire two years earlier, had been restored during her absence. It struck ten as she parked. Still clutching her bag, she went into a telephone booth to make a phone call. She was pretty sure they wouldn't be able to pick up her conversation if she was quick. In any case, it was a risk she had to take. She spoke for no more than a minute – nothing emotional, all matter-of-fact – ignoring the man in a suit who had materialized out of thin air at the end of her conversation and was loitering next to the booth. *Not close enough to hear,* decided Hella. She hung up and pushed past him, then went into a neighbouring café to buy something to eat. She then marched back to the car, with the same dark-suited man watching her, put her bag on her lap, and waited, all the while nibbling at the turkey sandwich she had bought. She didn't have to wait long. Less than ten minutes later, a squat little woman dressed in an ankle-length sheepskin coat and a garish headscarf emerged from one of the side streets and made her way inside the station. Walking behind her was a tall, gawky man lugging a heavy suitcase.

Hella, who was still eating, glanced at her watch, then, with the sandwich bag in her left hand and her shoulder bag worn across her body, she hurried across the square. Once inside the station, she went straight to left luggage. She loitered in the room until there was no one around, then she stuffed her shoulder bag inside one of the lockers and walked out quickly. The gawky man was standing next to the train schedule, beads of sweat rolling down his face, his black coat open. Hella looked away, bumped into him and would have fallen if the man hadn't caught her. He looked astonished as Hella slipped her hand into his pocket briefly, but before he could say anything she had excused herself and hurried away. She attempted to throw her half-eaten lunch into the overflowing bin by the exit but missed, then ran across Elielplatsen to her car. If she had turned to look, she would have seen the gawky traveller being roughly handled by two square-jawed young men while passers-by watched and commented. She would have also seen the squat little woman, who had been standing by the exit eating an apple, pick up the sandwich bag containing the key and shuffle back inside, and then, less than a minute later, come out of the station, her heavy sheepskin coat bulging at the front.

# 56

She had no more coins left, so the first thing she did when she got back to Unioninkatu was ask Irja to lend her some. Then she telephoned Kyander. Kalle squeezed into the telephone booth with her and Hella, holding the receiver between her ear and shoulder, stroked his reddish-blond mane with her left hand as she dialled with her right.

The man picked up after two rings. She would have bet her red Christmas sweater that he had been sitting at home the whole time, waiting for her call.

"Kyander. Listening."

"I have proof," said Hella. "Tangible evidence."

"Then you'd better hand it over."

Hella smiled. There was a man standing next to the telephone booth, ostensibly waiting to make a call. He was wearing a cable-knit sweater and fishing waders, but his hands were small, white and delicate and there was a faint dent on the bridge of his nose, most likely left by reading glasses. He must have taken them off right before changing into fisherman's garb. She had second-rate spies watching over her. Either that, or their standards were slipping.

"Sure," said Hella. "No problem. As soon as you recognize in writing the SUPO's role in this affair and provide satisfactory medical assistance to my friend."

It was Kyander's turn to laugh, and it was not a friendly sound. "You must be delusional. I've heard that lack of sunlight can drive people crazy. You're a good example of that. Do you think we didn't have you followed? As we speak, my boys are breaking into locker number 7 at the railway station. I had them on the phone less than a minute ago. They have obtained the authorization of the station's security service. And let me tell you one more thing, young lady. Our friends – you understand who I'm talking about, don't you? – our friends are very unhappy with this turn of events, with your obstinacy and your decision not to be reasonable, and they have asked me personally to make sure you behave."

Hella gasped (*rather appropriately*, she thought) and hung up. She would call Kyander back in half an hour, once his "boys" had reported to him that locker number 7 was empty.

She pushed past the fake fisherman who was busy playing with his coins and returned to the table where Irja was sitting waiting for her.

"Did he refuse?"

"For now, yes. But he doesn't have a full grasp of the situation yet."

She hoped to God – in whom she didn't believe – that she wasn't mistaken. What if Esteri hadn't made it? What if there hadn't been two square-jawed individuals at the train station but three, and one of them had stayed behind in the locker room and caught Esteri red-handed?

"I expected him to refuse," said Irja. She smiled, a little smile of triumph that Hella found difficult to comprehend. "I've changed my mind. If you're still up for it, we can go to the Western Alliance."

Hella stared at her in disbelief. "Are you sure?"

"You were right when you said my baby's life mattered more than anything. I can feel him kicking, Hella. And I think the Western Alliance is a better choice than the SUPO. They conducted these tests. They're the ones who are responsible for this. They must have chloroquine."

Hella nodded, relieved. "Of course it's a better choice. The Western Alliance are the ones pulling the strings. Kyander is just executing their orders. Let's hurry before the fisherman over there casts his net."

They piled into the car, Kalle still clutching his toy bus. As the car pulled away from the kerb, they saw the fisherman run out and stop abruptly by the roadside, unsure of what to do.

Hella waved at him cheerfully and opened the window. "What are you waiting for? If you're going to follow us, go and get your car."

The young man blushed and turned away, ignoring them.

"All right," smiled Hella and sped up. "Time to get going."

"You didn't tell me what you did while you were away," said Irja. "You don't have your bag with you any more. Did you hide it? How did you manage?"

"I called someone from a café on Elielplatsen. She was rather good at it, given that she's just an old housewife."

"A relative?"

"On some days, it really feels like it."

She wondered if she could tell Irja the truth, but decided against it. It was not her secret to tell, after all. She doubted very much that anyone would ever arrest Esteri for killing her own son, the child-murderer, now that everyone believed that the man had died at the hands of an inexperienced police officer – herself – whose gun had misfired.

But it wasn't worth the risk. Esteri deserved to live out what remained of her life in peace, caring for her only remaining granddaughter, and if it did her good to think of Hella as a sort of guardian angel and lavish her with offerings of gherkins, so be it.

"I have one condition," said Irja. "I will be the one doing the talking now. I want you to remain silent."

*Here we go,* thought Hella. *She doesn't trust me to do the right thing. I've failed miserably in my negotiations with Kyander, so now Irja thinks she can do better than me.*

"As you wish," she said gloomily. "But if you intend to appeal to their better nature and talk about truth and justice and a safer world, my advice is to forget it. These people are not philanthropists, and they are certainly no saints. This is a business transaction we are proposing. They provide you with medicine, and they call the SUPO to tell them to drop the charges against your husband —"

"And you," chimed in Irja.

"And me, yes. And in exchange, we give them what we have."

"The results of the blood tests," said Irja. "And the Ysteria vials. Have you got all three in your bag?"

"No," explained Hella. "I separated them. One vial is in my bag. The other two I hid away before this even started, as insurance for all of us. I wanted to be sure I had some proof to fall back on if everything else was taken from me."

"So where are they? Didn't they find them when they searched the car?"

Hella waited while the traffic light changed to orange. There were hordes of people on the street – girls in silk stockings and flowery skirts despite the biting cold, men in double-breasted suits, with black coats thrown casually over their shoulders. Just two years in Ivalo and she was completely out of touch with this other, sophisticated, cosmopolitan reality. And the worst of it was, she didn't even care any more.

She turned to look at Kalle. "Does your bus have a baggage compartment?" she asked.

"It does, but the door's stuck."

Hella smiled. "I'll fix it as soon as Irja and I are done talking with one very nasty gentleman."

# 57

They had come to the right place. The receptionist, a sleek strawberry blonde wearing a demure white blouse and over-bright red lipstick, stared at them with undisguised fascination upon hearing their names. Hella wondered how this woman's bosses had described them: two weirdos from up north? One pregnant, flushed and panting, one dark and surly and unkempt. And a skinny boy – don't forget the skinny boy – with his beautiful gleaming toy bus.

"We've been expecting you," murmured the receptionist and pressed a button on her desk. Her nails were painted the same fiery red as her lips.

The Western Alliance outfit was not at all what Hella had imagined. From outside, the place was accessible through swinging doors. It looked like just another office, one selling agricultural machinery, or a law firm, maybe. It just stopped short of screaming *look at us, we're as inoffensive as one can get. We barely exist.*

Yet the ginger-haired young man who signalled to them from further down the hall had an unmistakable military bearing and an unfriendly manner. He was dressed in khaki fatigues, but wore no insignia.

"This way, please. I first need to make sure that you have proof of what you're accusing us of. Do you have anything to give me?" Hella pulled out of her pocket a sheet of paper folded in four and handed it to him. A copy of the blood test she had found among Kalle's paper planes.

The man nodded and walked away briskly, leaving them standing there.

He wasn't gone for long. "The Captain will see you now. However, we would prefer that the child waits in the reception area, if you don't mind." Then, without waiting for their response: "Greta, find him a comic book or some crayons, will you?"

Once Kalle took his place on the reception room sofa, the two women were marched down a narrow corridor painted institutional yellow, then motioned into a small, sparsely furnished room. There was nothing there but a metal chair and matching desk.

"I need to search you."

"Suit yourself," sneered Hella.

His hard, probing fingers ran over her body but found nothing except her car keys.

"Madam?"

Irja was blushing.

"She's a priest's wife, for God's sake," snapped Hella. "Get a woman to search her, if you really need to. Can't you see she has no weapons?"

The young man glanced at the door, visibly hesitating. Finally, he ran his fingers over Irja's arms; even then, he stopped at her elbows.

"All right, we can proceed."

Back to the corridor, retracing their steps, then up a flight of stairs. They stopped before a big oak-panelled door. The man knocked.

"Captain, your visitors."

The occupant of the office was sitting at his desk, supposedly reading but most probably just pretending to be busy while he waited for them. The black name sign on his desk gave his name as Captain Y. Hobbs. He was a big man, a well-fed man. He had light-brown hair cropped short over a high forehead, steel-grey eyes and was clean-shaven. *Yared?* wondered Hella. *Yehu? Yorick? Or even Yago?* Behind him, the tall windows revealed a panoramic view of the harbour. He rose from his seat, his eyes never leaving Hella's, and came towards them.

"May I offer you a seat, ladies?"

There were four matching office chairs set around a table by the window. They took their seats, and the ginger-haired assistant retreated after whispering something in the captain's ear. The man took a chair opposite them, his back to the window and harbour. *They're not afraid,* thought Hella. *They feel at home here.*

"What can I do for you?"

His Finnish had no trace of an accent. Hella opened her mouth to speak, then remembered her promise. She glanced at her friend. Irja was flushed, her hands wrapped tightly around her belly. Would she be able to get her message across? Hella wondered, not for the first time, how they had wound up in this place, and what the future held for them. This was a tipping point, she realized. Their future – Irja's, hers, Timo's, even Kalle's – was at stake in this room.

"I want to ask you a question, Captain Hobbs," said Irja, and to Hella's surprise her voice was strong and clear. "This is what I came here for, all the way from Lapland. To get answers. What is the Western Alliance doing in this country?"

The captain laughed, genuinely amused.

"Since when are ladies interested in such matters? Geopolitics! You Finnish women are surprising, surprising indeed. But I'll answer your question. The Western Alliance opened a representative office here in Helsinki to share our expertise in dealing with the Soviets, with the Finnish people."

"So it's purely a consultative role, is it? All perfectly above board? Nothing to hide? You can scream it from the rooftops, even?"

"Of course we can," smiled Captain Hobbs. "What a question!"

"Good. I'm taking notice. So would you please tell me about Project Ysteria?"

The captain looked down at his hands. He wasn't wearing a wedding ring, but there was a band of white skin on his left ring finger, which he was now rubbing, as he must have rubbed his wedding ring when he still had a wife.

"I just got off the phone with a man who introduced himself as Colonel Kyander from the SUPO. Must be someone from Headquarters. I don't know him, have never dealt with him before. Anyway, this man tells me that you're going around town, screaming about the Western Alliance poisoning civilians. Well, I must tell you this much. You are lucky that you're living in this country. One hundred and thirty miles to the east, you'd would already have been on your way to the Gulag, assuming they hadn't just shot you outright. But this is a free country, and its citizens are allowed to express themselves."

From the way the captain said this, he seemed to bitterly regret their tolerant Finnish ways very much indeed.

"I'm glad to hear you say that," started Hella, but Irja laid a hand on her sleeve, urging her to stop.

"So what is Ysteria, exactly, Captain Hobbs?" asked Irja again. "As you can see for yourself, I'm dying to know. And my child is dying inside me, too."

The Captain frowned, clearly finding Irja's words in poor taste. "I saw the blood test results you came with. Are they yours?"

"No, those belonged to Anna Jokinen. She died from complications of malaria. Pulmonary oedema and organ failure. But I'm suffering from the same illness as Anna."

"Don't worry, we'll get you chloroquine. I've already sent for a doctor. We're not monsters; all we want is for this thing to remain nice and quiet. The SUPO overreacted. I'm sure you wouldn't have had to come here if they had just arranged treatment for you in the first place. Overzealous bastards, if you'll pardon the expression. We never asked them to cover for us. They did it of their own accord."

"Does Ysteria come from Hysteria?" persisted Irja.

Hella frowned. Something was wrong here, but she couldn't quite put her finger on it. Irja was leaning forward, her eyes gleaming, holding her breath. She was still, yes, she was very still, she was barely moving, not making any sound other than speaking. And was there something on her neck, inside the collar of her shirt? Hella's heart leapt, but she forced herself to remain calm. No, that just wasn't possible. She was delusional. A Käärmela housewife would never dream up a thing like that.

"Project Ysteria no longer exists, it might please you to know," said Captain Hobbs. "It was a promising project, but it never lived up to its promise. Too difficult to put in place. It has been aborted." He paused, looking at them thoughtfully. "Yes, it does come from Hysteria. Our mad scientists called it Project BW54M, but that didn't satisfy my artistic tastes, so I renamed it. You see, mass hysteria is the main benefit of bioweapons, much more than direct casualties. The Soviets are testing their own weapons of mass hysteria, and we're testing ours. It's the rules of the game." He looked at them. "We all agree, yes? That this testing was a necessary evil? We can't all have the luxury of living out our days like Snow White. Some people have to get their hands dirty – for the greater good. Humanity needs to be managed; only here, in the West, we can't use brute force. That is the prerogative of our Soviet friends." Hobbs brought his hands together and placed his fingers under his chin. He could have been praying. "We civilized nations have to be cunning. You are educated people" – he glanced doubtfully at Irja – "and you can understand that. But not everybody can. So, once you leave this room, you will never, ever, talk about Ysteria to anyone. We'll deny it. That man Kyander said you had proof?"

"A vial full of malaria-inducing agents. The word 'Ysteria' is printed on the side."

"I'll need you to hand it all over to me, along with your notes on the case, after I telephone Kyander to call off the dogs but before I let the doctor in. This is the best I can offer."

Hella nodded. It was a reasonable offer. It was almost *too* reasonable. An easy victory, if one could call it that. Truth and justice in exchange for one family's life and happiness. And what about her? What would become of Sergeant Hella Mauzer after all this? Heaven only knew. Still, it was worth it. And they still had two other vials, so for them the risk was limited. But Irja was not quite done yet. The fever was speaking for her. Fever … or something else?

"Do you know where Käärmela is?" asked Irja, leaning towards the captain.

He looked at her, annoyed. "Of course I know where Käärmela is. For the past four days, I've kept hearing this name over and over again. But, my dear lady, you need to realize. Käärmela" – he pointed to the big map of Finland hanging to the right of the window – "this is Käärmela. That tiny dot over there. You can barely see it. And this is only the Finnish map we are talking about. When you get to the scale of the world map … People are dying all the time, all over the world. Think of that train crash in Harrow and Wealdstone in England last week. Do you know how many people died? How many good, ordinary citizens, hurrying to work, travelling to see their families? One hundred and twelve. They died for nothing. When you compare that number to one sickly woman and one unborn child … their deaths were not useless, at least. They died for the greater good."

He paused, looking at them. *He's not sorry at all,* realized Hella. *He's convinced that he's doing the right thing.*

Captain Hobbs' voice cut across her thoughts.

"Don't you realize there's more at stake here than just a few lives? It's us against them! We're at war, ladies. A war that doesn't speak its name, a cold, frozen, dreadful war. There are casualties, yes. Sometimes even our own citizens, or citizens of satellite nations. But we are doing this to protect you. So that you don't end up like the Baltic states."

The telephone rang and Captain Hobbs went to answer it, turning his back to them.

"Yes," he said. "We're almost done here. Please ask him to wait downstairs."

He hung up and turned towards them. "All the proof you have gathered, ladies, now. Let's not keep the doctor waiting."

"Call Kyander first," snapped Hella. "No, wait. I'll call him. I'd like to be sure that you're speaking to the right person."

She dialled the now all-too-familiar number, which was immediately answered by the all-too-familiar voice.

“This is Hella Mauzer. I’m with Captain Hobbs. He wants to talk to you.”

She passed him the receiver.

“Kyander, it’s Hobbs. It’s all settled. Tell your people to free the priest. Yes. Yes. Thank you for your assistance.”

# 58

"You will find the evidence at Ekberg Café," said Hella. "Bulevardi 9. The head waiter has a letter addressed to a Mr Evil. Your people will find a key to a locker inside the envelope."

"What locker? At the railway station?"

Hella addressed him with her sweetest smile. "I'll tell you once the doctors take Mrs Waltari away. I'm not sure I can trust your word."

Captain Hobbs barked his orders into the receiver. His people must have been primed, because ten minutes later – which they spent waiting in uncomfortable silence – the phone rang. Hella's spirits lifted as she saw the confirmation in Captain Hobbs' eyes. So Esteri had made it. Amazing, that woman!

"All right, they have the key. Where's the locker located?"

"The doctor first."

They waited some more, Hella's heart pounding. If she'd gauged this right, all hell would break loose any moment now. It was a miracle they hadn't heard already. But they were serious people. They didn't listen to the radio during their working hours.

The doctor came in, a short, wiry man, trim and efficient. A Finn. He went straight to Irja.

"Where will you be taking her?" asked Hella.

"University Hospital."

Hella sighed with relief. University Hospital was good. It was not an army hospital, but of course they would never dare admit a civilian there. It would be tantamount to a confession.

"Will she be all right?"

"With the right treatment, yes. But you people should think twice before travelling to Africa. And pregnant at that! Can you walk?" he asked Irja. "I have two nurses with a stretcher downstairs."

"I can walk." Irja got to her feet slowly. "I'll just say goodbye to my friend."

Captain Hobbs cut in. "You need to tell me now where the locker is located."

"The General Post Office."

Hella wondered if the police would be dusting for fingerprints. She hadn't told Esteri to wear gloves. And what if they did get her fingerprints? There would be other prints on that locker, a whole lot of them. All belonging to ordinary, law-abiding Finns. She doubted very much someone would take pains to compare the prints to a case the police had closed and archived years ago.

She looked at Irja. They moved into a corner of the room.

"Take care of yourself … and the baby. I'll come and visit. If I can."

"I have something for you," murmured Irja. "Something you forgot back in Käärmela. I'm sorry, I read it."

Irja pulled a letter out of her pocket. Shivering, Hella recognized her own handwriting: MR STEVE COLLINS, YLE RADIO, UNIONINKATU 20, 00160, HELSINKI. The letter she had put under her pillow in Käärmela and forgotten all about.

"I think he still loves you," Irja said. He was worried about you when I saw him just now, while you were out and about." She took a deep, shuddery breath. "I recognized the address as I was walking around with Kalle, and then I had this idea … I had to try. There's more at stake here than just us. The whole country. Innocent people. I don't think it will start a war. Both parties are guilty, after all. A Soviet captain crossed the border. They'll never admit it. I had to try."

"You succeeded," smiled Hella, her first real smile in weeks as she saw the ginger-haired young man appear at the door, out of breath and waving frantically at Captain Hobbs. She steered Irja towards the doctor. "Go now. Get out of this building."

From that moment on, time folded back on itself; or so it seemed to her. But maybe this was only her impression because things started moving at a terrible speed but she could hear nothing, only the deafening beating of her own heart.

Hobbs was gesticulating wildly, almost foaming at the mouth, the hapless messenger standing dumbfounded, the microphone that someone had torn off Irja lying on the floor in a heap while the doctor whisked her away. The pale Finnish winter sun, finally deigning to appear over the steel-grey waters of the bay. Kyander materializing out of nowhere, apparently screaming at her, with his very red mouth wide open so she could see the rotten teeth at the back. And all the while, her heart sang. Irja had done it, she had got justice for Anna, for Aleksi, and for all the others, the innocent, the victims. The corrupt state, that above-the-law mortal god, had just been kicked in the teeth. It couldn't have gone any better. And even if what Irja had said about Steve wasn't true, it didn't matter. But maybe it *was* true. A priest's wife wouldn't lie, would she?

At some point, someone – maybe even Hobbs – switched on the radio an assistant had brought him. The men gathered around it like crows. Hella breathed in deeply and willed her heart to calm down. She wanted to hear. To hear it like the rest of the country had heard it.

They were all over the news. She recognized the bellowing voice of Ahti Linna from Radio Finland.

*… an unimaginable crime, all the more so because it was committed by our own government, and its partners in crime, the Western Alliance. What cynicism, what contempt for human life! Just listen …*

And Hobbs again, a disembodied Hobbs, a pompous fool, declaring, "There's more at stake here than just a few lives."

The man was slumped behind his desk now, his head in his hands. The white band of skin on his ring finger trembled.

Quietly, Hella got to her feet and made her way out of the room and down the stairs.

Kalle was still sitting on the sofa in the reception area, pale and scared, clinging to his bus.

Hella waved at him. "Come on, sweetie. Let's go. Have I told you that I know a shop in Helsinki that only sells Fazer Blue chocolate? They have mountains of it, all different flavours, shapes and sizes. I bet you won't even manage to try it all!"

# *Author's Note*

While many elements of Finland's history are real, this novel is ultimately a work of fiction, and I have taken certain liberties in telling Hella's and Irja's story. For example, while the city of Ivalo does exist, there is no Käärmela village in Lapland; the name comes from Käärme, meaning "snake", with the suffix -la, meaning "place". In the same manner, the Western Alliance does not exist outside the pages of this book, other than as the name of a US bank, although the term "Western alliance" has also been used to refer to a certain intergovernmental military partnership between North American and European countries.

Kerry Segrave's book *Policewomen: A History* shows that Finland appointed its first two female police employees in 1907. However, their presence remained marginal; twenty years after this, there were still only five female police employees. By 1950, according to Statistics Finland, this figure had risen to a mere forty-seven.

From 1944, these women, called *polissysters* in Swedish and *naispoliisi* in Finnish (Finland's two official languages), started to receive formal training. As I mentioned in the Introduction, at the beginning their work concerned only women and children. The fact that one of them finally managed to join the homicide squad as early as 1948 is fiction – even though many surely wanted to.

# *Acknowledgements*

I owe enormous thanks to a lot of people:

My agent, Marilia Savvides, for her breathtaking faith in this book, her unfailing kindness and enthusiasm. To all at Peters, Fraser and Dunlop, especially Alexandra Cliff, Silvia Molteni, Rebecca Wearmouth and Laura Otal – it has been a great pleasure to work with you.

My editor extraordinaire, François von Hurter, who took my book and made it a million times better. Thank you also to Laurence Colchester and everyone at Bitter Lemon Press – I couldn't have dreamt of a better home for Hella.

Sarah Terry, my eagle-eyed copy editor, who ironed out a myriad of inconsistencies and was incredibly patient and kind.

Eleanor Rose, for the time and skill she put into designing a perfect book cover.

Madlen Reimer and everyone at btb, an imprint of Random House; everyone at W. F. Howes.

Father Denis, for answering my questions, and Maritta Jokiniemi, curator of Finland's National Police Museum, for pointing me in the right direction. Any mistakes are most definitely mine.

My friend Alina Mauchamp, for her invaluable support.

My family, for being patient and helping me keep everything in perspective – you know how much I love you.

Finally, there wouldn't be any books without readers, booksellers and bookshops – so thank you all!